I0534373

Books by Steven Jaeger

Awaiting Arrival

From The Depths: The Awakening

From The Depths: The Confrontation

Coming soon

The Eternal Experiments

The Climb

FROM THE DEPTHS

The Confrontation

Book 2

Steven Jaeger

From The Depths: The Confrontation
Copyright © 2023 by Steven Jaeger

All rights reserved. No part of this publication may be reproduced or transmitted in any form or by any means, electronic or mechanical, including photocopy, recording, or any information storage and retrieval system, without permission from the author.

For information about permission to reproduce selections from this book, write to author@stevenjaeger.com.

First edition: 09 2023
Printed in the United States of America
ISBN
Paperback: 979-8-9864112-4-8
Ebook: 979-8-9864112-5-5

Book design by Steven Jaeger

For everyone along for the ride.

Chapter 1

Brenda nudged Shannon gently to wake her. Shannon opened her eyes more easily than she had anticipated. It was still dark, but she felt rested enough to continue on.

The blue of the moon outlined Brenda's dark skin, her lean muscular figure, and revealed her hair, which had grown out slightly into a short afro. Her eyes were wide and alert. Though they had just escaped camp, leaving Billy and Jenny behind, Shannon got the impression that Brenda was not nervous or anxious, but excited and energetic.

"How'd you sleep?" asked Brenda. "Have any dreams?"

Shannon reflected for a moment, rubbing the magnetic headband she wore—in hopes that it would shield her from the aliens that invaded her mind—thoughtfully. "No, I didn't. At least not that I can remember," she said in amazement.

Brenda smiled at her. "Let's play it safe and not take the headbands off for a few days. At some point we'll have to test that they are working by taking them off, but we can save that for when we have less concerns that are more pressing."

Brenda extended a hand to Shannon and pulled her to her feet. She helped Shannon get her pack on and then handed her a protein bar.

"If at any point you want to stop, just say so," said Brenda. "As long as you don't say anything, I will assume you can keep going. Sound fair?"

"Yes," answered Shannon. She stepped into a lunge to stretch. She had thinned out a bit after escaping the bunker that saved her from the comet. In addition to less food intake, she had spent much of her time resting on a boat, or later sitting on the beach when the fishing crew would travel. Her limited exercise had started to bother her. She knew she would recover her athletic physique quickly if she had the chance. She placed her long blond hair into a ponytail so it would be out of her way.

Brenda bounced on her feet as she adjusted her backpack on her shoulders and prepared to hike. "Great. If we keep a strong speed, I think we can make the trip in ten days."

Brenda started walking, slowly at first and gradually picking up the pace. They continued for several hours without stopping. The sun slowly rose into the sky, revealing the gulf and the mountain ranges on the other end of the gulf. Though the area had been stripped of trees, Shannon found the view quite beautiful. She spent much of her time thinking about what the world around her would look like in a few years as plants began growing again and as the water potentially brought sand from the ocean to the beaches in the gulf and covered the current soil and dirt.

After six hours they stopped to eat lunch and rest. When Shannon sat down her muscles felt a wave of relief and she instantly worried that she wouldn't have the willpower to get up again. Her body had become numb to the exertion of hiking after a couple of hours, but ached the second she rested.

"Are you doing okay?" asked Brenda.

"Yeah," answered Shannon. "I'm a bit sore now, but I've done enough running in my life that my body bounces back quickly after times like this. Tomorrow will be tough, and then after that things will get easier each day for me."

"The joys of being young." Brenda chuckled to herself. "Anything I let go of for a while, I have to fight tooth and nail to get back. Though it just forces me to stay focused and keep my time organized so I don't quit anything I still consider important."

The two fell silent as they ate their lunches. Looking out to the water before her, Shannon remembered how she felt the first time she reached the beach after escaping the bunker. The hurt of losing her dad flowed over her as though it had just happened. She wondered how Billy, her brother, was handling her being gone right now, and if he had taken time to mourn the loss of his father yet. Shannon remained quiet as tears gently streamed down her face.

"It's a lot to take in sometimes," said Brenda, softly.

Shannon nodded.

"Do you mind if I ask what happened to your husband?" asked Shannon.

Brenda pursed her lips in a half-smile and shook her head. "I don't mind," she answered. "Just don't apologize once I tell you. He killed himself."

Shannon fought her gut reaction to apologize for asking, swallowing the words as they bubbled up her throat. "Most people say they're sorry after you answer?"

"Yes. Every time."

"Did you feel guilty afterward, like you should have done something about it?" asked Shannon.

"I definitely spent a lot of time being angry, at myself and others. You see, my husband, Sam, was a surgeon. One day there was a six-car pileup and there were more people that needed help than there were surgeons to help them. My husband was given two kids that were both impaled by a pipe that fell off of a truck. He essentially had to choose which one he thought was more likely to survive and let the other one die since no one else was available to help. He spent hours trying to put that kid back together, but unfortunately he died from complications."

"When the mother comes in to see the bodies, she is irate that he chose the wrong child. My husband tried to explain that he picked the person who appeared to have the best odds of survival, but she would have none of it. She apparently had her favorite child and believed that kid would have lived if helped."

"Sam took it hard that he had let those two boys die. It became significantly harder when the mother sued. During the trial, I unfortunately found out first hand that surgeons have one of the highest suicide rates of any profession."

"That's awful," responded Shannon.

"Yeah. At first I was angry at the mother, but the mother lost her two boys. She should be allowed to lash out in anger, whether it was my husband's fault or not. He was there at the end of all of the events, and was the easiest to be angry at. Once I came to peace with that, and I learned how often surgeons kill themselves, I became angry at myself. I was angry for not knowing that truth, and for not seeing the change in him before it was too late."

"I feel that way about my dad," responded Shannon. "I'm angry at myself for not preparing better and preventing his death."

Brenda smiled gently and nodded. "Then maybe you need to learn the same thing I did; you can't be angry for the things you couldn't have known. Sam and your dad, they both died trying to do the right thing. They didn't die because of our neglect. We tried our hardest, and sometimes things simply aren't perfect."

"I guess," responded Shannon, doubtfully. She knew she was far from ready to consider forgiving herself for not predicting the issues that cost her father his life.

"Well," said Brenda. "Do you think your dad was angry with you when he died?"

"No." Shannon quietly admitted.

"Do you think that if he were standing here right now he would blame you?"

Shannon held on to her answer as long as she could, unwilling to hear the word. "No."

"So the only person blaming you, is you. It's okay to want to do better. It's okay to want to learn from the past, but even if it *was* your fault, the only thing you can control is now, not the past or the future. Do your best now. I know your dad must have been proud of you and would still be. He wouldn't want you to be suffering now because of him, just as I know Sam wouldn't want that for me either."

Shannon struggled to absorb what Brenda said. She appreciated Brenda's help, and the weight on her shoulders lessened as she calmed down.

"Thanks," said Shannon.

"Normally, in times like this I would say that half the battle is mental. However, we are dealing with an enemy that can enter your mind, so it's probably a lot closer to a hundred percent. With that in mind, I think it is important to deal with your inner demons on your own terms, rather than waiting for the aliens to bring them up, and I'm here to help you through that in whatever way I can."

When they finished their food Brenda stood and gestured to continue.

Chapter 2

Brenda and Shannon walked along the edge of the water where the land was flattest. They had traveled for five days, and had seen no sign of land demons, giving them the courage to venture closer toward the water over time.

Brenda stopped and faced the water. She let out a relaxed sigh. "When I forget what we are doing here and I just focus on the walk, it's actually pretty nice."

"Yeah," agreed Shannon. "It's nearly impossible for me to stop thinking about what is going on and what we should do next, but for those brief moments when I zone out, I do enjoy the exercise and the view."

Brenda breathed deeply, closed her eyes, and enjoyed the smell of the water and a gentle breeze that continually swept in from the coast. She remained silent for a while. "What's on your mind?" asked Brenda.

"I'm just concerned about what we are going to do once we get to the planes. Do we have the tools necessary to fly to Hawaii safely? If we somehow manage to get to Hawaii, what then? I know we don't have enough information to form a solid plan, and we likely never will. Either we move blindly forward with what little information we have, or we make no progress at all. But that just isn't how I normally work. I'm here, obviously, so I can do this. However, that doesn't mean that I won't spend every waking moment trying to figure more things out."

Brenda looked at Shannon and smiled. "You and I work similarly. I wish I had more answers for you. My fear is that the water has risen enough that any military bases on the islands would be far under water, if the tsunami hadn't just completely ripped them apart. So I don't know if there will be any salvage possibilities. But that's the thing; I don't know. You want to gather more info to make a decision, that's what we are doing. We are the scouts. Maybe we get there and find a ton of options and answers. Then we can come back and figure out how to get more people there. We'll see."

"Reconnaissance." Shannon nodded her head. "I hadn't thought about it like that."

Brenda watched Shannon's face intently. The time they had spent together had already allowed her to get a good read on the way Shannon worked. "What else is on your mind?"

Shannon looked out at the water. The glow of the morning sun shined on it brightly, hiding the mud and debris that lay just beneath the surface. She followed little ripples in the water as they made their way to shore. The water was just feet from them.

"We've gotten pretty comfortable next to the water, but we still haven't tested if it is the headbands keeping us safe, or just coincidence," said Shannon. "When is the right time to figure that out, and how?"

"Those are the questions I've been asking myself," responded Brenda. "I think I know the how. I'll be honest that the best solution I have does put you at risk, but I'll do everything I can to protect you."

"Just me at risk?" asked Shannon.

"I think only one of us should take the headband off," answered Brenda. "I believe you will be most enticing to the aliens."

"So I'm the bait?" interjected Shannon, grimly.

"Yes, but I brought weapons, and will guard you from a distance," assured Brenda. "It will entirely catch them by surprise. The second we see them, you will put your headband back on. I kill all the ones I see, and we make a break for it to lose them again. I know it may seem a bit crude, but it is also the best option I've come up with so far."

Shannon thought it over a bit. "Okay. So when would we do it?"

"Because I am asking you to put yourself at risk, I will let you decide, but the sooner the better. The longer we go, potentially working under false assumptions, the more at risk we will be."

Shannon exhaled deeply. "I'm ready when you are."

Brenda looked at the morning sun as it sat upon the nearby hill, flooding the area with light. "We have enough sunlight to do it now. Let me get my guns ready and I'll let you know when I'm good to go."

Brenda ran off a small distance from the water and dropped her backpack. She quickly unloaded two guns and assembled them. She placed extra ammunition nearby.

Shannon walked over and examined the guns and ammunition.

"I sure hope you don't need all of that," said Shannon.

"They would have to send a small army after you," said Brenda as she worked, not taking her eyes off of what she was doing. "But just in case..."

"Where would you like me to be?" Shannon asked.

"Anywhere that feels comfortable to you that isn't directly in front of me. I want to make sure that I have a clear shot."

Brenda finished assembling her equipment and then sat down. She pulled a protein bar out of her backpack and ate it calmly. Shannon watched from a distance as she waited for her cue. Brenda lowered herself into a prone position and peeked through the sight of her gun. When she had finished preparing herself, she looked at Shannon and nodded.

Shannon took off her headband and gripped it tightly in her hand. Nothing happened.

If it was working, then we just tipped our hand. They know we can go dark, thought Shannon.

Several minutes went by as Shannon examined every wave and shadow on the water. Still nothing happened. She began doing math in her head. Just from the distance they had walked for the past five days, she knew that land demons, if they started from the ocean, would have two hundred miles to travel, plus however deep the gulf was from the ocean. Even if they somehow swam at twenty miles an hour, it would take at least ten hours.

"If they started from the ocean, then I think we are going to be waiting here for a long time," yelled Shannon.

"Yep," responded Brenda, casually. "This will be our day, but hopefully when we are done we will have valuable answers."

"Should we keep walking then, so we can still cover more ground?" asked Shannon.

"No. If anything, we should start going back the way we came. I don't want to give them any indication as to which direction we are going."

"Okay," said Shannon as she leaned back enough to rest her head on her backpack while still being able to watch the water.

Shannon ate quietly. She had held out for as long as she could, but after seven hours, her stomach grumbled loudly. She was amazed by Brenda's ability to remain in one position for hours as she watched the water. Despite Brenda being easily visible, since there was no where to hide, she insisted after five hours had passed that Shannon was no longer to talk to her. She didn't want there to be any extra indication of her existence to anyone that might be watching Shannon.

Shannon looked at her MRE with disinterest. She was currently eating the spaghetti, which, of all the MREs, tasted closest to an honest meal, yet still ended up slightly dry, and artificial tasting.

A rock whizzed by Shannon as she poked her food with her fork. She turned and looked at Brenda, who was gesturing to the water. Shannon looked toward the water, but couldn't see anything note worthy. She reached for her headband, just in case.

Suddenly the water swelled as it rushed toward the shore. As the wave of water reached land, six land demons rushed out and charged at Shannon. Before she had a chance to react, Brenda fired off three consecutive shots, all hitting their targets. Shannon sat stunned as the remaining three charged at her on shore. Another shot and another land demon dropped; two remained. They both jumped into the air to attack Shannon as she watched in terror, helplessly frozen.

Time slowed as Shannon beheld the two animals hanging in the air as they rushed toward her. A fifth shot rang deafeningly, and one of the beasts flew to the side, tumbling to the ground limply. Before Brenda could take another shot, the final beast landed on Shannon, throwing her onto her back. Without thinking, she threw her hands into the air to beat at the animal with her fists. Her right hand struck the creature with no noticeable impact. Then she swung her left at the beast while she still clutched the headband. The moment the magnets reached the head of the animal, Shannon's vision was consumed and she found herself standing in snow near a vast ocean.

Shannon swept her gaze across what looked like Antarctica. *This was from my dream*, she thought to herself. *This is Alaska.* She looked around frantically in an attempt to find any clue that gave the vision importance. The ocean was behind her and she saw islands in the distance, but nothing that gave her a clear indication of where she was. Everywhere she looked on land she saw only ice and snow. In desperation, she got down on her hands and knees to dig in the snow around her. She dug quickly, but found nothing. Then she looked around from where she was on the ground, and noticed mounds of snow a small distance away; small bumps that stood out perceptively from the smooth, wind-swept snow that surrounded them. She crawled to them and began digging at the mounds.

Eggs.

Shannon's vision shot back to reality as the beast on top of her rolled off and she was no longer in contact with it. Somehow freed from its mental bondage to the aliens deep in the ocean, it sheepishly backed away from Shannon as she lay on the ground. It turned to run away, but before it reached the water one final shot rang in the air as Brenda blasted the animal, sending its body toppling over until it rested just inside the water.

"Get your headband back on quickly!" shouted Brenda.

Before Shannon had time to think, Brenda was helping her to her feet and handing her bag to her.

"We need to run before they send reinforcements," said Brenda as she took off as fast as she could while carrying her hiking backpack. She had shoved her pistol into her bag, but carried her rifle under her arm, not taking the time to dismantle it.

Shannon adjusted her backpack and ran as quickly as she could to catch up with Brenda. After they gained some distance and it became clear that they were not being followed, they slowed their pace.

"When I hit the land demon with the magnets in my hand, it got rid of its mind control, the same way that it removed the alien from my head when you put the magnets next to me," said Shannon after she caught her breath. "The animal seemed scared. I don't think you needed to kill it."

"I did notice that," responded Brenda. "It looked like the light had come back into its eyes and it was confused, but I still had to kill it."

"Why?"

"Because the aliens would have just taken control of it again," answered Brenda.

Shannon shook her head, not that she disagreed with Brenda's assessment, but because she now had reason to believe that the alien she had talked to had lied to her. The land demons might not have been attacking people on the beach because they were inherently violent, but because they were being controlled and forced to do so. What she had experienced wasn't enough to make a definitive conclusion; but it was enough to doubt what she had previously assumed to be true.

Chapter 3

The sun cast its warm rays upon Shannon as she watched its light slowly rise into the sky and shine on the water before her. She ate her protein bar, oblivious to her fatigue of the flavor. For the past three days, her thoughts had been consumed by what she had experienced when she was attacked. Everything she had gone through felt connected. Her dream, which she now viewed more as a vision, revealed everything she was currently doing, but not why. Yet, despite her confusion, what stuck with her most was the idea that the land demon that attacked her didn't need to die once it had been freed.

"Ready when you are," said Brenda as she stood with her backpack shouldered. "I think we'll be to the airplanes by the end of tomorrow."

Shannon was slow to respond as she struggled to draw her thoughts back to the task at hand.

"What's up with you?" Brenda asked as she extended a hand to Shannon. "You've been out of it the past few days. What happened to you when you were attacked? I know you like to work things out on your own, and I've given you time for that, but now you have to clue me in."

"Sorry," responded Shannon as Brenda pulled her to her feet with ease.

Brenda gestured for them to start walking, but she maintained a slower pace so Shannon could talk.

"When I hit the animal with the magnets and got rid of its possession, I immediately had a vision like I had with the alien. This time I was in Alaska and unburied eggs in the snow. That, in and of itself, is interesting. I did not get the impression that it was a voluntary link between us, and it ended when it rolled off of me, as though it were a connection through contact. I wonder why I didn't experience some other memory. I wonder if that was a coincidence, or if the aliens keep the land demons under their control most of the time and only let them go when it is mating season. Maybe I experienced that memory because the animal doesn't have many others to pick from, or it was the last one it had."

Brenda looked Shannon over, took in her posture and tone, and noticed her expression. "You mentioned that as though it was a side note," pointed out Brenda. "So what's actually on your mind?"

"When I was coming back from picking up the cache from the beach, I fell asleep and I think I had a vision," said Shannon.

"Like... of the future?" asked Brenda, skeptically.

"I know it sounds odd, even with everything that has happened," acknowledged Shannon. "I can't remember any of the details. I couldn't even remember them when I first woke up. But four things lingered in my mind. I remembered a plane, a submarine, Hawaii, and Alaska. Keep in mind, this was before you mentioned the planes we are now traveling to."

"You knew about Hawaii before this vision," said Brenda as she worked through what she had just heard. "That could potentially explain that." She paused as she seemed to evaluate her conclusion. "I'll admit that the plane and Alaska seem like very strange coincidences. Maybe I had mentioned the planes at some point and we just don't remember it. Are you sure it was Alaska? Was there a sign that said, 'You are in Alaska?'"

"No," admitted Shannon. "In fact, it looked like pictures I've seen of Antarctica. But in my dream, I just *knew* that is was Alaska. What little I remembered of my dream, though, looked exactly like the environment I saw in the vision that I had from the land demon."

Brenda let out a deep sigh. "I don't think you're lying or anything. This is just one more thing we have to wrap our heads around. Let's just say for a moment that the dream you had wasn't just by chance. Do you think it's possible that the aliens gave that to you to try and steer you?"

"At this point, anything seems possible. If they did give me the vision, then I don't know how to respond to that. Should we keep moving forward with what they are telling me is going to happen, or try and act unpredictably? If they can see the future, I'm not sure it will be possible to fight against that. Any change we make, they will already see the outcome. If they can't see into the future, and it was just their best guess, then it reveals a level of knowledge that I don't think we can overcome. Most of my vision I could understand them already knowing. Like you said, I had already thought of Hawaii. You already knew about the planes. Maybe someone else knows about submarines," Shannon said with a shrug. "But how could they have predicted that I would have a vision of Alaska from the land demon? At the same time, if they didn't give me the vision, and I simply had a glimpse into the future, how did that happen? Is it a side effect of linking minds with them? If it is a side effect, does that mean they too have the ability to get visions?"

Shannon walked in silence, overwhelmed by the questions that bombarded her thoughts.

"Do you think it was from them?" Brenda calmly asked.

"I have a hard time trying to figure out what they would be attempting to accomplish if it was. It also wasn't anything like previous interactions I've had with them. In the past, I always remembered my dreams with them as though they were real events. They don't fade away upon waking like an actual dream does. This was very different."

"Okay. So what if it was a vision and it *wasn't* from the aliens?" asked Brenda.

"That's what I've been trying to figure out for the past three days, but I'm not sure how we would be able to survive in Alaska."

"That should be the building with the airplanes coming up," said Brenda. Her voice clearly lacked enthusiasm.

Shannon could see the remains of a building in the distance. Her heart sank. The building was half submerged into the side of a hill, which Shannon guessed had once fully covered the structure until it was ripped apart by the megatsunami. Even from a distance, Shannon could see that the building was in poor shape. One corner of the concrete structure was missing, exposing the black of the building's interior, and presenting menacing claws of rebar. The large doors for the hangar looked as though they bowed outward at the top.

"Let's not draw any conclusions until we get in there and assess the damage," said Brenda, addressing Shannon's concerns before she could voice them. "Considering how much of the building is still intact, there is a chance that some planes survived, or that we can piece a couple together."

They walked the remainder of the way quietly and quickly. As she approached, Shannon could see that the walls were nearly six feet thick, which made the missing corner with exposed rebar more impressive. The metal doors to the hangar were three feet thick and Shannon could immediately tell what had happened to the building.

"It looks like the megatsunami ripped away the hill that covered the building and tore away the corner of the structure, allowing water to rush in with a force that bowed the doors open when the bunker became full," said Shannon.

"I genuinely can't imagine how much force that would have taken," responded Brenda. She moved closely to the doors and examined them. She found an opening near the door with an exposed valve covered in rust.

"How could that have possibly survived?" asked Shannon.

"I'm guessing the thick security panel that is now long gone took the bulk of the impact," answered Brenda.

Brenda pulled on the three-foot wide valve with all of her strength. It budged minutely at first and then locked up.

Shannon moved next to her and helped turn the valve. An ear piercing squeal rang into the air as the valve slowly turned. The massive door to the hangar slid open gradually. They continued to turn the valve until the door's movement became blocked from the portion of the door that had bowed out.

"That should be enough space to get our planes out and let light in," said Brenda. "It will have to do."

They moved away from the wall where the valve was and looked inside the hangar. Shannon felt a rush of defeat. The hangar was thirty feet tall, two hundred feet deep, and eighty feet wide. Debris, from what she could only assume were the planes they had hoped for, covered the ground.

"So much for that plan," said Shannon in defeat.

Brenda said nothing. Without acknowledging Shannon's comment, she moved into the hangar and began climbing around, examining the debris and the hangar. After several minutes, she gestured for Shannon to come to her.

"Help me move some of this," said Brenda.

Shannon chose to not ask questions while they worked to expose the ground where Brenda was. She was too defeated by what she saw to inquire as to what Brenda was doing, and Brenda seemed too focused and determined to divulge the information without being prompted.

After they had finished, Brenda set her backpack on the ground and began rifling through it. She found a metal rod that was a foot long, the width of a finger, and bent at a ninety-degree angle at the top, giving it a five inch handle. She took the long end of the piece of metal and placed it in a small hole in the ground that Shannon had not noticed. She then began turning the tool, and a rectangular section of the floor, a foot wide by two feet long, began raising next to where she had placed the tool. As the floor produced a crack from where it was raising, Brenda would occasionally attempt to lift it without success. After the floor panel lifted two inches in the air, Brenda gave it another tug and the panel lifted up, exposing a set of valves.

Brenda began turning one of the valves and a fifteen by fifteen foot portion of the floor sunk down before sliding to the side, revealing a dark and massive hole. Brenda then turned the other valve and a platform slowly raised out of the darkness. It dripped large amounts of water as it rose into the air, signifying that much of the space below was under water.

"Considering that the floor and machinery are still perfectly intact, I'm guessing the water down there was from a slow leak and not the destructive force that obliterated everything up here," said Brenda.

"Are there more planes down there?" asked Shannon.

"Yes."

"Will they still work if they have been under water?"

"When I'm done with them they will."

Chapter 4

Thunder cracked loudly overhead as rain poured from the sky. Shannon sat in the hangar eating her lunch while she watched the rain fall. It had been raining heavily for more than a day now, and showed no sign of lessening. She bundled herself tightly in a large coat that Brenda had retrieved from the lower hangar, which had many useful things for them to sift through. They had spent their first two days at the hangar replenishing their supplies. Brenda had found several planes that she believed would be in working order, but they were half submerged in water and they were currently unable to move them.

"Catch," yelled Brenda from the hole.

Brenda had spent the past four hours of the morning attempting to float the planes they wanted so they could move them to the lift. Shannon looked down just as Brenda threw a large rope to her. She caught the rope with one hand as she set down her food with the other. Brenda braced herself against one of the poles that rose into the air for the lift.

"Let's start gently," said Brenda.

They both began tugging on the rope. It moved slowly. Brenda moved below as she tried to steer the plane they were pulling. They continued to pull for several minutes, until the plane was positioned on the lift. Brenda gave a thumbs up when she was pleased with the plane's placement.

Shannon moved to a nearby valve and began raising the lift. Brenda had a look of triumph as she came up on the lift. The plane, which was almost entirely made of carbon fiber poles, had wings that could fold up toward the plane and was currently collapsed into a teardrop shape and dripped water. Shannon could see that the wings were covered in a navy blue paint that had an odd shimmer to it, as was the tail fin on the sides. The cockpit —which had two seats, yet appeared only slightly larger than what one person would need—was surrounded in domed acrylic glass that led to the propeller at the front of the plane. It sat inside a wood and metal frame that Shannon guessed was the majority of the weight they had struggled to move.

"Unfortunately, I think I have to break apart the frame before we will be able to move the plane off of the lift," said Brenda as she held a large ax. "The whole thing is screwed together, but I would have to unscrew it manually and I think it would be easier to just chop it up."

Shannon drew close as she examined the small aircraft. She ran her fingers over the wings. The paint had a slight texture to it.

"Hmm," said Shannon.

Brenda grinned. "It's solar paint. It has the function of a solar panel, but without the weight or wind resistance."

Shannon massaged her sore hands as she watched the sun set outside. They had worked tirelessly to lift up three planes, and remove them from the frames that had protected them. The cold and the moisture in the air from the rain made her hands feel especially painful from her exertion. Brenda continued to work on the planes while the sunlight had not yet fully retreated.

Rain came down in sheets of water, reminding Shannon of her vision of the aliens walking around on their home planet. Panic raised in her as she tried to think of a way to defend herself against them. She needed an army. Yet the people she had access to were disjointed and belligerent.

An army.

Shannon rested her head in her hands as she dwelled on the words. Her fingers touched the magnets in the headband that she had begun forgetting that she was wearing. *When the land demon was released from its mental prison, it seemed non-hostile. We have a way to neutralize their army,* she thought to herself. Brenda's words ran through Shannon's head again. *The alien would have just taken control of it again.* She knew they would always take control of their army again. *I know where the land demons make their nests. I could destroy their eggs before the aliens could take control of the next generation.* Shannon felt uncomfortable with the idea of killing land demons just to prevent them from being used as an army against people.

"You seem deep in thought," observed Brenda as she sat down next to Shannon. "What's on your mind?"

"I'm just thinking about how we need an army to fight against the aliens, but no one seems too eager to work together. Everyone just wants to find a way to seize power. The aliens, on the other hand, have the land demons under their control." Shannon paused as she worked through her frustration. "There are all these pieces we've figured out, but I just don't know how they all work together."

"Well, lay them all out for me, and we'll see if we can work through them as a team," said Brenda.

"I think we know we can free the land demons with magnets, but we don't know for how long. I believe we know where the land demons make their nests, though I don't know what we would do with that information other than kill off the eggs, which feels wrong to me."

"Why is that?" asked Brenda, curiously.

"The land demons are just a tool to the aliens. I don't think they would actually be aggressive toward us if not for the aliens. We also don't know anything about their life cycles. Killing off these eggs could be devastating to their survival, and I'm not comfortable making them go extinct just for our benefit. Plus, in a world with limited life on it now, eliminating an entire species seems reckless."

"You wouldn't kill puppies just because an owner was training dogs to fight. I get it," responded Brenda. She reflected on her own words. "The aliens are using the land demons as their army. What if we did as the Mongolians would do and just recruited our enemies?"

Shannon gave her a questioning look. "Explain."

"I'll admit that the analogy may have been a bit reaching. But the idea is this; they would accept those who had surrendered and now had no home—since the Mongolians had just conquered their land—into their ranks to fight for them, rather than forcing them to become nomads. My thought is, if we can figure out how to raise the pups of these animals, we may be able to train them like dogs to serve as our army rather than for the aliens."

"If we can figure out how to feed them and keep them alive while we train them..." said Shannon as she contemplated Brenda's proposition.

"It may be wishful thinking to create an army of these animals, but even just studying them and attempting to tame them could give us valuable information on how to protect ourselves from them."

"I wonder if making collars with the magnets in them would be close enough to their heads to prevent the aliens from possessing them," mused Shannon aloud.

"Only one way to find out," responded Brenda.

Shannon nodded. She worked through everything in her mind. "Then I think we should go to Alaska."

"Do you have any idea what part of Alaska?" asked Brenda. "It's a third the size of the continental United States, or it used to be, at least."

"I know that in the vision I had I was in the most southeast portion of the state, on the coast."

"That does narrow it down quite a bit," said Brenda. "It's the most we have to go on at the moment and definitely a solid direction to go in, but we may need more guidance if we don't want to just wander off and freeze to death."

"I'm open to suggestions, if you have any."

"Do you think you would have another vision if you touched a land demon again?"

Shannon became concerned. "I'm not sure I want to find out," she said with tension in her voice. "While you were an amazing shot, and I did end up unharmed, I'm a bit afraid that I wouldn't be so lucky a second time."

"To be honest, I was thinking we could try capturing one. We wouldn't have to use you as bait in the same way as before."

"I'm not sure if it will even work a second time. We tipped our hand to them the first time. They may assume that us jumping back onto their radar is a trap, especially since we have been off of it for so long. I'm not trying to say that it's a bad idea. I just don't know how we would make it work."

Brenda ate a protein bar casually, not trying to force the issue with Shannon. "I was just thinking that we might be able to tap into their memories and pinpoint where exactly we should be flying to. However, we have plenty to do before that is an issue. Take some time to think it over, and we can come up with the details later. If you would rather be the one holding the gun while I'm the bait, I would be willing to give it a try."

"How will we capture one if we are shooting it?" asked Shannon. "Don't we risk killing it?"

"Well, it would be a bit tricky. If they attacked like before, then the first thing you would have to do is kill all of the ones you don't want to keep. I found a net gun in the hangar which was meant to be used for escaping livestock on the farms."

Shannon laughed. "That seems a bit extreme."

Brenda shrugged. "Times are extreme. It's not like you can just run out and catch more animals if the ones you have escape, and the majority of the people running the farms have military backgrounds, not farming. Plus, there are a couple other locations that have larger animals that can utilize the net guns. It's perfect for deer."

Shannon didn't like the idea of sacrificing more land demons just to acquire one, but the ability to capture one so that they could hopefully experiment with it safely was enticing. Though is seemed like all she was doing lately was thinking, she now had even more to contemplate.

Chapter 5

Shannon came to a stop outside of the hangar and wiped the sweat from her forehead. Her chest heaved as she gulped in air. For the past three days, the rain had let up enough that she could go out running. It helped her gain energy throughout the day, and gave her something to do while she waited for Brenda to finish working on the planes. She returned to the hangar just as Brenda was about to start one of the aircraft.

"Are you going to be ready to leave soon after I take these things for a test run?" asked Brenda. "I know the chances of anyone seeing or hearing me while I fly around aren't very high, but I don't want to risk someone hunting us down thinking that they have better plans."

"I've had three days of nothing to do except get ready," said Shannon as she continued to catch her breath.

"I'll take each plane up, circle around a bit, check that everything is working properly, and then bring them back down. After that, we will have about an hour to load everything up and make sure that the batteries are recharging properly."

Shannon nodded and then made her way to the items she had gathered for loading. She stood out of the way and watched as Brenda climbed into the cockpit, which was narrow and looked cramped, but was big enough for her and one seat directly behind her. She pressed the button for the ignition and the propeller lurched forward, paused, and then fired into full rotation. She wiggled the rudder, elevators, and ailerons—the various flaps that controlled the plane's position in the air—one last time to make sure everything was working before finally moving forward.

Shannon watched as the plane went down the path they had taken to get to the hangar and it eventually lifted off of the ground. She was shocked by the amount of noise that such a small plane made. As it flew around, she stopped watching and began loading all of Brenda's gear and supplies onto the other plane.

Among the supplies buried in the hanger they had found winter clothes for extreme weather that Shannon placed on top of the other gear for easy access. Brenda had explained that several simulations had predicted the comet to trigger an ice age, so they had provided clothing that far exceeded the weather they were currently experiencing. Shannon was grateful.

After several minutes, Brenda circled back around and landed. The plane bounced as it touched the ground and quickly came to a slow taxiing speed. Brenda brought the plane back to where it had started, once again checked the rudder, elevators, and ailerons, and turned the engine off. She gave Shannon a smile and a thumbs up before exiting the cockpit.

"You ever flown a plane before?" asked Brenda.

Shannon shook her head.

"Hopefully the fun of flying these things will last long enough that we won't mind the ten or so hours of flight each day for the next five or six days," said Brenda with a smile. "You will have a blast."

"You aren't worried about me crashing?" asked Shannon.

"We will be flying pretty low with an average cruising speed of thirty-five knots, or roughly forty miles an hour. Unless you nose dive the plane into the ground, you should be alright."

"Scientifically speaking, it makes perfect sense, but I had never really thought about the fact that I could fly at a slower speed than I would drive," said Shannon with relief.

"You have nothing to worry about. We will be able to talk to each other the entire time with radios, and I will fly ahead of you so you can just follow my lead. That way, you don't have to worry about elevation or direction at all while you become familiar with everything."

Brenda made her way to the other plane.

"Let me check this one out real fast and then when I'm back I will give you a quick flying lesson," said Brenda. "You will be shocked by how easy it is."

"Sounds good," said Shannon as she went back to the items she had gathered for the other plane.

Brenda jumped into the other aircraft, which Shannon had already packed. She checked everything, just as she had with the other plane, and then took off into the air.

Shannon placed her gear onto the plane that Brenda had tested first. She had a hard time believing that she was going to spend over forty hours of the next five days in such a tight space. She laughed at the idea that she was nervous to do something for such a long period of time that she had never done before; yet, had she been given the same opportunity simply for fun as a kid, she would have likely flown just as much, if not more, in the same amount of time. "I guess it's all about perspective," she said to herself with a smile.

Shannon sat in the pilot's seat and tried to imagine what she would want most easily accessible. She placed water and snacks in a bag nearby and again put jackets and warm clothing on top of the pile behind her. She also put a hand-warmer inside the bag of food and water. Shannon still sat in her plane as Brenda landed and pulled her plane next to Shannon's. She again gave a smile and thumbs up to Shannon before jumping out of her plane.

"As long as you're in there, I will show you how to fly it," said Brenda.

Brenda stood beside the plane and leaned over next to Shannon.

"These truly are the basics," said Brenda. "There was a more capable plane down there, but it was not electric and was only meant to be flown to locations where you knew you could refuel. An ultra-light-weight solar plane obviously has more freedom with some necessary concessions, or limitations. Obviously, as you can see, there is no speedometer, altimeter, gyroscopic pitch-bank, or even a radio. The implication there is that you should always be flying low enough that you don't need those things. You don't really need them when you are flying low enough to always see the horizon and your plane goes slow enough that you are always flying as fast as possible."

"I wouldn't know what those things were even if I had them so I guess I won't worry about it. They still could have provided a compass and radio, though," lamented Shannon with a shrug.

"Consider it two less things to distract you with," responded Brenda while smiling. "Of course, we have our own of those things, though it wouldn't really be an issue. We are just flying along the coast the entire way and we could easily land at any moment if we needed to talk. Anyway, what you do have in front of you should be easy to understand. The console in front of you only has two things. I guess the logic was that the less electronics you have, the longer the battery would last. You have the power switch and a poorly back-lit display that shows you how much juice the battery has left."

Brenda gestured to a lever to Shannon's right. "That controls the wheels of the plane. If you pull it back until it clicks in place, it will lock the wheels, like a parking brake. If you push it down very far, again until it clicks, it will fold the wheels in and allow you to easily land on water."

"This plane can land on water?" asked Shannon.

"Yes," answered Brenda. "They may look cosmetic, but the large casings around the wheels are actually small pontoons. Since the majority of the plane is just framing, it doesn't take much to keep it afloat. I will say though, since we are talking about the wheels, that landing is probably the one somewhat tricky part. Because the plane is essentially a tricycle on the ground, and it has most of its weight in the front, when you land, you will need to point your nose up to the sky a bit to force the tail end down. It will feel a little unnatural since it requires making the plane not level and takes your eyes off of the ground a bit. But all you need to remember is that the plane should feel exactly how it does right now when you are landing."

"So, like I am pointed at the sky, ready to take off," observed Shannon.

"Exactly. Also, when you first get off the ground, keep climbing for a bit. Your first instinct is going to be to level out so you can see the horizon, but it can be tempting to point your nose down too much so that you have a better view of the land below. Follow my lead and climb until I level out. I will make sure we are high enough that you can play around a bit and get a feel for what you think the plane is doing versus what it is actually doing."

"You sure you don't want to fly me around a bit and teach me while we are both in the same plane?" asked Shannon, anxiously.

Brenda let out a small laugh and looked at the pile of items behind Shannon. "Even if you hadn't already packed the planes, I don't think we both could fit in here. I also don't think you could see what I was doing, even if we could both fit. We have the headsets, and I will talk to you the entire time. Now, for the rest of the controls. You have the stick between your legs. Move it forward or backward and it adjusts the elevators on the tail so you can raise or lower the nose of the plane. Left to right adjusts the ailerons, which are for banked turning, specifically when combined with the rudder pedals at your feet. Left foot forward moves the rudder left and so on. The ailerons by themselves will just make you spin while continuing in the same direction. Kind of like a barrel roll. The rudder by itself is like holding your hand flat and just changing the direction your finger tips are pointing. A smooth turn needs both. We'll practice at a high altitude, where you'll have plenty of time to straighten out if things get weird. Though most of our flying will be in straight lines.

"Last, you have the throttle on your left," continued Brenda as she gestured to a short lever with a large, black rubber grip at the end. "You pretty much just have four positions to worry about. All the way forward and you have your flying speed. Like I said before, you will just want to go as fast as possible when flying, nothing to think about there. Half way is a good landing speed. A quarter forward will be your taxiing speed. Pull it back to its current position and you kill the engine entirely. Once the engine is dead, use the hand brake to gently bring the plane to a complete stop. Don't pull it too quickly, unless it's an emergency, because it could tip the plane forward."

Shannon examined the controls around her. "How will I know when I'm ready to take off if there is no speedometer?"

"You'll notice that, as you get to full speed, the plane will start to feel like it is floating a bit. At that point, you just need to gradually pull back on the stick and you will take off. Before you get too nervous about this, remember that you are never going more than forty miles an hour.

Not that you couldn't get hurt at that speed, but as long as you never overreact to anything, you should always be able to bring things around."

"This is nothing like flying a real plane, is it?" asked Shannon.

"It's a bit like driving a go-cart compared to a car," said Brenda with a shrug. "The risk is low enough that planes that fall under the ultra-light-weight classification don't require a license in the United States, or well, didn't. There's no one to issue licenses anymore. So take that for what it's worth. You can hurt yourself if you are really stupid, but you should otherwise be completely fine." Brenda leaned in closely to read the display for the battery. "Ninety-nine percent, great. It's apparently charging properly. Let's eat and go to the restroom while we wait for the other plane to finish charging, and then we will go."

Chapter 6

The engine of the plane whirred to life, and the blades outside the window spun into a blur. Shannon's stomach was filled with butterflies. She struggled to see the path ahead of her over the front of the plane, which only made her nervousness worse. She watched as Brenda's plane reached full speed, bouncing over the dirt until it finally tilted back and went into the air.

"It's as easy as it looks," assured Brenda over Shannon's headset.

"Hopefully I don't prove you wrong," quipped Shannon. She wiped the palms of her hands on her knees, removing the excess sweat.

"You'll be fine," responded Brenda. "First release your brake, and then put the throttle all the way forward."

Shannon leaned forward in her seat and looked toward the sky to see Brenda circling overhead. She let out a deep breath. Shannon pressed a button on the end of the handle for the brake and it popped forward a little until clicking in the upright position. The plane lurched forward slightly. She then pushed the throttle forward completely. The noise from the engine grew significantly, a high pitched whine, and the plane began moving forward at a quickening pace.

The plane bounced wildly as it picked up speed, tilting left and right under the influence of uneven ground. Despite the low speed that Shannon knew she was traveling at, it felt to her as though the ground was speeding by her rapidly. As the plane sped up, she noticed that the drops from bouncing were diminishing.

The floating feeling she had described.

She waited a moment longer to be sure that the plane was ready, and then nervously she lightly pulled back on the control stick. She was surprised by the resistance the stick gave her.

I'll have to be more deliberate than that.

She tugged harder on the stick and the front of the plane shot into the air. The angle felt too sharp to her, but she fought the urge to correct it.

"Perfect!" Brenda triumphantly shouted.

"Can I level out yet?" asked Shannon with panic in her voice. Seeing only the sky in front of her immediately made her feel disoriented. She jerked her jaw in a yawning motion to try and pop her ears as she rose.

"Just a little higher," responded Brenda in a calming voice.

A few seconds passed, which felt like minutes to Shannon.

"Okay, now you can level out," said Brenda.

Shannon gradually brought the control stick forward, lowering the nose of her plane, until she could see the horizon clearly.

"Not too much," corrected Brenda. "If you center the horizon in your view, you are actually pointing down a little bit."

Shannon adjusted her angle and then looked around. "I don't see you anywhere. Where are you?"

"I'm behind you. I wanted to make sure I had a good view while you were taking off, in case anything went wrong."

"Can you get in front now so I can follow you?" asked Shannon, her voice shaky.

"I know you are nervous to lead, and it would probably be easier if you could follow me and see what I'm doing. But these things don't exactly have rear view mirrors, and I think it would be better if I could watch what you are doing. It will be fine, though. We are just heading to the coast right now, and then heading north. You are maintaining your height well at the moment, and you will slowly become familiar with where the horizon is in your view."

Shannon took a deep breath and let it out slowly. Her anxiety lessened. "Okay."

A moment passed where the two women said nothing. Shannon looked around and was surprised by the world she could see around her. To her left and right she could see for miles. Most areas around her looked barren, except for the debris that littered the landscape, and the peaks of brown hills and mountains where the debris had struggled to stick. However, she did see small patches of green that she had not expected. She was also high enough up that she could see the ocean in the distance, through a thin haze obscuring the details of the water.

"How high up are we right now?" asked Shannon.

"I would guess we are cruising around two thousand feet," responded Brenda.

"Are we going to stay at this height, or does the plane fly faster at higher altitudes?"

"We likely could fly a little higher and see very small gains from the thinner and colder air, but I don't know if it would be worth the extra trouble."

"It just now occurred to me that this plane is not even remotely pressurized," said Shannon. "How high can we fly without that?"

"We could fly as high as twelve thousand feet without supplemental oxygen, though we will never get that high in these things."

Shannon blew a sigh of relief as her plane, after many bumps and a lot of wobbling, came to a complete stop. The sun hung low in the west as night quickly approached. She yawned hard as she eagerly exited her plane and prepared to setup camp. Despite having landed and taken off several times throughout the day, she was not entirely comfortable flying yet, and was relieved to have a long break from it. She gathered supplies quickly to build a fire before all of the sunlight was gone.

"Grab extra wood for the fire," said Brenda. "It will likely be noticeably colder tonight because of how much farther north we are."

Brenda made a large fire as Shannon gathered extra wood. The fire served as Shannon's only light as she continued to work after the sun had set. They continued to set up their camp for several minutes before quietly settling down and eating food they had packed.

"How are you doing?" asked Brenda, breaking their silence. She sat with her long slender legs crossed. Her food rested on her lap.

"I'm doing fine. I got used to flying after a while. There were times when I forgot about everything and was just excited for the new experience, though I'm glad to be on the ground for a bit." She held up her hands in the light of the fire. Shadows danced over the delicate skin of her hands. Even through the chaotic illumination of the fire, she could see her hands still shaking from the vibrations of the plane.

Brenda ate more of her food before speaking again. "I know you are very particular about planning everything. It must be tough for you right now since we don't know a lot of details about what we are going to do."

"My biggest concern," responded Shannon, "is not the parts I don't know, but the parts I do."

"How so?"

"When we get closer, we are going to have to make contact with the land demons again so we can pin-point the location of the nest. Considering how the last time went, I'm not too thrilled to try that again. We also need to do more testing next time. We need to know if you have visions when touching them. We need to figure out how long they are free from mind control after we remove the magnets. We need to understand what the creatures are like that we are dealing with. And we will have to find a way to trap one. I can't know for sure how long my ability to sense the location of a nest will last. If we can trap one of the animals so I can regularly make contact, then our chances of success will be higher."

Brenda nodded. "When the time comes, we will not move forward with that part of the plan until we are both completely satisfied with our preparations. Telling you everything will be fine obviously won't make you feel better, and wouldn't be honest since it is not entirely within our control. But I can tell you that we will try our hardest, and plan thoroughly before executing. I have confidence in our ability to succeed."

"Fortunately, we have a few more days of flying. That gives me plenty of time to iron out the details in my mind." Shannon cracked a disingenuous smile to show Brenda that she was okay.

Brenda returned the smile and quietly finished her food.

The two laid out their sleeping bags and climbed in without any more conversation. Though she was heavily inflicted with mental exhaustion from flying all day, Shannon had not moved much, and her body refused to sleep for a while. She gazed at the stars and listened to the comforting crackle of the fire for some time before finally drifting into a deep sleep.

Chapter 7

Shannon found herself deep underwater. She was cold to her bones. She could only see three feet ahead of her, as far as the headlamp she wore could pierce through the water. Her vision went just far enough to see the land demons that were next to her. There was one under each of her hands as they carried her downward. In the dim light she could just make out collars around their necks.

Shannon struggled to look around. She wondered how many land demons may have been hidden in the darkness that surrounded her. She felt disoriented and her lungs were beginning to burn.

No. They aren't taking me down. They are taking me up.

Shannon started thinking that she was likely having a vision. As if peering into a window, she lacked the omniscience she associated with dreaming. While a dream often made perfect sense while dreaming, she was completely confused about the events that were unfolding. She also lacked the ability to move or change her situation in any meaningful way. She was stuck observing.

Shannon held onto the land demons, her arms slung over their shoulders. They swam with fierce strength, a perfect unison of movements between their powerful arms and odd behinds. She was beginning to wonder how much longer she could hold her breath. As her lungs began to ache with the last fleeting pangs that indicated that she would soon suck in water involuntarily, her grip weakened. Before she had a chance to lose her grip, another creature swam up beneath her feet and pushed her ever upward toward the surface of the water.

The water remained black as she climbed, refusing to reveal her progress. Just as Shannon was convinced she could hold her breath no longer, and would be forced to inhale water, she breached the surface with such force that she flew into the air. She gasped urgently before crashing back into the water.

Shannon trod water as she looked around desperately for any sign of rescue, but the dim light of the stars above were of no help. Suddenly, there was a tug on her leg and she was yanked into the dark depths below.

Shannon woke, her heart pounding as it raced in her chest. *Another vision,* she thought to herself. *And the land demons were helping me.* Her mind swirled with ideas of how she had gotten into the situation in her vision, and how she had gotten out of it. *If* she got out of it. She eventually conceded to the fact that she couldn't know more details without another vision, or simply living it. Through long lingering distress, she eventually went back to sleep.

Chapter 8

Shannon tugged on her headband, which currently hung around her neck uncomfortably. She had worn it that way for several hours to test how close the magnets needed to be to her brain to interfere. So far she felt no intrusions, and the land demons had not yet found them. She adjusted in her seat. She had remained in her plane while it was parked on the ground as she did her test. She wanted to make sure she could make a quick getaway, if land demons were to attack at some point.

"It would appear that the collars will work just fine," said Brenda from behind her gun as she noticed Shannon's uncomfortable adjustments to her collar. She lay a distance away, her eyes only taking brief glances away from the water to check on Shannon.

"I think you're right, which is good, because I don't think the headbands would have stayed on them well. This also makes our lives easier and more comfortable." Shannon spoke through her radio from inside her plane. She then removed her headband completely.

"Are you sure you want to be the bait again?" asked Brenda. "We can trade places."

"We both know you are the better shot. Plus, I had a vision of things to come, and I was still around. So I feel pretty safe."

"Not that I doubt the sincerity of what you are saying, but how do we know—if you are in fact having visions—that the aliens aren't having them as well, and predicting your moves?"

"I can't explain what is happening to me, and it is entirely possible that I'm wrong, but it wasn't like any dream I've ever had before. I also think that the aliens either don't have visions at all or don't have control over them, just like me. If they could control seeing the future then I think they would have caught us by now, and that the magnet headbands would not be nearly as effective."

Brenda shrugged. "As long as you're comfortable with your decision, I will back you on it."

"Just use the net gun first to capture one. Once you have one caught, I will start up my plane and fly away. If we are lucky, I can fly off before you have to kill one to protect me. You'll stay clear of the action and hopefully go unnoticed by the land demons during all of the commotion."

Just as Shannon was talking she felt a twinge in the back of her mind.

"They know I'm here," said Shannon, more ominously than she had intended. She relegated the presence to the back of her mind with ease, but tried to remain alert. She sat patiently and waited for any sign of approaching land demons.

She examined the water that was a hundred yards away. A cold breeze would occasionally blow in from the ocean that would force Shannon to huddle in her blankets more. They had flown north for five days, and had gone far enough that there was now snow that covered the ground by several inches. While it did make landing and taking off in the planes more difficult, it was only a minor concern because of their low speed.

Eight hours had passed since Shannon had removed her headband entirely, and there was still no sign of land demons. Her initial anxiousness had worn away into boredom. Watching the nearby water move rhythmically with soothing sounds, and no indication of danger became a painful exercise as it attempted to lull her to sleep. She fought to keep her eyes open. Every time her head would momentarily drop as she started to fall asleep, she would shake her head, wiggle her legs, and talk to herself. Her attempts to stay vigilant for the past few hours had left her increasingly exhausted. As the sun shined dully in the west as it became evening, she closed her eyes against her will and fell asleep.

Lincoln stood next to Shannon's plane and spoke loudly so she would hear him and wake up.

"What are you doing here?" he asked with a slightly harsh tone.

He stood with a posture and expression of disappointment. Shannon lazily opened her eyes and turned to face him. His demeanor was not something that she had ever seen from him before. It both hurt her to see it, and helped her realize that it wasn't really him. Her mind went to his question. Before she had a chance to steady her thoughts from the alien's prying that she knew it was doing, she thought about her attempt to find a nest.

Lincoln laughed before she had a chance to speak. "You found a way to hide from them. That is very impressive. After the way you killed the creatures they sent to investigate you the last time you reappeared, it should be no surprise that they didn't show up this time. Had they known that you simply wanted to capture one of the land demons, they would have helped you."

"Why?" Shannon asked doubtfully.

"They would love nothing more than another chance to unite," answered Lincoln. "As a sign that they are willing to work with you..." Lincoln gestured to the water in the distance as a land demon sprang out of the water and slowly made its way toward her. "They will give you one without contest."

Shannon watched for a moment as the beast continued forward, walking with its arms.

"Just remember—"

Lincoln was cut off before he could continue. Shannon felt an explosive pain in her head and her vision shot completely white and filled with stars. An instant of agony.

49

"I don't know if it was dumb luck, or what, but I bagged one that just jumped up here by itself," said Brenda enthusiastically as she adjusted Shannon's headband.

Shannon struggled to wake herself. She shook her head and wanted to speak, but her mind was still split between the dream she had and the reality she was processing. Her ears rung from the pain of her sudden awakening and escape from the alien's intrusion. "They gave it to us," she finally got out.

"What do you mean?" Brenda asked, her excitement tempered.

"I mean," said Shannon with frustration. "They visited while I was accidentally sleeping and read my mind. They figured out that we were trying to capture one so we could find a nest, and somehow use them to get to the aliens."

"So..." began Brenda.

"When they realized what we were doing, they gave us that thing for you to capture," said Shannon.

"While it does seem a bit defeating that they are so not threatened by us that they are willing to help us, I have to ask, how are we going to do it?"

Shannon thought for a moment. "I have no idea."

"For once I'm happy that we don't have a solid plan," said Brenda with a smile. "How much information could they have really gathered from you when you don't even know what you're doing?"

Shannon considered Brenda's argument. A tired grin grew on her face. "I guess you're right. Knowing that we are trying to use the animals to our advantage is like knowing that an army is going to use guns. That won't tell them where, when, or how we will actually attack."

"And if they are willing to help us, then they hopefully don't take us seriously enough to fortify against us," added Brenda.

"You don't think this changes things?"

"Of course it does," responded Brenda cheerfully. "We now know what they think they know, which can easily become misinformation. We can now misdirect them and play against their expectations. The key is that we can't tip our hands again. Right now we are early enough in all of this that we have options for changing things. Farther down the road, and it could be impossible to recover if they learn our plans. Now, let's figure out what to do with our gift."

Shannon climbed out of her plane and walked to the animal as it lay still under the net that Brenda had shot at it. The creature watched her intently as she approached and she could sense the aliens watching her through its eyes. She hid her hand that held the collar of magnets behind her back. Some details she didn't know if they had learned from her dream or not, but she wanted to keep as much of her actions a mystery to them as possible. She leaned down over the beast and met its gaze. As the two locked eyes, she moved her hand just out of view of the animal's head. It lurched forward as the magnets forced the presence of the controlling alien out. The animal jerked around in a panic, as it came to. Its head shot back and forth between Brenda and Shannon. Then it began to move around with growing urgency as its breathing quickened. Knowing of nothing else to do, Shannon placed her hand on its head.

In an instant, she was swimming under the water and attacking fish with other land demons. Shannon was living through a memory from the land demon, and while each moment felt real to her—the feeling of the water, the sweet and refreshing taste of the fish—she knew that it was not her memory. She also felt a strange power, that she could control where she was in its memories while touching it. Swimming in the water had been mere minutes earlier, before the aliens had taken control of the beast. She could tell when it had been under the control of the aliens because its memory was fragmented. Their possession of the land demon left gaps.

Her connection with the creature created layers in her mind and an awareness she could never have known before. She felt its past as though she were living through it, but could also observe it objectively. Simultaneously, she could feel and identify the creature's current state. With a naturalness akin to intuition, she moved back through its memory in search of the nest that she hoped it had interacted with.

While probing the memory of the land demon, Shannon could sense its tension and stress. She soothed it the best she could with her thoughts. Speaking to it not with words, but with energy. The stress of the animal lessened with Shannon's effort.

Finally, Shannon found the nest she had been hoping for. Her sense of location was heightened by her connection with the beast, and she immediately knew the nest's location. However, she didn't seem to have the ability to know where others were, and she got the distinct feeling that she only knew the location of the nest because this one had been there.

Shannon removed her hand from the beast and was brought back to her own vision. Unlike before the connection, it now lay still and calmly watched Shannon. She carefully placed the magnetic collar around its neck and it did not resist.

"I'm not sure what you did, but I saw it become calm as you touched it," said Brenda. She examined the creature closely. "He almost looks tamed."

"Why don't you give him a touch and see what happens?"

Brenda took a deep breath and let out a sigh. She leaned over and tentatively reached out her hand. Her stare became vacant as she held her hand on the animal. A moment passed, and then she removed her hand and furrowed her brow.

"What did you see?" asked Shannon.

"All I saw was you, right now," answered Brenda. "I could see you through his eyes, but as far as I could tell, it was only what he was seeing in that moment. What happened for you?"

"I had a glimpse of the ability that I think the aliens have," said Shannon. "I could control which memory of his I was viewing, and experience them as him. I could also sense his feelings at that moment and was able to calm him down."

"The aliens must have really done a number on your brain, because I think I just experienced a living periscope, and that's it." Brenda looked at the now docile animal. "Now what do we do with him?"

"I would hate to hurt him if we did somehow happen to tame him just now. I also don't think removing the magnets is an option if we are trying to keep our actions a secret. I say you get a distance away and set your sights on him. I will let him out, and if he starts to go wild you can do what you need to. Though, hopefully he will just run away."

Brenda nodded and quickly moved fifty feet away before crouching and aiming her gun. She nodded again to Shannon when she was ready.

Shannon carefully removed the netting from the land demon while attempting to not block Brenda's aim. When Shannon had fully removed the net, the animal sat up and continued watching Shannon. It did not run away as she had hoped, but instead watched her, showing no intentions of leaving.

"Well," said Shannon, awkwardly. "I guess we can just leave now so the aliens won't know where we are anymore."

Shannon backed away from the animal slowly as she made her way to her plane. The beast continued to sit where it was, leaving its attention on her. She finally turned away so she could climb into her plane. After getting into her seat, she saw it still not moving. When she had entered her plane safely, Brenda finally lowered her gun and quickly walked to her own plane.

"Do you think we broke him?" asked Brenda over the radio.

"I have no idea," responded Shannon as she started up her plane. "If they can't survive without the aliens controlling them, then they are in trouble either way."

Shannon found her gaze fixed on the land demon as her plane lurched forward. The plane picked up speed, all the while the animal followed its movement with its head. Just as Shannon's plane lifted off the ground, the land demon burst into a full sprint and dove into the water. Its movements were so sudden that Shannon gasped.

"Hopefully that means he'll be okay," said Brenda.

For several hours they flew. Shannon spoke very little as she thought about her interactions with the land demon. They eventually landed for the evening and set up camp. Shannon remained deep in thought as they ate around the fire they had created. Though everything was covered in snow, they were still able to find wood in the piles of debris nearby for their fire. She bundled herself in blankets to stave off the increasingly cold weather as she sat on her sleeping bag.

"I've been thinking," said Shannon. "Both times that I touched a land demon with the magnets, it turned into a completely different animal. Each time they seemed to become scared and appeared to want to retreat. I think they are only dangerous when they are possessed, so I think we should give them a proper name, something more appropriate."

"Like what?" asked Brenda.

Shannon shrugged. "Something that doesn't sound so superstitious." She fell silent as she struggled to think of a name. Her hand ran over the magnets around her neck, the same kind of magnets that now hung around the animal's neck. "How about Collara?"

Brenda frowned as she pondered the word. "Collara, collara," she repeated as she mulled it over. "That works for me."

The two spoke only a little before climbing into their sleeping bags and falling asleep.

Shannon tossed and turned as she slept, too excited from the day's events. Her dreams were chaotic yet unmemorable. She was asleep for no more than an hour when something warm blew on her face and woke her. A shadowy figure leaned over her and panic left her frozen as her eyes struggled to adjust and see what was towering over her.

A collara!

Before she had a chance to react, she noticed a glint around its neck.

The collara from earlier today followed me here.

She carefully sat up. The animal stepped back just enough to allow her to do so.

"Brenda!" whispered Shannon harshly.

"What?" she asked groggily, without rolling over or opening her eyes.

Shannon watched the light of the dimly lit fire dance across the collara's face, casting harsh shadows. Its expression was indistinguishable. "We have a visitor," she said calmly. Shannon heard Brenda roll over. "It's the same one from earlier today."

"How did it follow us?" asked Brenda. Her voice was instantly clear and awake. "Do you think it can swim fast enough to keep up with us?"

"There's only one way to find out." Shannon reached out her hand and placed it gently on the collara's head.

She traveled backwards through the animal's memory. It was intact from when they had seen the collara last until now. Besides the occasional break to eat, there was no indication that the animal had done anything other than swim. Yet, as Shannon experienced the surge of water around her as she swam through the cold ocean, she felt a sense of herself elsewhere, and a desire to find herself. She removed her hand.

Shannon reflected on what she had experienced, pausing for a while before talking. "I think," she said hesitantly as she processed her thoughts, "that he could sense where I was and followed me. I don't think he followed our planes by sight, though, because he never left the water, or looked up to see where we were."

"So he can just *sense* where you are," said Brenda to herself. "For now, let's pretend that sufficiently explains the how. But, why?"

"All I could tell was that he felt a compulsion to follow me. There was no reasoning that I could deduce."

"Hmm," responded Brenda. "So, I guess I was right. You tamed him, and now he follows you because you're the new pack leader."

"If that's the case, then recruiting an army may be easier than I had anticipated."

"Don't get ahead of yourself," interjected Brenda. "You still have to learn how to tell him what to do."

"True, and now is not the time to do that. Hopefully he will get the hint and get some sleep. If not, then I guess he will be our guard dog, of sorts."

Chapter 9

Shannon awoke to the sound of Brenda rummaging through her bag for breakfast. Brenda had started the fire up again, and waves of heat hit Shannon in between the icy gusts of ocean air. She looked around and saw no sign of the collara.

"Did you see where he went?" asked Shannon.

"No. He's been gone for as long as I've been awake."

As if on cue, the collara jumped out of the water and came bounding toward Shannon. Though recent events told her not to be afraid, she felt a rush of fear as the animal approached quickly. It stopped just short of barreling into Shannon, and stood strong with its chest puffed out proudly.

"He seems like he is waiting for a command," observed Brenda.

Unsure of any other method of communication, Shannon reached out her hand. She touched the collara and thought about laying down. She removed her hand and found it still in a strong stance.

"What did you just do?" asked Brenda.

"I think I just told him to lay down."

"He doesn't seem like the 'lay down, roll over' type," said Brenda. "Dog, he is not."

Shannon thought for a moment, and then reached out her hand again. She thought about how hungry she was, since she had not yet eaten. She released her hand.

Immediately the collara turned around, and quickly made its way to the water. Without hesitation it leaped into the air, gracefully diving into the water and out of view.

"What did you do this time?" asked Brenda in astonishment.

"Rather than telling it what to do, I thought about how hungry I was," responded Shannon.

"I'm not sure I understand how that worked. What made you think to do that?"

"When I had viewed his memories before, I got a strong sense of this desire, or compulsion, to follow me. It was this feeling of desire that drove him to follow us. A feeling of instinct, in this case to follow the pack leader, was what he felt. I imagine it is a similar compulsion that people who struggle with addiction feel. So I tried to emulate that the best I could. At the moment, the most pure desire I felt was hunger since I just woke up."

"In a day you figured out how to traverse through their memories and give them commands, assuming he comes back," said Brenda. "What originally seemed like an impossible task suddenly seems far more approachable. There are still a million things to figure out, but you've made amazing progress."

"I'm okay with things going our way for once," she responded as she reached for a protein bar from her bag. Before she had a chance to eat it, the collara returned with a large fish in its mouth.

Brenda gave a look of complete disbelief. "Wow. He did that in no time. Too bad you probably can't eat that. Who knows what kind of alien bacteria he may have in his mouth that our bodies would freak out about."

The collara ran to Shannon and dropped the fish near her feet.

"If I'm to believe my visions, then I know it won't kill me," said Shannon.

"Your vision may have shown you still alive, but that doesn't mean that sharing their bacteria wouldn't put you on bed rest for a month, or give you diarrhea for a week."

"If we are building an army of these guys and training them, I think it is only a matter of time before we would get contaminated. If they have something our bodies can't handle, we'll find out eventually. Not to mention the time and energy we would save if we could have them do our fishing for us."

Shannon picked up the fish and took a knife from her bag. She cut the fish in half and threw half back toward the collara. The animal pounced on the fish and ate it greedily, its teeth chomping loudly.

"It's better that we find out now, rather than during a time-sensitive moment in our mission. Plus, I'm tired of protein bars." Shannon picked up some wood and placed it on the fire.

"Fine," conceded Brenda. "Just you will eat it, and I will take care of you if you get sick. Please make sure to at least cook the hell out of it first."

Shannon nodded. She skewered the fish and held it over the fire for several minutes. When the fish looked thoroughly cooked, she pulled out her knife and cut out slices to eat. It was a relief to eat something different from her routine. Brenda watched her intently as she ate.

"Let's wait for a little while and see what happens," said Brenda.

"How long do you want to wait before you think it's okay?"

"We can wait an hour before we travel. That will at least prove that there is not an immediate reaction. If five hours go by and you aren't sick, then I will believe it doesn't give you food poisoning. After two days go by, I will entertain the idea that you aren't going to die. Of course, you cooked it, which could have killed off anything dangerous. If that collara licks your face like a dog and you don't die, then I'll really know they are safe."

"Alright," said Shannon with a mild groan. "This is at least a start. Cooking it may change things, but at the moment, that is all we need from them. If they are gathering food for us, then our lives will be significantly easier and more productive."

An hour passed quickly and Shannon felt no different than when the hour had started. Momentarily satisfied, Brenda agreed to continue on with their journey. Just as last time, when Shannon's plane began lifting into the air, the collara ran into the water and disappeared.

The two women flew their planes in silence. With all they had been through, it was easy for them to get lost in their thoughts, and they often did. Shannon thought of her dad and it brought a familiar pain to her chest. She heard a click of static as she activated her radio.

"How long ago did you lose your husband?" Shannon realized how blunt her question was after she asked it, but did not apologize.

"Seven years ago," responded Brenda. Her voice was calm and unflinching to Shannon's sudden question.

"Do you still think of him often?"

"Every day when I wake up and he isn't there. Every dinner I eat and I don't have him to talk to. Every night when I go to sleep alone."

"Does it at least hurt less now than it used to?"

"Yes and no," replied Brenda. "I've become immune to the every day pain that I used to feel, but if I dwell on it, it hurts like it was yesterday. Plus the occasional feeling of guilt over the fact that it doesn't hurt like it used to."

Brenda fell silent.

"I know it's not the same for me," said Shannon. "We grow up knowing that our parents are going to die some day. Barring some tragedy befalling us, there will more than likely be a time in our lives when we live without our parents around. Sure, I've heard of women that live into their hundreds, and outlive their children who simply die of old age, but you don't expect that." Shannon paused. "I wasn't ready yet."

"The second parent is always the hardest," added Brenda. "I remember the feeling when my mom died. It was years after my dad had passed. I felt pretty alone. I also felt like everyone was now looking to me to die next. There was no one from the older generation left to expect to die first. I was the oldest generation now."

"That's definitely part of it, but there is something much more for me. My mom died while I was still young, but my dad became my hero. He did his best to cover the gap that my mom left behind, and I really depended on him during that time to help me get through it. I hadn't given that up yet. He was still my hero."

"Don't worry," said Brenda in a comforting voice. "That will never change."

In an effort to get Shannon's mind on other things, Brenda changed the subject. "It's been over four hours. How is your stomach feeling? Are you sick yet?"

"Nothing yet," answered Shannon. "I'll try it a couple more times by myself just to play it safe, but I'm beginning to think it will be okay."

"That's good to know. So, we should be able to use them to help us gather fish, which is absolutely a boost for us, but that still doesn't help us much with the problem we are currently facing. Any new ideas about how we are going to use the collara to attack the aliens?"

"So far, what I know is that we need to gather the collara and train them to listen to our commands. We need to get to one of the islands around Hawaii. I had a vision at one point which had some sort of a submarine. Hopefully we can figure that one out on the island we get to, since I can't imagine it coming from somewhere else. Once we get in closer proximity to the aliens, we can use the collara to do reconnaissance. Once we can pinpoint their location, we will probably have a better idea of whether or not we can use the collara during the attack or not. I don't have the ability to see the whole picture at this moment, but I have a rather clear path to follow. I'll just have to take it one step at a time."

"My guess is that the collara that is currently following us views you as a pack leader," added Brenda. "If that is the case, then I bet he will defend you, even if you can't figure out how to command him to attack when you want."

"Yeah, and, if nothing else, the more of them we have on our side, the less the aliens have access to."

Shannon removed her hand from the collara. "We only have two more miles to go until we reach the nest."

"We have to bunker down," responded Brenda. "We don't have a choice. The storm is too strong."

Brenda finished tying down the airplanes as Shannon entered the tent that she had assembled. Her hands were bitterly cold from digging through two feet of snow to properly secure the tent. She rubbed them together before grabbing her hand warmer. Several minutes passed before Brenda entered. She gave a slight shiver and then removed her jacket and shoes so she could dust off the snow they had collected.

"It's going to drive me nuts if this storm lasts for a while when we are so close to the nest," said Shannon with mild frustration.

"We've worked this hard and traveled this far; a little longer of a wait won't change anything," responded Brenda calmly. "Plus, with your collara retrieving food for us, and our ability to melt the snow for water, we can survive for a while. I wouldn't mind the rest, even if it is forced."

"It's funny," began Shannon. "When I was in the bunker, all I could do was worry about how I was going to survive and start a new life. It seemed like such a daunting task. Now, all I do is wish that the aliens could somehow be dealt with and done so I can get on with life and settle down. It seems like it would be such a treat to only have food and shelter to worry about."

"The joy of having perspective," said Brenda as she cracked a smile.

Chapter 10

The snowstorm raged for several days. Shannon remained in her sleeping bag most of the time to stay warm and to conserve the energy of the heaters they had. She sent the collara to get fish several times a day. She had attempted to send the animal to the nest to either confirm its current status or to retrieve eggs, but the animal was unresponsive to her request. She was struggling to find a way to give it commands other than fetching food.

"I honestly get the sense that he just doesn't want to do what I'm asking of him," said Shannon in frustration.

Brenda shrugged. "Maybe collara are like wolves. It could take a few generations to domesticate them. Or maybe if we raise them from birth, they will be more inclined to obey."

"I've had a vision of them rescuing me, so I don't doubt their importance. I just have to figure out how to get from this point to that one."

"Maybe you can't teach old collara new tricks."

Shannon threw up her hands in defeat. "I guess not."

"Fortunately, I think the weather is lessening, and we should be able to hike to the nest tomorrow morning."

"You don't want to fly the rest of the way?" asked Shannon.

"There is too much fresh snow to take off or land on the ground, so anything we do will have to be by water, but the water has been too choppy to feel comfortable landing on it safely. If we are going to fly again, I am going to want it to be away from this weather."

Shannon shrugged. "I guess a couple miles, even in this weather, won't be that bad on foot."

Brenda nodded and crossed her fingers.

"So," began Shannon with excitement. "I was trying to see how far back the collara's memories go, and I was actually able to see pretty much everything. All the way back to when it hatched."

"You said before that there were no memories when it was possessed by the aliens?" asked Brenda.

"Yes."

"Were there a lot of memories to sift through to get to the beginning, or did the aliens control him most of the time?"

"There were definitely large gaps, but this collara at least, had control during mundane life events like eating, and sleeping."

"Interesting," said Brenda. "I apologize for taking you off topic. What were you trying to say?"

"I was able to figure out the life cycle of the collara after they are born." Shannon's face lit up with enthusiasm. "They are a weird amalgamation of earth animals. But before getting into the details, I wanted to say that this plan is totally possible. I was originally worried that I would have no idea what to do with the eggs after they hatched."

"Me too," added Brenda. "Though, winging it has gotten us this far, so I wasn't going to panic about it."

"As it turns out, when they are babies, they are fed just like birds. An adult collara will throw up into the babies' mouths. What's interesting though, is that they don't follow any form of parental structure. Any female adult will feed any child that is in need. Oh, and our collara is female, not male."

Brenda gave an exaggerated expression of surprise and then grinned. "So we just steal some eggs and tell Gwen to sit on them until they hatch. And she will just choose to feed them after that?"

"Gwen?" asked Shannon, momentarily lost.

"It was the first name that came to mind for our collara friend. *Collarian* friend?"

Shannon gave a look of irritation as she pondered the question. "Collarian," she said with a nod. "*Anyway*, we don't need *Gwen*," she rolled her eyes as she said the name, "to sit on the eggs. They will hatch and the baby collara will make their way toward the water, just like sea turtles. This is where Gwen will hopefully play a role. The adults will return to the water near the nest around the expected time of hatching and will wait for the babies to eventually enter the water. The adults will then catch the babies and place them on the adult's back where they will hold on for as long as they are in the water, similar to koalas. From what I saw, it appears that a single adult will at times carry up to six babies on her back."

Brenda gave a large smile and shook her head. "Your research really paid off. We have more answers than I even knew I wanted. We know we should grab six eggs; we know what they will do when they are first born; and with any luck, we will have Gwen take care of them while they grow up."

The snow crunched loudly under each step. Nearly an hour had passed since they had started walking, and Shannon's legs were burning from how high she had to step to walk over the snow. According to Gwen's memories, they should have been where her nest was, but all Shannon could see was fresh snow.

"This should be the area," said Shannon, "but it's not obvious where a nest would be." The mounds of snow she had seen in the collara's memories were long gone. The snow was deep and smooth.

"I guess we should start digging through the snow," responded Brenda. "Just make sure you don't accidentally step on an egg."

Shannon dropped to her knees and began sweeping her hand under the snow. Snow piled around her, working its way through her clothes until it was falling down her neck and working its way up her sleeves. The two searched for nearly thirty minutes in complete silence before Brenda called out with a holler as she found a nest. Almost immediately after Brenda's discovery, Shannon found a nest of her own.

The eggs were as large as an ostrich's egg and were very heavy. They wobbled in Shannon's hands as she examined them. She got an odd sense when holding the eggs, as though the telepathy the animals possessed was stronger in the infants. She could sense that it would not be much longer before they hatched. She looked around cautiously as she picked up three eggs. Brenda did the same. When they had secured the eggs safely in their backpacks, they gave each other a nod and began heading back.

The return seemed much quicker to Shannon. She wondered if it was her excitement of finally feeling as though she had made progress, or if it was her fear of getting caught by the collara, that spurred her on with haste. When she had returned to camp, she made a nest in the snow near their tent and buried the eggs.

"Do you feel anything weird when you hold the eggs?" asked Shannon.

"No. Do you?"

"Yes. I can tell when they are going to hatch."

"How long do we have to wait?"

"If I'm properly understanding what I'm feeling, then I would say three days."

"Great," responded Brenda. "That will give us time to fly south and escape this freezing weather."

"I hadn't thought about that, but I guess you're right. We don't really have what we need to be able to stay here much longer."

"We sure don't," agreed Brenda. "In fact, I will prep the planes so they are properly charged before we leave tomorrow morning."

Brenda promptly left the tent and began cleaning the snow off of the planes and expanding their wings so they could properly absorb sunlight. Tomorrow would begin their journey south.

Chapter 11

"They are going to hatch any minute," said Shannon.

She watched intently. Her eyes were wide, unwilling to miss any details.

Brenda laid down a pile of sticks and debris she had been collecting, since they were unsure of how long they would be staying in this location as they raised the baby collara. She walked over and watched, clearly not as invested as Shannon, but still intrigued.

"Are they all going to hatch at the same time?" asked Brenda.

"Not exactly, I don't think, though they must be in sync with each other a bit, nonetheless. I don't know if it's some telepathic thing, or if the eggs are producing a chemical that would let the other eggs know what is going on. Somehow, though, they do seem to be on the same schedule."

A couple minutes passed and the eggs began to wobble. Slowly, the chaotic movements transitioned into an almost rhythmic rocking until a faint cracking sound could be heard as the first egg began to splinter. Shannon fought the urge to move in too closely as the first egg continued to break open. Finally, a small hand broke through the shell and revealed the small collara that was inside. It was covered in down that was white and made the baby collara much cuter than its adult form. It moved silently as it emerged from its shell. Shannon guessed that it was quiet to avoid the attention of predators. Tumbling out of the egg, it weakly tested out its arms, working to coordinate the limbs into a fluid walking motion.

As the little creature began to feebly climb over the other eggs to get to the ocean, Shannon reached out her hand to attempt to imprint herself on the animal. She could sense the energy of the animal before her hand even made contact. The second she touched it, her vision was washed away into darkness. The only moment she could see was from inside the egg and faint blobs of light that fought to penetrate the surface of the egg. She did her best to feel calm and to soothe the collara. Unlike with the adult, Shannon could feel herself less while touching the baby. She struggled to remove herself, but was unable to move. Suddenly, she was pulled from the black void she had been consumed by and collapsed to the ground that she sat on. She looked up to see Brenda holding the collara in a blanket. A look of concern on her face.

"You were unresponsive for a moment," said Brenda. "Are you okay?"

"Yes," answered Shannon, quickly shaking the alarming feeling of having her consciousness trapped. "They are like scorpions. The mental connection is much more potent when they are young. I can't really feel or sense myself when I am connected to them." She took deep breaths to try and tame her raised heart rate.

"That sounds dangerous."

"I think it is okay. I also think this has to happen so that they will build a bond with us. However, I will need you to physically remove them from me a few seconds after I touch them."

Brenda had grown confident in Shannon's judgment, and had become impressed by Shannon's uncanny ability to be successful. Though she kept having a lingering feeling that their luck may run out soon, she nodded, reluctantly.

One by one Shannon connected with each collara, and each time Brenda would rescue her from the bondage she had placed herself in. By the sixth one, Shannon felt weak and drained, her nerves fried from the uncontrollable tension that her entrapment caused. Brenda had released each collara before picking up the next and held onto the last one as she looked at Shannon to make sure she was okay.

"Are you going to be alright?"

"Yeah," answered Shannon. "I might have a headache for a while and need some water, but I'm sure I will be okay."

"I sure hope Gwen is in the water receiving these little guys as they jump in."

"Yeah, I have no interest in doing this again any time soon if it didn't work this time."

As if to answer their question, Gwen burst out of the water and charged toward them. Unsure of her intent, Brenda and Shannon froze, surprised by her behavior. Gwen reached Brenda and gave a loud, coarse bark before snatching the remaining infant from her arms in a swift and sudden movement. She placed the last baby collara onto her back with the others, and then carefully made her way back into the water. She climbed into the water slowly—unlike her usual dive into the frigid ocean water—carefully ensuring that she did not lose any of her precious cargo. Brenda looked at Shannon, stunned.

"At least we know she has all of the babies," said Shannon.

Brenda nodded. "So, what now?"

Shannon scratched her head, still looking in the direction where Gwen had last been. "I guess we just wait here and hope they come back."

Brenda returned to camp with four freshly caught fish slung over her shoulder. Shannon quickly prepared them for cooking and placed them over the waiting fire. The aroma of fish filled the air.

"All this fishing reminds me," began Brenda, "not that I haven't enjoyed the rest, but it's been eight days since the collara hatched, and we haven't seen anything from them since." She delivered the statement as mere observation. Her expression was neutral, hiding any concerns she might have had about their current attempt to raise collara having failed.

Shannon's expression was one of exhaustion and disappointment. She knew that they both thought about the collara throughout the day, and as casually as Brenda attempted to deliver her comment, it spoke of a growing concern they both had that they had made a mistake.

Shannon chose to be direct so Brenda didn't have to. "How much longer do you want to wait before we start heading south again? I know we can't wait much longer, since winter seems to be growing rapidly."

"Is it possible that they haven't returned because they have already begun migrating south?"

"Unfortunately, I didn't do enough research when I had access to Gwen's memories to know. I was so focused on finding the nest and how to take care of the baby collara that I didn't pay attention to any form of migration pattern. Plus, who knows how my actions may have interfered with what they would have usually done?" Shannon sighed with defeat. "As much as I'm afraid that they may come back here just after we leave, I don't think we should stay here any longer. They obviously move south eventually, and I have no idea how long they keep their down after they are born so they may retreat to warmer weather immediately."

Brenda nodded in agreement. "If we are to believe in your visions, then we should assume that things work out somehow. So, the best option, I think, is to make our way south and start figuring out how we get to Hawaii. Anyway, you had previously described with Gwen that she just had a sense for where you were, so I'm sure they will know how to find you once they decide they are ready for that."

Relieved by Brenda's willingness to accept her vision without questioning her sanity, Shannon was happy to follow along with Brenda's plan.

After three days of flying, Shannon and Brenda had flown as far south as they could to be closest to Hawaii. Though Shannon preferred the sparkling white snow to the brown and muddy dirt, the snow had lessened as they traveled south until it eventually disappeared. The warmer climate was, however, a welcomed change for Shannon.

Brenda stared out at the ocean after quickly setting up camp. Their routine was so ingrained within each of them that they rarely communicated while they arranged their camp, and they consistently got the camp setup faster each time.

"Even if we do make contact with the collara again, are we sure we want to fly to Hawaii?" asked Brenda. "It's going to be a grueling trip."

"I'm open to suggestions, if you have any better ideas. It just seems like we need to be in close proximity to the aliens if we want to be able to attack them."

Brenda continued looking out at the endless water before her, imagining the trip they were considering. "You're not wrong. It's just going to be at least a six day flight, and unlike the trip we just took, we won't have the luxury of getting out and stretching our legs whenever we want."

"I'll admit that the logistics of going to the bathroom into the ocean without getting out of our planes does seem nearly impossible." Shannon gave an exaggerated shudder.

"I wish that were the worst part," replied Brenda, unresponsive to Shannon's humor. "My biggest fear is when we land the planes and need to sleep, but won't be able to throw down an anchor of any sort. At best we risk getting turned around a bit; at worst we could encounter bad weather and our planes could get washed away or crash into each other. Regardless of safety, we will have to tie our planes together when we sleep, because I'm terrified of the idea that our planes could drift out of sight of each other. You can just collara whisper up some directions and get to where you are going, but I would be on my own in the middle of the ocean. I would be screwed."

"You seem to be quite useful with your sextant. I mean, you were able to find our latitude rather easily, which will make flying west toward Hawaii easier. We also have our radios, so at no point will you of all people be helpless, but you're right, we don't want to get separated."

Shannon watched the final rays of the sun cast their warm, orange glow over the ocean as the sun disappeared beyond the horizon, bringing morning to a different part of the world.

"As urgent as all of this feels at times, there is no rush," said Shannon. "We'll hammer out these details before we ever consider leaving."

"I'm not too worried about it, but you're the one that stays up at night trying to figure everything out," responded Brenda. "Don't let this keep you from getting a good rest."

"For now, I still have something to keep me distracted. I'll make magnet collars for the collara while I wait for their return."

Shannon woke to the feeling of her ear being pulled. To her surprise she found herself surrounded by the baby collara. In the days that they had been gone, they had shed almost all of their down and grown nearly double in size. They barked a high pitched wheeze that Shannon knew would grow deeper and eventually be the bark she was familiar with, and snorted playfully as they bound around her.

It took her a moment to realize that she wasn't having any visions, despite the fact that the collara were touching her. She reached out her hand and gently touched one of the creatures and immediately was sucked into its world. She pulled her hand away, confused.

"Brenda, we have company."

Brenda opened her eyes slowly as she turned to look at Shannon. Her eyes shot open when she realized what she was seeing.

"Well, that's a relief," said Brenda. After a moment, she noticed that Shannon was touching the collara. "How are you touching them without me needing to pull them off of you? A few days ago I had to save you each time you came in contact with one of them."

"They've already learned how to control it, I guess," she answered. "It's crazy. When they touch me, nothing happens. When I touch them, I immediately connect with them, though I can get out of it on my own now."

"Do you think you could control it like they do?"

"With enough practice I probably could. I was able to figure out how to keep the aliens subjugated when they entered my mind. I can probably do this too."

Shannon placed her hand on one of the collara, her vision went blank, and then released her hand. She did this several times.

She shrugged. "I'll get it eventually." Shannon said, reassuringly.

"I'm sure you will. You just figure out how to tame them and put them to use, and I will get us ready to travel to Hawaii."

Chapter 12

Shannon watched as Brenda flew overhead. She was returning from her trip to the hangar that the planes had been stored in. In the past month that Shannon had been training the collara, Brenda had made several trips to the hangar to retrieve all of the tools and supplies she thought they would need to get to—and survive on—Hawaii. Brenda landed quickly. Her plane looked completely full of new supplies.

"Is that the last of it?" asked Shannon.

"Yes," said Brenda with a nod.

"Are we going to be able to carry everything you brought?" Shannon looked at the pile of supplies they had amassed skeptically.

"With the bags I have designated to carry things on the outside of the planes, I think so."

"And the planes can handle the weight?"

"I believe so," said Brenda as she examined her plane from a distance with a critical eye. "We will fly low to play it safe and will likely have to stop more often so the planes can recharge since we will be pushing them harder than normal, but it should be fine. Worst case scenario, we just drive the planes on the water and don't force them to carry the weight."

Shannon gave a worried look. "I definitely want to keep my distance from the water, especially while in something that makes so much noise, but at least you have a good backup plan."

"How are things coming with the collara?"

Shannon placed her hand on one of the nearby collara. "I think I've mastered touching them without making a connection."

"What's the secret?"

"I have to specifically be thinking about not connecting."

"How did you figure that out?"

"I had to work my way up to it. I started by touching them accidentally. If I was able to touch them without thinking about it at all, then I wouldn't link with them. It evolved into being able to choose to touch them, but simply refusing to connect by thinking about refusing the connection."

Brenda shrugged, acknowledging her limited understanding of the situation. "As long as it works."

"That's not even the best part," said Shannon with a smile. "Check this out." Shannon placed her hand on a collara and closed her eyes for a second. The collara quickly jumped into action and charged forward until it reached a small rock. It picked up the rock and returned it to Shannon.

"It may seem like I just taught him fetch, but it is more important than that."

"How so?" asked Brenda with genuine curiosity.

"With Gwen, the only things I could get her to retrieve were things that I could convey to her as an actual need. If I couldn't impress upon her a physical feeling like hunger or thirst, then she wasn't interested. With these new collara, I can actually communicate simple thoughts or directions to them and they seem to understand."

Shannon again placed her hand on the collara who had retrieved the rock. She closed her eyes for a second, and then the collara began to bark.

"So it can fetch and speak," said Brenda. "That is actually quite impressive. I don't know what exactly I was expecting, but in a lot of ways I wasn't really getting my hopes up."

Shannon lifted her hand and the collara stopped barking, picked up the rock the animal had given her, and threw it out into the ocean. As soon as the action was over, the collara returned its attention back to Shannon and seemed completely docile and happy.

Shannon gave a contented smile. "They may be simple commands at the moment, but even simple commands can have a powerful impact if used correctly. I don't know if I could ever train them to fly the plane for me while I sleep, but they can still be extremely valuable."

"Do you think they will follow us all the way to Hawaii? Can they even make it that far?"

"Yes. I think they will follow us just like Gwen did, and from what I have seen of Gwen's memories, they seem to be able to travel great distances without stopping. They may even get there before we do."

"Aren't they going to follow us so we can have them fish for us and so we don't get lost?"

"I'm going to test out a few commands with them. I will send four of them to the island and keep two with us for fishing. Two of the four I send will come back as scouts so I can get a better idea of what to expect. Since they have never been there before, the two that return to us will also help us properly navigate. If all of that works, then I will feel pretty confident in any future missions we try to accomplish with them."

"What about Gwen?"

"If she follows us, that's great, but I still can't control her like I can the others. If she doesn't make it, then I hope she just runs away and is happy not being controlled by the aliens."

"And you think you're ready?" asked Brenda.

"Yes."

Brenda gave an excited grin; her dark brown eyes lit with anticipation. "Then we'll set off tomorrow morning."

Despite Shannon's nervousness for the trip ahead of her, she had slept quite well, yet awoke with an anxiousness to begin her journey. Brenda took extra care this morning to make sure that everything was packed properly. Whatever they needed during the trip was within reach, either inside or outside of the plane. Everything on the outside was placed into waterproof bags and safely secured.

Shannon fought every desire she had to linger at their current location. She wanted to keep combing the area to make sure they weren't forgetting anything. She was afraid that maybe she had not properly tended to the seeds she had planted of various trees and bushes, something she had done all along the coast as they had traveled. What if her collara weren't trained well enough yet to make the trip? Every question that refused to accept a reasonable answer persisted in her mind. Ignoring her hesitation, she pushed forward. One by one she placed her hand on the collara and gave them their instructions. She thought clearly of the island she was hoping to land on. Four of them sprang into action and dove into the water to begin their long journeys. The remaining two, who would remain close to her, continued to wait for her to leave first.

"We'll do this exactly like we have done everything else up 'til now, one step at a time," assured Brenda, noticing Shannon's look of concern.

Shannon forced a smile and nodded in response.

"Let's just jump right into this and not draw things out," continued Brenda as she gestured to the planes.

They both climbed into their planes and strapped in.

"Let's keep it low at first, to make sure everything feels alright with the extra weight," said Brenda over the radio.

"Sounds good."

Shannon's plane lurched forward as it began accelerating. She looked out her side window and saw the remaining collara run into the water. The plane bounced as it reached top speed until it gently rose off the ground.

Shannon matched Brenda's altitude of forty meters off the ground. As the plane flew peacefully in the air, Shannon tried to imagine that she could notice the difference in the weight that her plane was now carrying, but she knew she couldn't. Having primarily flown straight, and only on a few occasions turning the plane more than for minor corrections, she had no real idea of the performance of the vehicle or how it may now be different.

"Long flights over endless water like this can be difficult," chimed Brenda over the radio. Her voice was thin and full of static. "If you need a break at any time, just let me know. Fatigue can set in suddenly. If you head-bob but think you can power through it, you will be putting yourself at serious risk."

"I'll be careful. Though, I think I'll be fine for the first day since I'm pretty anxious. Once we figure out how long the planes can fly with the additional weight, we can set up a schedule for breaks so we don't get too exhausted."

"Great idea."

Shannon looked out at the ocean and wondered how much life still existed in it. She knew some fish had survived but wondered how many, if they had adjusted to recent changes, and how many of them the new creatures ate.

Hopefully they can find a new balance that allows most, or all, of them to survive.

"In an hour we'll land to eat lunch and take a thirty minute nap," announces Brenda.

"Sounds good," responded Shannon.

"How are you holding up?"

"I'm doing fine. I just keep watching the water, hoping I'll see an animal I recognize. I haven't seen anything yet."

"Neither have I. However, we have been eating fish, and there is some sort of food for the collara and colossal sharks to survive on. We aren't seeing animals right now, but I'm sure they are out there, possibly thriving, now that there aren't people to fish them into extinction."

"Do you think we will get to a point that moves beyond survival, where we can spend time studying and doing research again?" Shannon asked.

"That's an interesting question. There are obviously times when survival and research overlap, like when you visited the aliens. They are clearly beings that impact our lives, and we need to know how and why. Beyond that, however, life is very much about survival right now, and it will take longer than our life times to simply rebuild the things we already know. It won't leave much room, or need, for researching new things. But we have an advantage compared to any other group of people starting out with as little as we have throughout history; we still have the knowledge of everything that can be achieved."

"I guess we wouldn't have the means to do the research I would want to do now anyway, since everything is destroyed." Shannon could hear the defeat in her own voice.

"Well, the smart ones figure out how to do their research while maintaining their daily lives. They live around the things they study, and incorporate it into their world. I've never met someone with more passion for knowledge than you. You'll find a way."

"I know you're right. I'll always have things around me to figure out. I just really wish I could visit the impact site and study it."

"Me too!" responded Brenda with sudden enthusiasm.

Shannon laughed. "Where did that come from?"

"You just reminded me! With everything we've been doing, I've been completely focused on each day as it comes. I completely forgot about life before all of this until just now. There were things that were completely baffling before the comet hit that... are still completely baffling, but somehow make more sense."

"*Like?*" asked Shannon in frustrated excitement.

"Everyone kept asking why we didn't just blow the thing up before it got close enough to us to do damage, but we did. Well, we *tried* anyway. In fact, a few countries had tried. Everyone wanted to take credit for saving the world. But time and time again, as a missile neared the comet, it would stray off course and miss the comet entirely. A onetime accident I could understand, but the missiles had the ability to course correct when something changed their trajectory. It's not like the comet was somehow in the wrong spot and we missed it either. The comet was exactly where we thought it should be, when we thought it would be there; and yet every missile that was sent missed."

"Given what we know now, about who, or what, was in there, you have to wonder how they did it. While the idea of them having telekinesis is alarming, it only gets worse. The reality is that an object as large as that comet colliding with Earth should have produced results far worse than it had, but the thing was actually slowing as it neared Earth."

"Slowing?" asked Shannon in disbelief.

"Significantly. And people had no idea why. Most assumed that there must have been some element within the comet that interfered with our ability to properly observe or measure the comet. That seemed so obviously wrong, yet it was the best guess anyone had."

"I have no idea how that will play into things, but it obviously makes our situation far more complex," responded Shannon.

"I wonder if they viewed that as a sign of aggression, us sending missiles, and that is why they seem to not be friendly toward us."

"That's a good theory," agreed Shannon. "But I also get the impression that they simply consider themselves superior to us. Whether it was aggressive or not, they seem to look down on us, and I don't think they want to share with us. They want to be top dog here."

Chapter 13

The planes rocked gently on the water. Shannon looked around nervously at the vast ocean that surrounded her. Brenda collapsed the wings of the planes and then tied a pontoon from each plane together at multiple points so that the aircraft moved together as the water pushed them back and forth. Only a light creaking could be heard from the ropes as the planes bobbed.

"Let's just eat from our rations tonight and cook fish for dinner tomorrow, when we've taken more breaks," said Brenda. "I'm exhausted."

"Sure," responded Shannon.

Though she was anxious to be on the water, Shannon allowed herself to lean back in her seat and rest. She closed her eyes and listened to the sloshing of the water around her.

"Any other circumstance and this would be enjoyable," said Shannon.

"Yeah," agreed Brenda. "I've noticed you looking around nervously. I don't know who has it worse, though. You know what these colossal sharks look like, and have interacted with them. I've only heard stories. You know what to expect, while my imagination runs wild."

"If one finds us that is controlled by the aliens, then I think we will be alright. My fear is that we will come across one that has free will. You ever see one of those pictures of a shark jumping out of water?"

"Unfortunately," groaned Brenda.

"Imagine that, but a hundred times bigger. I've seen that from a distance."

"I'd rather not." Brenda took a bite of her food as she sat sideways in her plane, her feet dangling freely. "How about, whoever wakes up first, gets the other person up, and we leave as soon as possible? The less time we spend on the water, the better."

"That's fine with me. I've hated the ocean ever since I saw *Jaws* as a kid."

"That's funny," responded Brenda. "You seem to be so fascinated with the world. I would have assumed you loved the ocean for all the mystery it has."

"I do," confessed Shannon. "But I would want to explore it from within the safety of a large steel submarine. I would also pick outer space over the ocean any day of the week."

"That's something we can agree on. It just seems so peaceful when you look up to the stars, and even though you may be confined to a space ship, it still seems so open and free."

"It does seem limitless." Shannon agreed.

Shannon ate her final meal for the evening and then leaned back in her seat. The sun had just set completely, allowing the stars to reflect on the water around her. She imagined herself floating in space peacefully, surrounded by stars, and was quickly asleep.

"Wake-y wake-y," said Brenda.

The gentle movements of the planes on the water threatened to lull Shannon back to sleep. Though she quickly oriented herself to her surroundings and remembered her desire to get off of the water as fast as possible. She had spent the night dreaming about Billy and Chris, and missed the comfort and security of being part of a larger group. She fought back her feelings of worry for them and her concerns about how they were doing, knowing that it would only give her stress for a situation that she had no control over.

"It's about 5:30 right now, so we have a half hour to get ready before the sun's up," said Brenda.

"Okay."

Shannon yawned hard enough that she almost hurt her jaw. Though she had gotten plenty of sleep, her dreams had been frantic, and did not provide her with the rest she had needed. She stepped out onto the pontoon and stretched out the ache in her legs and mid-back from sleeping in a sitting position.

"One night on the ocean, done," said Shannon with excitement.

Shannon looked into the deep ocean below her and was startled, letting out an audible gasp. She noticed moving shapes beneath the water, dark shadows that moved around quickly, making her think of swarming sharks. Her fear subsided when she realized it was her collara.

"They have been circling for as long as I've been awake," said Brenda.

Shannon reached her hand into the water, and one after the other the two collara sped toward the surface and shot out of the water onto the pontoon. The planes rocked forcefully, and Brenda shot a glare at Shannon. She pet them and then scanned through their memories. Neither of them had seen anything suspicious while traveling. She also used them to get her location and adjusted their direction based on how much they had drifted through the night.

"We did alright last night," said Shannon as she looked at her compass. "We only need to course correct by five degrees. We will travel at 265 degrees now instead of 260."

"So we drifted south in our sleep… It's nice to have something work in our favor, for once. Now let's get off of this water for a while."

"Sounds good to me," said Shannon as she climbed around to the side of her plane that was tied up against Brenda's.

Brenda let the two planes loose from each other and gave Shannon's plane a push so that they drifted away from each other. Shannon expanded her collapsed wing and then carefully maneuvered back to the side of her plane that opened. The plane rocked more severely when it was by itself. Her two collara dove into the water and disappeared immediately.

They both started their engines, and Brenda gradually moved herself farther from Shannon so they could take off safely at the same time. After a few bumpy moments,

Shannon breathed a sigh of relief as she distanced herself from the water. She examined the ocean beneath her as she climbed into the sky and saw nothing suspicious.

The sky was clear and the weather was calm. The flying was smooth and peaceful. Shannon and Brenda would take turns initiating conversations that would run their courses and then settle into quietness. As much as she could, Shannon tried to force herself to enjoy the experience she was having, and remove it from the circumstances she was forced to have it in.

The next two days would end up being as uneventful as the first.

Chapter 14

It was just before nightfall. The sun was casting its long warm rays, providing Shannon with her last strong sense of direction before the ocean was blanketed with darkness and her view was consumed with stars and the reflection of stars. The two collara that Shannon had sent to the island with the intent of reconnaissance had finally returned. She scanned through their memories and found nothing unusual upon a light investigation. The island they were planning to land on did not appear to have any aliens close to it. She was confident that they should be able to arrive with relative secrecy. She conveyed her appreciation to her capable spies and then sent them back to the island to wait for her.

Shannon looked at the stars through her window as she leaned back in her chair and attempted to fall asleep. She was full from the fish that Brenda had cooked on their solar cooker and was eager to sleep. Yet, as she had become accustomed to, she struggled to turn her mind off. She listened to the sounds of the water around her and tried to connect the movement of her plane with the noises she heard, but there wasn't much correlation. The wind came in random gusts, carrying with it a cold mist. Over time she had gotten used to the quiet of the night. No electronics, no cars, no humming of electricity, or the buzz of human life outside her window. Having recently spent so much of her time on or near the water, she hadn't even heard bugs much since her birth into this new world from her shelter, what seemed like a life time ago.

The silence was what always struck her as the most different. So much of what she had done recently could feel like a camping trip, and her mind, tapping into those deep seated memories, could confuse everything she was currently going through as something temporary. But the silence was inescapable. She spent many of her nights listening to the water, focusing on the rhythms of the waves. As her mind started to drift and the sound of the water around her dulled to white noise, she faintly heard a familiar noise, a distant moaning. But before her mind could register how it was familiar to her, she fell asleep.

The plane rocked sharply and Shannon woke as she slid from her seat and banged her head against the wall of the plane. Shock and sleep fought within her as she looked out of her plane and struggled to gain awareness. It was still night, and looked darker outside her window than she had remembered it being. She couldn't see rain, but heard water pouring. She looked at Brenda and saw her looking out of her plane, completely stunned.

Slowly, the stars in the sky revealed themselves as the black veil that covered them pealed away, descending into the water. *A colossal shark*, she thought to herself as panic began to pour into her.

They had seemed curious but not dangerous before, but what if this one is being controlled by the aliens? Or maybe the aliens will find us because of this. We need to leave.

The fin of the shark was underwater, and Brenda was busy scanning the surface of the water for any sign of the beast's return.

"We have to go," yelled Shannon, even though it had become quiet again on the water. She was unable to control her fear.

Before Brenda could acknowledge what Shannon had said, the large fin breached the water next to Brenda's plane, quickly ascending into the sky with a rush of water that then came pouring down. The two planes buckled inward toward each other as the fin moved forward, away from the planes. It was immediately clear that they needed to separate their aircraft or they may crash into each other and both be destroyed if that happened again.

"Cut the planes loose," screamed Shannon, but Brenda continued to look out at the water, paralyzed by shock.

Shannon grabbed a knife from her bag, jumped out of her plane onto the pontoon, and swung around the outside of her plane. She went to the farthest knot first, and slashed at the rope with her knife. It frayed mildly, but stayed intact. She slashed again and again, each time fraying the rope a bit more. Finally, recognizing that she needed to change techniques, she sawed at the rope until it popped away from itself and the tension loosened. She worked to unwrap the rope, and, without thinking, threw it into the water as she was turning around to start working on the next rope. *We still needed that!* She suddenly realized. She knew it was too late to do anything about it now.

Shannon felt a brief moment of relief when she turned around and saw Brenda had snapped out of her stupor and was almost done removing the other rope. When she had finished, she smartly threw it into her plane before climbing in. With Brenda out of her way, Shannon climbed around her plane and climbed in the cockpit. She scanned the water as she got into her seat and saw that the shark had once again hid under the black mass.

The planes' engines roared to life simultaneously.

"Get into the air!" Brenda screamed. "I'll move out of your way. Just go!"

Shannon threw the plane into full acceleration. The plane lurched forward, slowly, unaware of her urgency. As the plane gradually gained speed, Shannon could see Brenda attempting to turn her plane so that she could take off safely away from Shannon. Her efforts to gain a better position was slow moving. Shannon reached top speed. Her plane bounced on the choppy water until finally climbing into the air. She scanned to her side, but saw no sign of Brenda yet. Unwilling to continue without Brenda, Shannon swung her plane to her left, away from where she knew Brenda should be, to circle around and see what was happening.

As she faced away from the action below, the water and sky seemed to blend together, creating an endless sky that engulfed her. She focused intently on the rippling of the water beneath her to keep her bearings. She flew in a wide circle so she knew she could safely avoid whatever Brenda might be doing.

She had hoped that by the time she had swung her plane around Brenda would be off the water, but that wasn't the case. Brenda was still attempting to gain speed for takeoff. Shannon watched impatiently. Brenda was beginning to bounce on the water when the shark fin quickly emerged to her right, sending a large enough wave toward her that it threw her plane to the left and she lost momentum. She changed direction away from the colossal shark and again fought to gain speed.

The shark had gone underwater again, and Shannon raked her vision back and forth, trying to find a sign of the animal. With each scan of the water, she would look at what Brenda was doing. She jumped in her seat when she saw Brenda's plane finally leave the water.

As if to make one more attempt at sinking Brenda's plane, the fin shot into the air one last time as Brenda made her ascent. The fin clipped Brenda's right wing and the plane darted to the left, weaving back and forth as she struggled to straighten out her aircraft. She arched her plane up as much as she could to gain height, and Shannon felt immediately exhausted from relief when she knew that Brenda was safe.

Several minutes passed without a word. Shannon did not want to risk distracting Brenda, if she was in the middle of an emergency from the impact.

"I have no interest in landing any time soon. Are you good to fly for a while?" Brenda sounded as though she were forcing herself to be calm. The static from the radio did little to mask her fear.

"Yes. Are you okay?"

"I'm fine, but I would rather not talk about it. If I think about this too much, I'll never be able to land on the water again. But we simply can't make it to land on our current charge, so I would like to forget this happened."

"Yes, ma'am." Shannon was surprised by how truly shaken Brenda seemed.

Just then, Shannon remembered the collara that had stayed with her for the journey. She hadn't seen them during the ordeal, but became worried that the colossal shark may have been acting the way it had in an attempt to attack and eat her collara. Sadness hit her as she feared that she may never see them again. She would have to wait and find out later if they were still following her.

Chapter 15

"I see land!" Shannon screamed as she scrutinized the horizon intently. Visibility had decreased significantly as they had neared the islands. A gray haze of ash hung in the air from the volcanoes that had erupted recently. Only the peaks of the mountains could be clearly seen above the ash. One of the peaks still bellowed plumes of smoke into the air.

"That looks like Hawaii from here," said Brenda. "We will want to pass that and a couple other islands before we reach Oahu."

They followed along the curve of the islands, flying low for visibility. Shannon looked out her window in amazement. Despite the carnage she knew the islands had endured, they had already grown back a large amount of vegetation. After flying for several days without feeling safe to leave her plane, her legs ached with anticipation for landing on the island.

When they finally reached Oahu, they landed their planes on the water and then beached them. Disregarding any responsibilities she might have had, Shannon jumped out of her plane and flopped onto the sand. She closed her eyes and enjoyed the warmth of the sun on her face, and the heat of the sand on her back.

"I know we have a lot of work ahead of us," said Shannon, "but it's still nice to be here."

Brenda nodded. "I've been here a bunch throughout my life and it looks very different, but after living in a bunker and traveling through absolutely freezing weather, this is still a dream."

Brenda unloaded her plane before allowing herself the opportunity to enjoy being on land again. Shannon appreciated how hard Brenda worked, but appreciated even more how, like a loving parent, she did not prevent Shannon from enjoying the moment every now and then. As Shannon sat, the two collara she had sent to remain at the island came bounding toward her. She greeted the animals joyfully, but did not bother seeing their memories for now, and continued to rest.

After Shannon had taken some time to stretch out her sore body, she and Brenda set out to find wood for a fire. The amount of vegetation they were finding was shocking to her. Many trees had begun to grow, including plants she did not recognize. She wondered if they were original to the islands, or if they had been brought here by the ocean. They arranged their camp more thoroughly than they had before, since they anticipated being there for a long time. They even found large logs to use as chairs. They set the logs around a second fire they had created away from the center of the camp, which would be used for cooking. By the end of the day, Shannon was feeling very confident in the foundation for their camp that they had created. She also felt completely spent. She had not gotten the exercise she needed while flying her plane for so long, and her muscles needed to stretch and regain some strength.

As the sun began to set on their first day on the island, Shannon dug her toes into the sand and settled into her comfortable habit of planning. She recalled her dream of a submarine and wondered how they would ever climb that hurdle. At this point, she believed in the vision she had. She knew that the moments she had experienced in her visions would come to pass. However, knowing where she would end up made her more concerned about the journey than she thought she would have been otherwise. She couldn't see how to get from point A to point B, but felt a burden to fulfill the things she had seen, and an urgency to do them quickly.

"I recognize that face," said Brenda, noticing Shannon's unknowing look of concern. "What's troubling you?"

"I'm just wondering how we are going to find a submarine." She couldn't help but say the line with a laugh. The idea seemed preposterous to her.

"Everything has worked out so far, much to my amazement. I'm sure this will work out also. I know that the bunker the military had set up for us in California with planes and supplies was not the only one they made. I'm sure there is one here as well, since they did have a military base here. If your vision is accurate, then I'm guessing that is where we will find the submarine you saw. My biggest concern is what depth the aliens may be living at. Depending on how deep they are under water, we may not be able to do anything other than look at them, or maybe run into them with the submarine."

"You don't think we could just fire a missile at them or something?" asked Shannon.

Brenda let out a laugh. "Is that the kind of submarine you saw? Any submarine we find that we can operate by ourselves would not have the ability to fire anything. At this point, I'm not sure what exactly a submarine could do for us, other than reconnaissance, though that is still extremely valuable."

Shannon shrugged. "I didn't actually see a submarine, or at least I don't remember seeing one. The idea, or concept, of one was just lingering in my mind in an unfamiliar way. I guess we just have to find a thing that would in some way be classified as a submarine and figure out what our options are."

Brenda worked hard to cook the fish that the collara provided while Shannon prepared additional MREs to complete their feast. They didn't usually eat so lavishly, and at any other time Shannon may have remembered that she was growing tired of the food they were eating. However, tonight they chose to celebrate their victory over their travels. Shannon was also grateful for being near the equator and the laziness that the sun had in setting. Her body was exhausted, but her mind was not eager to sleep yet, so the extra light was appreciated.

The two ate, laughed, and talked lightheartedly. The sun set casually, but they hardly noticed as they sat at either end of their fire and relaxed. For once they did not pay attention to the time, or plan for the coming day, but simply enjoyed themselves. If they had been more focused, they may have noticed the darkness on the horizon, and Shannon might have been less surprised when she heard the first crack of lightning.

The rain had waited just long enough for Brenda and Shannon to prop up a tarp over their fire and inch their tents closer to it before pouring down on them with startling strength. Shannon's tent *thwapped* and shook like the head of a loose drum as the rain pelted it. The noise of the rain and thunder gave her a nice distraction from her thoughts and was a welcomed change of pace. The excitement she had from reaching her destination and momentarily ending their traveling carried on regardless of the weather. She happily climbed into her sleeping bag and calmly fell asleep.

Chapter 16

Shannon woke to the continuing sound of the storm. Peeking out of her tent, she could see that it was in fact morning, and the rain was continuing with the same strength as last night. Brenda crouched under the tarp they had hung and tended to the fire.

"I don't think the storm is planning on letting up any time soon," said Brenda.

Shannon shrugged. "At least we can still use the collara to explore the island a bit."

Brenda nodded to something behind Shannon. "The others showed up last night."

Shannon turned to see four collara playing, tackling, and fighting each other while brandishing their teeth, but not actually inflicting harm. A moment of sadness took hold of her as she accepted that the other two had succumbed to the colossal shark's attacks. She whistled, and they came bumbling toward her. She pushed them around and played with them like she would with dogs.

Quickly she viewed the memories of the two collara that had just returned. Their trip to the island was uneventful compared to the last time on the ocean that she had seen them. She more thoroughly examined their memories as they approached the island, but found no signs of the aliens below.

"Anything good?" asked Brenda.

"No," answered Shannon. She then remembered that she hadn't examined the memories of the collara who had stayed at the island. She reached out and placed her hand on one of the animals. It had explored one side of the island they were on and provided no new information. She then went to check the memories of the other collara, hoping that it had explored the other side of the island.

Inside the mind of the collara, Shannon found herself swimming around the islands. Her speed and mobility were liberating. She looked around and saw the same things she had seen with the other collara, a muddy ocean floor and ash covering the water. She gained momentum and burst onto the beach. Sand plumed under her fists as she bound across the sand.

For a couple of hours she climbed the mountains and examined the island as she ascended. She was amazed by how far and clearly she could see through the eyes of a collara. Their vision was far better than human eyesight. When she reached the top, she could see dark clouds approaching. She could also see the nearby islands. They were more green than her island, and the plants seemed more dense, possibly even taller. She looked around her own island once more. Much of it was beginning to regrow, but it was disorganized, and in many places sparse. There were a few spots that seemed to contain the remains of buildings, debris from a world that was becoming more and more distant. There were areas of the island they would investigate more thoroughly later, but her interest remained on the vegetation of the nearby island.

Shannon made her way back down the mountain she had climbed. She jumped, bounced, and at times rolled as she raced back toward the ocean. As she reached the water, the sky overhead became dark, as ominous clouds brought flooding rain. The water jumped under the pummeling of large drops of rain landing on it. Shannon leaped in and swam with ease.

Though she was quite comfortable in the water, it took some time to reach the next island. Her uncontrollable hunger didn't help, forcing her to get distracted eating fish along the way. The surface above her danced with excitement from the rain. As she neared the next island, she noticed a portion of the ocean floor that was clear of debris and plants had started to grow that she did not recognize. Finally, she reached the next island and emerged on to land with a bit more subtlety than she had used before.

She immediately noticed the difference on this island from the one she had been on. The vegetation was thicker and seemed organized. Moving up the beach beyond the sand, and drawing closer to the vegetation, she could see distinct rows of plants.

These plants were intentional.

She examined the plants closer and was shocked to see many of them bearing fruit. There were berries, tomatoes, and fruit that she didn't recognize.

Succumbing to her hunger, she ate them with satisfaction as she made her way down the rows, away from the water.

With the thunder and rain that poured down around her and the distraction of the plants, it took her a moment before she noticed movement as she turned around to head back toward the water. It was difficult to see at first, but she could make out figures moving in the distance. She got low and lay below the height of the plants. Slowly she crawled farther from the beach and the new entities.

Are there more things to be worried about on this planet?

She hid behind a plant that had no fruit on it. She had moved slightly higher, and could see the rows of plants and the shadowy figures moving. After watching for a moment, she realized what she was looking at.

The aliens can come on land, but how is that possible?

Her visibility was low in the rain, and she struggled to watch them among the plants.

The rain! Of course. Just like the memory I experienced of their home planet.

She hid for an hour while the aliens walked around. Eventually the rain let up and the unwanted visitors retreated to the ocean. When the coast was clear, she ran to the water, making sure to avoid the area she had seen the aliens retreat to, and made her way back to the island she had first been on.

Thunder cracked overhead and the fading glow of lightning could still be seen as Shannon emerged from her connection with the collara. She thought about what she had just seen.

The aliens are farming on the island next to us.

As she reflected more on her new knowledge, something else nagged at her mind.

The collara did exactly what I wanted in the memory.

The more she thought about it, the more it had felt to her that she had been in control of what she had experienced.

Shannon turned to Brenda, who was still tending to the fire. "I have bad news," she said.

"What?" Brenda asked cautiously.

"The aliens can come onto the islands when it is raining heavily, and they are farming on the next island over." Shannon pointed.

Brenda's expression fell flat as shock set in and she worked to think it over. Eventually she shook her head.

"That isn't necessarily a bad thing," said Brenda. "The more we know, and the more we have access to them, the more options we have for fighting back. Maybe they are even dependent on that food somehow and they will be unable to escape us. Learn anything else?"

Shannon shook her head. She would wait to reveal her theory about the experience she just had of controlling the collara until after she had done more research.

Brenda gave Shannon an encouraging smile. "Well, that still gives us plenty to start with. If they are farming on land, then they likely aren't going very far away. They are probably very nearby in the water. That does also mean that we were at risk of being spotted as we flew around the islands before landing, and that we may want to move farther from the water, in case they decide to come exploring this area while it is raining."

"I think we are okay for now," responded Shannon thoughtfully. "They still have plenty of room for growth on their island, and I went through the rest of the collara's memories and didn't see any evidence of them coming over here."

"The first thing we need to do is have the collara swim around and make sure there aren't any aliens nearby that we should worry about." Brenda spoke firmly and made Shannon imagine Brenda's military days.

"Okay, I'll do some reconnaissance," responded Shannon.

Shannon knew this was her chance to test what her abilities were when viewing a collara's memories. She placed her hand on one of the collara and gave it the order to swim around the island. The collara jumped up from the command and bolted for the water.

"A few hours or so and we'll have some answers," said Shannon.

As she waited, Shannon grew excited for the collara's return.

Enough time went by that Shannon had a growing fear that the collara she sent may have been caught. The animal came merrily bounding up the beach after three hours.

"Your scout is back," announced Brenda.

Shannon sat up from inside her tent. Her excitement to test her theory was palpable. She opened her tent, and the collara ran directly at her. She outstretched her hand as the animal came to a halt in front of her, just making contact. She was immediately back in time.

Shannon was looking at herself from the perspective of the collara. She attempted to look away, but her view was rigid. It felt different than last time. Her view turned as the collara made its way toward the water. It ran quickly and dove into the ocean.

As if the water had washed away her restrictions, she was suddenly able to look and move wherever she wanted. She turned away from the island she had just moments earlier directed herself to circle around and swam out toward deeper water. After swimming for five minutes, defying her own directions, she knew she was in control. She swam back and began making her way around the island.

Shannon swam in a large circle, following the edge of the land just before it dipped into deeper ocean. She kept a close eye on anything that might look like alien activity, or signs of previous activity. She saw nothing of note. Significant debris from buildings had built up around the island, and she feared that any potentially hidden submarine would be entirely out of reach.

After some time, she had made it all the way back to where she had started. She emerged from the water and heard Brenda announce her presence. Shortly after, she saw herself come out of a tent and she immediately felt the loss of control over her actions that she had just had.

I've made it full circle.

She had one more test to do. She rewound the memory to before she had gone around the island. Now as she moved forward in time and swam in the water, her vision was fixed. Her movements were in sync with everything she had done the first time.

I only get one try. Once I know what the collara has done, I can't change it.

Chapter 17

Brenda studied the maps of Oahu on Shannon's tablet intently.

"I think there are three primary places to investigate," said Brenda as she surfaced from her maps. She spoke in a near yell to be heard over the still pouring rain.

Shannon moved closer and looked over Brenda's shoulder.

"Pearl Harbor seems like an obvious spot to the west of us," began Brenda as she pointed to the map on the tablet in front of her. "To the north is the Marine Corps Base, which may have facilities—under water now—that could have housed equipment that might have survived. The third option is that they did like us and found a high place with an underground bunker, which would unfortunately be much harder to locate. I don't honestly have any idea where a bunker could be if it was hidden on the island."

"We obviously aren't going anywhere with this rain, but I can send the collara for us." Shannon hesitated. She knew this conversation had to happen eventually, but she was concerned that eventually it would be too much for Brenda to believe. She combed her blond hair behind her ears nervously. "So, I know things keep changing, but I have something I need to show you."

Brenda cocked an eyebrow; her expression was one of half concern and half amusement. "What now?" she asked dryly.

"Write down three things that you want a collara to do. Think of unique things, but don't tell them to me. Just write them down and put them in your pocket." Shannon turned away so she couldn't see anything.

"Okay," responded Brenda with growing curiosity.

Shannon summoned a nearby collara, closed her eyes, and plugged her fingers in her ears for good measure. She waited for the collara to complete the tasks until the animal bumped into her, indicating that it was done. Shannon turned around and saw Brenda completely shocked.

"How did you do that?" asked Brenda.

"What happened?"

"Everything that I wrote down. Exactly as I wrote it."

"Can I see what you wrote?" asked Shannon.

Brenda tossed her the piece of paper, still stunned.

Draw three lines in the sand. Roll over twice. Jump five times.

"Here's the thing," said Shannon. "You're in shock that the collara did everything you wrote down, and in order, but I haven't actually provided the direction to do those things yet."

Brenda's eyes squinted in confusion. "What do you mean?"

"I never touched the collara before it did those tricks. It hasn't received any directions from me yet. If I never saw the paper, though, I wouldn't be able to tell it what to do, and I *do* have to tell it what to do."

Shannon touched the collara, instantly jumped back a few seconds ago, and followed through with the requests that Brenda had written down.

"I don't know the details. I just know that when I view a memory of a collara that I haven't already personally seen, heard about, or experienced in any way, I have the ability to control what happens. If I had watched the collara while it stood in front of you, then nothing would have happened. Also, I can only do it once per time period. Once I know what happens, I can't change anything." Shannon shrugged, indicating that she didn't have any more details or understanding of how it worked. "Anyway, my point with all of this is that we can send them out, and when they come back, I can connect with each of them and make the journey as though I was actually there. This may be the only way things are getting done until this rain lets up."

"I'm not going to pretend like I fully understand what just happened. It mildly sounds like you can time travel inside the collara's body. At this point, I just don't know what to make of that. It's magic. You're magic. I'm talking to a witch." Brenda let out a snort of a laugh, gave a defeated smile, and shook her head. "Alright, send them to the areas I showed you on the map. We'll save the mountains and the rest of the island as a last resort."

"Okay."

Shannon gave the four collara their commands and they quickly disappeared into the rain.

"Any idea how long they'll be gone?" asked Brenda.

"Not really. I would imagine at least most of the day. Though, maybe they'll come back quickly, if they find what we are looking for."

"I guess we'll just settle into a nice lazy day in the rain then."

Brenda sat in the sand, leaning back on her hands. She was clearly in deep thought. "How much control do you have over the collara when you control them? Like, how are your fine motor skills? Do we need a submarine to allow us to go into the water if we have them?"

Shannon thought about it carefully. "I would say it's like trying to carve wood with a chainsaw. You could cut and carve large trees, but you wouldn't be able to carve something small enough to hold in your hand. Controlling their bodies, arms, and fingers is like that. It feels natural in the moment, but all of their movements are big and powerful. I don't think I could get them to hold a pencil and write, or collect samples of the vegetation on the other island or from the water."

"So any research we want to do in the water, we need a way for us to do it ourselves." Brenda concluded.

It was a day and a half before the first collara returned. Shannon looked at her watch, 10am. She was curious how long it would take to create nearly thirty-six hours of memories that had technically already passed. She knew from previous experience that it was not one-to-one. She experienced the collara's memories much faster than her own, even when she was making them up as she went.

"Is there anywhere that you recommend that I look while I'm gone?" asked Shannon.

Brenda shrugged. "If you happen to see anything that looks like a building, then I would recommend that. Otherwise, underwater?"

Shannon nodded. She reached out her hand and the collara submitted peacefully.

Shannon struggled to wrap her head around the idea that she was back in her own body, despite being gone for more than a day in the collara. She glanced at her watch, 10:30am. *It only took thirty minutes to live a day and a half in the collara's body.*

Shannon collapsed onto the ground and listened to the rain landing on her tent. Her mind was exhausted and had not yet adjusted to the lack of fatigue that her body actually felt.

"You were gone for quite a while," said Brenda. "Are you okay? Did you find anything?"

"Nothing." Shannon let out a sigh. "I looked all around on land and in the water. If it is buried under the water, then it's staying there, because we wouldn't be able to move the debris I saw. Though I will say that the debris was sparse enough in most areas to know that there wasn't much chance of anything hiding underneath."

Throughout the rest of the day the remaining collara returned, and each time Shannon failed to find anything that seemed promising. As the day came to an end, she fought the mental fatigue of living four days through the collara, plus her own, without sleep. She needed to rest her aching head. Tomorrow, after a long night of sleeping to recover, she would try to think of what to do next.

"Searching this island will be impossible if we have no idea where to look," said Brenda, acknowledging the concern that Shannon had expressed about the tole that living out the collara's days had taken on her.

Shannon shook her head. She knew Brenda was right, but she had no idea what their options were. "When the weather clears, we could fly around and look for an entrance somewhere."

"It's worth a shot, but there's enough greenery and debris all over the island that an entrance could be quite hidden."

"What other option do we have? We know what the next step in our journey is; we just have to find it."

"Well, we don't actually know that this is the next step, it's just the next clue, with no indication of when we will actually need that clue. Don't get me wrong. I'm not saying we shouldn't look, but we may come up empty handed here because now isn't the time to be searching for that. I still think this is the most likely place to find what we are looking for, but there is always that chance we are wrong." Brenda shrugged. "Is there any way that you can trigger another vision? Maybe get us closer to the submarine we are looking for?"

"The only thing that seems to give me visions is having contact with the aliens."

Brenda sighed in defeat. "Connecting with them obviously puts you at risk, and would give away our location. I know it's probably too risky at this point, but you did somehow use them to find me, back at the compound. Let's put a bit more time into our search. If we don't have any success, then we go about doing the other things that brought us here, like research. When all of our other goals have been met, then we will revisit the idea of connecting with them."

Shannon's stomach turned at the thought of letting the aliens connect with her again. "We should definitely exhaust all other options before we resort to desperate measures."

Her gut told her she was only delaying the inevitable.

Chapter 18

It took three more days before the rain let up enough that they had skies sufficiently clear for flying. Shannon had been awakened early by the silence brought on by the rain ending, and decided to release her restlessness by running. The morning was quiet, and the sunrise to her back broke through the cloud cover in rays that brought a warm glow, revealing the barren world around her.

She fought her way through her fatigue and settled into a steady pace. It was so rare that she did anything other than survive that she hadn't yet noticed how much she missed the wildlife that used to surround her. There were no birds or bugs to make noise or movement. She had often felt alone when she didn't see people for a while, which used to happen when she would study extensively in high school, but this felt far more surreal.

When the sun appeared fully established for the day, Shannon turned around and made her way back to camp. Brenda was ready when Shannon returned, and had prepared both planes for flight. Shannon ate quickly before boarding her plane.

"We'll fly around the outside, and work our way toward the center in a spiral," said Brenda. "Obviously be careful. We want to fly low for the best view, but you need as much of an eye on where you're going as you do on looking for any hidden facilities."

"I hear ya," responded Shannon. "We'll take it slow. I don't want to miss this place if we have a chance of finding it. The alternative method for finding the submarine is not promising."

"Yeah. If we don't find it, our options for data collection from within the water becomes rather diminished. But even so, connecting with the aliens may still not be an alternative worth the risk."

"Agreed," said Shannon as she climbed onto her plane.

They settled into a now unspoken routine as Brenda took off first and Shannon followed close behind. They began their trek around the island clockwise.

Over the course of the day, they circled the island dozens of times and marked the locations on a map that they would send the collara to investigate later. As the day came to a close and they made their final pass over the center of the island, they had made a list of twenty locations worth investigating.

Drops of water began landing on their windshields as they returned to their camp. The downpour ended its reprieve as they settled their planes on the ground. Shannon ran to the cover over her tent. The collara lay around the camp, unconcerned by the rain that was now covering them. Shannon sent three of the collara off to begin investigating locations and sent the fourth one fishing for dinner. Brenda began the fire in anticipation of cooking. As soon as the last collara returned with food, Shannon sent it to search a fourth location on their list.

Over the span of five days, Shannon had sent the collara to search sixteen locations. Living an entire day each time she scanned the memories of the collara, nearly four times a day, left Shannon exhausted, and at times, confused. It became harder to return to her own body and remember what she had been thinking before each scan.

Brenda handed Shannon a bottle of water. Seeing Shannon's obvious fatigue, Brenda was growing concerned. "We may need to concern ourselves with the lasting effects of your time traveling on your mind and body, if you plan on doing this much more."

"We've eliminated sixteen of the twenty locations we've marked. Hopefully we will get some luck with one of the remaining four and we can move on to something that doesn't require connecting with the collara so frequently, or for such long periods of time. I am concerned about what might happen to me if I keep this up, but it's a concern that is somewhat irrelevant given our limited options."

"Why couldn't they just be peaceful?" asked Brenda rhetorically.

"Maybe it's for the best. We see how they act with their powers. They think they are above the rest. When I interact with them, I gain abilities that they don't seem to have, in addition to many of the ones they do have. That could be a dangerous thing if they shared it with everyone and we played nicely with each other and took the time to develop our skills. We might end up being the ones crash-landing on a planet trying to take over an 'inferior species' next."

"You think people would eventually use the powers for evil?"

"Do you think there is any way that they wouldn't?" asked Shannon.

Brenda sighed. "I guess it only takes one bad egg to ruin it for everyone, and we've already encountered several."

Shannon nodded in agreement. "And unfortunately, in stressful times like these, people with ill intentions can more easily manipulate the general populace that just wants to do good and survive. If someone gains my skills, or even something far worse that we have yet to learn about, and chooses to use it to their advantage, it could be disastrous. Sure, given enough time, we might find a way to have these abilities while still protecting ourselves and others from bad actors, but that is under the assumption that those people don't destroy us first."

"That's a pretty dark view for you," responded Brenda. "I'm used to you being a bit more optimistic."

Shannon shrugged. "I guess I've just had run-ins with several dangerous people in a row recently, and I'm a bit demoralized at the moment."

Brenda gave a defeated smile in understanding. "Just don't stay that way for too long. Allow yourself to bounce back; have faith in those you know are good."

Brenda let out a long breath and slumped her shoulders. "Do you think the only answer is to eliminate the aliens entirely?"

"I hate the idea, but I don't know if they will give us a choice. So far, it does not seem like peace is an option that they are entertaining."

As they talked, the first collara returned from the final trip. Shannon quickly connected with the animal and for several minutes disappeared into the last twenty-four hours. As she returned from her trip inside the collara's mind, she collapsed to the ground from exhaustion.

Brenda stood over Shannon. "Are you okay?"

Shannon thrust her fist into the air. "I found them!"

"Where?" asked Brenda with excitement.

"Eighteen," answered Shannon as she pointed to the map that they had marked with all of the possible locations. "Pretty much everything was torn away, but there were a couple of places that went underground that were still somewhat intact. I found six vehicles that looked like single user submarines. They didn't even close around the driver completely."

"There used to be an army air field there. I'm guessing they knew that the beaches would be hit the hardest so they loaded up near the top of the island. I can't imagine why else they would have submarines at the center of the island. Do you think the collara can dig the submarines out?"

"They've already started."

"How is that possible?"

"I found the submarines before the other collara returned. That means there is no need for them to go anywhere other than to the correct location. They were with me—the collara I was in—the entire time. I didn't get it at first, why they hadn't gone to other locations, but when I got there and saw what was there, it made sense. The other three were still digging when I had this one return so that I could know what was going on. I don't think they will be much longer, actually."

"What exactly did you find?"

"Just like everything else we have ever seen, everything above ground is long gone. There was just enough debris, though, that I took the time to dig around and found a few locations that went underground. Eventually I found the submarines, and they seemed relatively intact. I'm going to send this collara back and help the other three carry one back to us."

Chapter 19

"It's absolutely amazing that the thing survived fully intact," exclaimed Brenda.

Shannon looked over her single-user submarine with surprise. She had never seen such a unique vehicle before, and couldn't believe that it was not even scratched. The second one, which had been retrieved for Brenda—despite her insistence that she would remain above the water—was in similar condition.

Brenda stood over one of the submarines with her chin in her hand as she examined it. A blueish gray color to blend in with the water, its shape, she had said, reminded her of a moped with an attached helmet. "I'm not getting in the water," reiterated Brenda flatly.

"I don't expect you to," responded Shannon without thinking. "I only expect you to do whatever it is that is needed at any given moment. Obviously, we will keep whatever is needed from you on land whenever possible."

Shannon knew Brenda was voicing her refusal to get in the water not for Shannon's sake, but for her own. The enemy was in the water, which had always out-ranked land on Earth, but even more so now. And direct confrontation, if necessary, would likely involve being in the water at some point.

"What's needed..." Brenda thought to herself. "What *is* needed? You've had this vision, which has gotten us this far, and I've been fine with having a bit of faith in all this, but now what? This is as far as your visions have come, isn't it? With no more signs to follow, we are going to have to figure out what is next. Do we wait for another vision or assess what we have and make our own calls?"

"We obviously have a lot of research to do here. These things will help with that immensely. Though, after that, I'm not sure. Then comes that tricky moment when we will have to decide if the visions I've had are things that will happen no matter what, a glimpse of the future that should be, or if it is a malleable thing that at times are not signs, but warnings of things that should be avoided. I still have one vision that has yet to come true. It is of me escaping the water with the aid of the collara. I knew during the vision that I was fleeing from the aliens, but I don't know exactly why I went down there."

"So you don't know if that is unavoidable, or a vision that serves as a sign that you are following the right path, or a warning of what you should avoid?" Brenda thought it through. "If I didn't know anything about your vision and was just suggesting what to do next, I would think that getting ourselves down there somehow to spy on them, or something like that, would be the best step. Research and reconnaissance. If we happen to find some way to gain leverage over them, I could see that as being a reason to go down and negotiate with them." Brenda paused, her face reflecting the feeling of defeat she was voicing. "My point is, I can think of a dozen reasons why the scenario you described might come to pass naturally, if we don't try to avoid it. I'm sure I could find ways it would come true even if we did try to avoid it.

"The good thing in all of this is that your vision ends with you escaping the water, and since I would have to be killed on land before I would let anyone throw me into the water, we can safely assume that I wasn't in the water with you. Scary things are not always deadly things, and in this case we happen to know that whatever you go through may be scary but not life ending, so we don't need to avoid it. Let's think positive and assume it is one of the first two options you gave, either unavoidable or a sign that we are on the right path."

Shannon nodded. "Then we just need to figure out how to connect the dots between now and then, and make sure that whatever reason takes me down there is worth it. The one thing I do know, is that it was at night, so I'll make sure I only use this sub in the water during the day time. That way, nothing can go too wrong."

Shannon stripped down to her underwear while Brenda stood anxiously in the water, holding the personal submarine upright.

Shannon shook her head. "With everything I knew about the comet, and the idea that I was going to be dealing with a lot of water from the very second I emerged from the bunker; it never occurred to me that I was going to need a swimsuit."

She folded her clothes neatly and placed them inside her tent. She ran back toward the water.

Brenda looked at her irritably. "The fact that these things were electric, *and* we were able to charge them with our solar panels is amazing, but don't go too far. We don't know how long the charge will last."

"Yes, ma'am," answered Shannon.

Shannon stood on the opposite side of the sub from Brenda, and the two of them walked it into the water, making sure to hold it upright. The helmet, which extended out from the front of the moped-shaped machine, had a thick acrylic glass front with the blue plastic covering the back and sides. The dome for the helmet extended over the shoulders of the driver. It trapped air as they submerged it into the water.

Sensing that Brenda didn't want to go any deeper—the water was up to their chests now—Shannon ducked under the water and placed her head into the helmet. With the help of the bubble of air in the helmet and her feet straddling the sub, standing on the ground, she balanced the sub just enough to turn it on. The two fans placed at the bottom of the sub, behind the driver, spun to life and the sub shot forward, pulling Shannon off of her feet and slamming her into her seat. She quickly tucked her feet in so she was sitting down.

It felt like her first time flying all over again. There was an elation for the new experience that struggled to ignore the risk she knew she was placing herself in. She felt a freedom that stemmed from her inability to explore the island on her own. Her collara swam around her, joyously, thrilled to have her in the water with them.

There were only two gauges, one for her power level and another for her oxygen. There also was no light on the vehicle. She had to remain fairly close to the surface to be able to see. She didn't mind not having a light. She didn't want anything that could give her presence away to others. She was also grateful that the fans seemed to be rather quiet. She couldn't know how good the aliens' hearing was, but she was hopeful that she wouldn't have to find out.

For now, all she had to do was circle around the island, staying close to land, and find out how far she could travel before she either ran out of oxygen, or electricity. She took the sub along a rather short path, back and forth, counting the number of passes she made so she could measure the distance when she returned to land. After an hour and a half, her oxygen was running low and she returned to land, driving the sub up the beach until it caught on the sand. She dragged it the rest of the way, with the collara helping her.

"That was quite a while, that you were gone," said Brenda. She handed Shannon a towel. "How far do you think you traveled?"

Shannon counted the laps in her head. "I did eight half-mile laps, so four miles. I think that is a pretty safe expectation for the future."

Brenda nodded. "That won't get you anywhere near the other island. We'll have to tie it to a plane and drag it over there. We'll use the pontoons and just drive the planes on the water rather than trying to fly."

"Okay. I'll use the collara to scout out a path that should be safe for us to travel without drawing attention to ourselves."

Chapter 20

The plane sped noisily along the water, kicking up mist behind it. Though Shannon had reassured her that the area they were traveling through was clear, Brenda ran the plane as fast as it would go. Brenda didn't want to be on the water any longer than she needed to be. She sat in the front seat, driving the plane. Her hands tightly clutched the stick between her legs, revealing the veins on the backs of her hands. Shannon was crammed into the backseat with her knees tucked high as she awkwardly straddled the seat in front of her.

They had spent a long while attaching the personal submarine to the back of the plane, tied between the pontoons. With the speed they were traveling at, and the bouncing they were enduring as they skipped on the water, Shannon hoped the submarine would still be there when they reached the other island. Shannon remained quiet. Brenda was far too distracted looking around at the water, her fear of an impending colossal shark attack too severe to hold a conversation. Shannon spent the time thinking about what she was going to do once she reached the island, thrilled by the idea of being able to research and study something.

Shannon jolted forward as the plane drove onto the beach and the submarine became an anchor in the sand.

Brenda promptly shut down the plane and let out a sigh of relief.

"Let's work quickly," said Brenda. "I don't want to be heading back in the dark."

"Okay," responded Shannon.

They jumped out of the plane and began untying the submarine. They carried it into the water. The process of lowering it into the water and mounting it had become easier as Shannon had practiced it throughout the past few days.

"We'll meet back here in six hours," said Brenda. "I'll unload the extra oxygen tank for you and leave it here."

Shannon looked at the clear sky above. The sun had just risen, and the day was promising to be bright and warm.

"Fortunately, you shouldn't have any risk while getting samples from their garden," said Shannon. "There is no chance of rain, from the looks of it."

Brenda looked concerned. "That may be true for me, but that means they will definitely be in the water, and you will have much more risk. Go slow, be cautious, and run away the second you even feel nervous. We can always try again later, inching forward as we gain more information. Don't rush things."

Shannon gave Brenda a smile. She liked how motherly Brenda was toward her. "I'll be slow and careful. You make sure to not leave any obvious tracks either, when you get your samples."

Shannon ducked under the water and fired up the submarine. It jetted forward casually. Brenda had explained how a lot of these personal submarines moved at rather slow speeds because they were seemingly invented for tourists. Brenda assumed that was how the military had acquired so many of them in a rather short period of time. She had used similar ones while sight-seeing when she visited Hawaii many years ago. Shannon couldn't help but think of the number of people that may have used her water vehicle in the past, and the joy they had to be able to explore the ocean. Even in their current circumstances, she couldn't help but enjoy being under the water. It felt a lot like flying, as though you were breaking into a world that was otherwise forbidden.

The sun broke through the water, casting rays that danced with the movement of the ocean. Her world was colored in shades of green and blue. The wreckage of the past, strewn about the ocean floor, gave the experience a haunting quality that made her feel as though she were exploring the set of a movie, the ruins of a distant past. The situation was made all the more tense by the fact that she had limited peripheral vision in her helmet. She remained very near land and attempted to see as far ahead of her as she could, to make sure she wasn't approaching danger.

Thirty minutes into her travels and she reached the outskirts of the underwater clearing she had seen previously through the collara. She idled from a distance and watched for movement. From her previous research, she had learned that the aliens lived farther in the water. She also noticed that the aliens did not appear to be active during day time. She wondered if they had a light sensitivity strong enough that they couldn't even be closer to the surface of the water during the day. When she had watched for several minutes, and felt confident that her previous observations were still holding true, she approached slowly.

Plants extended for several feet, reaching for the sky above. Many of them were like long ropes, their leaves poking out proudly. Some of the vegetation she recognized as seaweed. Other plants were entirely foreign to her, though she knew she didn't have enough familiarity with underwater plants to be able to identify what was normal or new. What she could recognize, however, was the uniformity of the plants' positions, the neat rows they formed.

She navigated around the perimeter of the underwater garden, slowing occasionally to collect plant samples. She also collected a small sample of the sand around the plants. The propellers of her submarine kicked up little air bubbles that rose in a steady stream. Time passed quickly as she worked, and before she knew it, her thirty minutes were up and she had to return to the plane for her next oxygen tank. She carefully placed her items into her pockets and began making her way back to the plane.

When she returned to where they had landed on the island, there was no sign of Brenda. She hoped Brenda was having success with collecting her samples. She quickly loaded the new oxygen tank onto the front of the submarine and then lowered herself back into the water. The process was difficult, and she almost tipped the submarine over, releasing the air trapped in the helmet, but managed to keep it upright.

For the return trip, Shannon lacked the nervousness that she had the first time. While she still remained vigilant of her surroundings, it was not with the same persistence that she had before. She once again reached the outskirts of the clearing and momentarily paused to make sure the area was clear. When she did not see movement, other than the gentle swaying of the foliage, she proceeded forward. She reached the outside of the garden and, having sampled all of the plants from the outside last time, now drove her submarine between the rows of plants.

It was when she had stopped to collect a plant sample that she noticed movement in the distance, a shadow that moved contrary to the movements of its surroundings. Without thinking, she shut off her submarine and gently dropped to the ocean floor. Sucking in a large gulp of air, she ducked out of her helmet and peeked through the plants down the next aisle. An alien floated in the water at the opposite end of the aisle. She watched as long as she could. The alien was examining plants casually. She impatiently waited—her lungs threatening to give out— for any indication of what the alien intended to do next. Just when she thought she would need to retreat to her submarine for more air, she saw the alien turn and begin swimming away.

She quickly jumped back into her helmet and swallowed the air urgently. The alien swam gracefully, its four arms working in perfect unison. It came into Shannon's view as it gained distance, fading into the darkness of the water. Suddenly filled with a desire for information that she would later question with disbelief, she brought her submarine to life and began pursuing the alien. It moved at a remarkable speed that Shannon struggled to maintain. The alien remained just at the edge of the distance that the water would allow her to see it. She hoped that the alien's vision would be just as limited as hers, should it choose to look back.

For ten minutes she followed the alien. She began to worry that she would not have enough oxygen to return to the plane. She debated with herself how much farther she should go, promising herself to turn back at various landmarks before inevitably going farther.

Suddenly, the alien slowed. Not noticing the alien's change of speed until she found herself approaching the alien quickly, she stopped her submarine completely. She sat on the ocean floor in water that had grown significantly darker as she had traveled, and rested from her sudden startle. With an awkward waddle, she carefully lifted and turned her submarine around. She then stood, attempting to hold herself over the submarine and test if it was stable enough on the ground to remain upright if she got out of it. When she was confident it would stay put, she exited and swam in the direction of the alien.

Dark mounds could be seen protruding from the ground. Their quality was difficult to define. Whatever material they were made of was markedly different from the sand around them. They seemed to shimmer and reflect the water, blending in with the water in an undefinable way.

Shannon's breath could hold out no longer. She was forced to return to her submarine. Knowing that she had already been gone longer than was safe, she sped as quickly as she could back to Brenda and the plane. She struggled to control her elation as she slowly traveled. Without having to give up her location, she had found where the aliens lived. That would provide significantly more opportunity for research. Though, she would do the rest of it through the collara, for safety.

Chapter 21

Four weeks passed as Shannon and Brenda researched the aliens. They learned about the aliens' routines, how much rain was required before they would surface out of the ocean, how much food they harvested from their crops, and many other details.

With the help of the collara, Shannon was able to get close enough to where the aliens lived underwater that she could tell they had created shelters for themselves. The shelters were made of a substance that looked to Shannon like a semi-iridescent blue pearl. Many huts, some as large as thirty feet squared, seemed to grow organically out of the ground in the pearl-like material that, in many ways, reminded Shannon of coral. The texture was smoother than coral, but was more wavy in its formation than a pearl. Openings to these huts were small and seemed difficult to enter. Though Shannon attempted to keep her collara unnoticed by observing these homes from a distance, she had seen on one occasion—after she had ventured more closely and was caught off guard when the aliens had returned early from farming—that they would swim toward the openings, yet glide in gracefully without additional movements as they neared the small entrances.

For several days after her close call, the two women discussed at length the chances that their collara had been spotted. The aliens' patterns had remained the same, and there did not seem to be any increase in distance that the aliens traveled from their camp, which led Brenda to believe that they were not investigating nearby areas for intrusions. She none the less recommended that Shannon keep her distance for a while so as to not further risk compromising their relatively close proximity.

"I'm going to begin preparing our planes for our return," announced Brenda casually as she ate her breakfast, her face down toward her food.

Shannon nodded to herself. "Okay."

Despite Shannon's agreement, Brenda continued her thoughts. "We've gathered every piece of information that we can about them." Brenda let out a sigh. "With our limited tools, and no additional help, I think we have just about reached our limit as to what we can accomplish."

This all sounded like familiar conclusions that Shannon knew they had come to from previous conversations.

Brenda looked up from her meal, directly at Shannon, her face somber. "I want to leave four days before you."

Shannon's stomach sank. This, too, was something they had discussed, but she had been unable to appreciate what it meant, until now. She swallowed her fear and nodded.

"We'll load up everything we've gathered for research into my plane, as well as tether up all of the submarines that we found." They had successfully retrieved six, and additional oxygen tanks. "I think four days will be enough time for me to pull everything with the plane on the water and not get caught up in the storm that you are likely to create when you try and connect with them." Brenda stopped and waited for Shannon to make eye contact. "Do not get in the water."

"Okay."

"Seriously," interrupted Brenda. "The second you think your position is compromised, you jump into your plane and get out of here. After two days of flying, you start trying to make radio contact with me. Look for me if you aren't being followed. Swing wide and keep them off my trail if they are chasing after you."

"Okay," replied Shannon.

"And don't dig for extra details. Find out where they all are, and get a sample of whatever their huts, or houses, or whatever, are made out of and then leave. If either of those things go wrong, then ditch them. We will regroup, get reinforcements, come back, and try again when we are prepared to handle them better."

Brenda stood up and walked into the rain that had relentlessly tormented them for the past three weeks. At first they had attempted to wait until the rain let up before doing things outside; but as the days went on, and the reprieves of the strength of rain became more and more infrequent, they gradually accepted their circumstances and began to ignore the downpour. The temperature remained fairly warm, regardless of the rain, so they grew used to simply being wet. She grabbed some rope from her plane and tied one end around the left pontoon. She then walked to Shannon's plane and tied the other end of the rope to her plane to use as a temporary anchor.

"The tide is low right now. Help me push my plane just far enough toward the water that when the tide comes in it will lift it. We can tie the submarines to the pontoons so they don't just sink or dangle loosely and risk catching something like an anchor. When the tide comes in and I can move the plane, I'll leave."

Quickly, Shannon ran to the plane as Brenda disengaged its breaks. Brenda could easily see the look of concern that was painted on Shannon's face.

"I know it feels sudden, but it is best to not let these things drag on. We've discussed all of this before. I also had a restless night to think it over, and decided the time was now to act. As we struggle to get answers and come up with strategies, our enemy is fortifying their position and gathering and developing their resources. We've done all we can do for now, other than the couple tasks that remain for you, and I have to get everything else away from you as quickly as possible so that our risk of failure diminishes significantly. I know you're going to be fine, and I'll see you in six or seven days."

One by one they attached all of the submarines to the pontoons. They placed all of the plant and soil samples from the aliens' farm inside the plane, and packed her tent and gear. When they were done, they waited for the tide to come in from inside Shannon's tent.

They sat silently with each other for a long while. Over their time together, they had become used to not talking to each other constantly. Finally, when Shannon's nerves had gotten the better of her, she spoke.

"What do you think our odds are?" asked Shannon.

Brenda shook her head for a moment as she thought the question through. "I don't honestly know. Humans have never been at a weaker point. There just aren't that many of us left, and many of the few who have survived are not in a great state of mind. Shock, fear, and survival usually mix with unfortunate results. Meanwhile, the enemy is largely unknown and has more and more time to organize themselves. However, they are in enemy territory, and at the moment, they don't seem to be able to do much to us from where they are. Meaning, if they want to attack us, they will probably have to come to us, which would give us a huge advantage. It could go either way, though I think whatever we can find out about the things we have gathered could make all the difference."

Shannon chuckled to herself. "My dad would have lost his mind if he knew we were being visited by aliens while we waited in that bunker." Her tone immediately became somber. "He was so close to finding out. If he had just survived a little longer," Shannon lamented.

"There are definitely nights I just lay awake struggling to accept the new reality we live in, that the things I've seen and done are not just dreams," replied Brenda.

Shannon fell silent as she dwelled on what she would have to do in the coming days. Brenda put her arm around Shannon.

"We've made it this far." Brenda said as she gave Shannon a squeeze. "Whatever visions or prophecies you've experienced have gotten us this far. We currently sit shockingly close to our enemy, and yet I feel completely safe leaving you here as I get a head start. Regardless of how you started having visions, if they were from the aliens, then I think they would have capitalized on us being here. The fact that nothing has happened, even though they seemed so focused on you, makes me believe they had nothing to do with your visions. So, if what you saw wasn't from *them*, then it seems reasonable to believe that you obtained from them the ability to see, or be sensitive to, the future. Within your own strength or effort, you saw what needed to be done to get us this far. I have no reason to think that what you've seen isn't for our benefit, possibly to prepare you for what is to come. With that in mind, I have no reason to believe that you won't get through this with success. Whether you had a vision or not does not change the fact that you are focused, careful, hard-working, and dedicated, to the point of being consistently successful."

For several hours they worked quietly to catch and prepare as much food as possible. They packed the food into Brenda's plane. Gradually the water rose up the sand until the plane began to tilt slightly under the waves. Brenda climbed in, checked her gauges, and then started her engine. The plane whirred to life as she continued to examine her plane in preparation for leaving. Shannon stood nearby as she watched the water rise faster than she had hoped it would.

As the plane stopped settling on the ground between each wave, Brenda cracked open her door, waved to Shannon, and shouted. "See you soon!"

Shannon waved as the plane slowly dragged the attached submarines into deeper water and it subtly sank from the weight. Careful not to overwork the engines, Brenda slowly began her journey. Her progress grew easier as she escaped the tumultuous water near the island. Shannon stood in the rain and watched as the plane grew smaller. When the plane had shrunk far into the distance, and her confidence had weakened more than she could bear, she turned around and made her way back toward her tent.

Shannon got dry, climbed into her tent, put on some pajamas, and, though it was still early afternoon, climbed into her sleeping bag. She knew how she worked. The hardest part of the next few days was going to be waiting for the time to take action. If she could sleep through at least some of that time, then she would gladly do so. As her emotional exhaustion fought to take over, she allowed her self to succumb to its grip and slept.

Chapter 22

The four collara bound happily across the beach, wrestling with each other in a playful manner. Sand shot into the air lazily under them, unable to overpower the rain that fell heavily. Her bond with the animals had grown over time, and now simply thinking of them returning to her manifested the action. She gently touched each of them and felt her connection with them grow. A subtle desire for them to go into the water was all that was required for them to run off and disappear into the ocean. Shannon examined the beach where her camp had been for several months and found no evidence of their presence remaining. Though she was happy to return to her brother, the barren camp brought a sadness to her. The time had been relatively peaceful and drama-free. She climbed onto her plane, satisfied with her preparations.

Taking a deep breath, she looked at her watch before reluctantly removing the magnetic necklace she had worn for so long.

12:38pm.

She fought the inherent panic she had previously trained her mind to feel for the absence of her makeshift jewelry. Leaning back in her chair, she closed her eyes, pushed her consciousness away from herself, and waited for the inevitable invasion of her mind. To her surprise, she could actually feel a presence approaching before it came knocking at the door of her mind.

My time with the collara has helped me more than I realized.

The connection she made with the alien felt far deeper and less one-sided than ever before. Her consciousness felt expanded. While she was still aware of her own body, she could also feel the water through the alien, and could sense a map of memories that were foreign to her. While much of the experience felt new, one thing was instantly familiar; the prodding and searching of her own mind. With much strain, she relegated the invading entity to a distant corner of her mind while still trying to discover what she needed from her enemy.

"What is it you think you are doing?" asked the entity in her mind. "You've learned some tricks, it seems, since the last time we met."

Shannon ignored the internal voice. Through this connection she could feel the other aliens, and she was desperate to know where they all were.

"You've grown in your abilities since working with our..." a slight pause as it searched her mind for the word, "collara. Despite what you've learned, you are far from being able to sneak around in my mind. If you want to know where we are, you can just ask. I've no reason to hide from you. In fact, the more you know, the more, I think, you are likely to admit to the impossible chances of your success."

Immediately, Shannon could feel a door being opened and she could sense the location of all of the aliens, as well as the other people globally. More powerful than ever before, and more of a feeling that they were her own senses, her connection with the alien was so strong—and therefore foreign—that it gave her fear. She was not stepping into the same situation she had experienced before. This was new, and as a result, unfamiliar. Instinctively she withdrew a bit. She was not afraid of what she would find out, but concerned that the alien might be drawing her out so she would leave her own mind unguarded.

The alien was tipping his hand in an attempt to get a peek at hers. This she knew. A certain amount of information she needed, no matter what. The location and number of the aliens was why she risked herself by contacting them. She moved forward in her mind very carefully, attempting to split herself, with much strain. Part of her sought out the information, while the other part remained and fought to keep her mental occupant contained.

As she cautiously embraced the connection, she felt herself, her awareness, split. She suddenly had a spatial awareness of others that gave her the sensation of looking down at a map with figurines as markers. It felt global. Simultaneously, she could sense, and even see, each entity, human and alien, individually. The dichotomy of these global and personal feelings was far more intense of an experience than Shannon's mind could handle. Maintaining this awareness required significant strain and was instantly giving her a mental nauseousness similar to the feeling of double vision.

The aliens had increased in number by eight and now totaled 155, though the offspring felt small and weak in their presence and capabilities compared to the adults. They were dispersed in groups of roughly thirty, each group close to major land masses around the world. There were nearly 12,000 people globally, though there did not seem to be any groups larger than 1,000. Most groups seemed to be between 200 and 500.

In addition to feeling the presence of the aliens, she could also sense their hierarchy. Though they were separated by distance, each of the aliens remained connected to each other, and there was a very clear distinction of importance among the different beings. There was also an indefinable string connecting them all, somehow empty in its quality. It felt to her as some sort of binding void between the aliens. She struggled to understand this void, and could feel it withdraw from her as she probed for it. The void did not feel like a lack of presence, but an awareness that was intentionally veiled. She immediately knew she had stumbled upon information that she would have to dissect later, but fought to conceal her reaction. When she felt she had gained the information she most needed, she then turned her attention to her brother and Chris. They were still at the settlement and seemed to be healthy, though she could not tell much more.

Suddenly the being she was connected to seemed to recoil, its attention divided. The magnets had protected the collara from mental detection, but clearly they had been noticed by some other means. Without waiting, Shannon retreated entirely, opening her eyes as she replaced her magnets for protection. She glanced at her watch, 12:46pm. Eight minutes had passed, which she quickly wrote down before firing up the engine of her plane. A minute later, Shannon was in the air and carefully following her compass. Her chest heaved from excitement in anticipation of catching up with Brenda, and hopefully seeing her brother again.

It was late evening when Shannon's collara caught up to her after her retreat. She had fought her anxiety that pleaded with her to keep going, and forced herself to rest and to connect with the collara. Three arrived and provided her with samples of the igloo-like homes that the aliens had made for themselves under water. She laid her hands on the first three and had a similar experience with each of them; covertly swimming up toward the alien community, snatching their samples, and then being alerted by the struggle and commotion of the fourth collara. Upon her noticing the trouble, she quickly retreated. She was unable to observe any form of pursuit from any of them.

By the time she was done with the three collara, the fourth had returned. Her heart beat in her chest, anxious to connect with the fourth collara. It had made it back to her safely, but even from the perspective of the others, this collara's experience had been rather startling. She laid her hand on the animal and instantly found herself in the same environment she had explored three other times. Having witnessed small portions of this collara's movements in the others, her control came and went with her visibility with the others. Eventually she reached a position near the mouth of one of the homes.

The colony was empty. The aliens had taken advantage of the rain to do their farming on land. Empty, Shannon assumed, except for the one that she was connected with as she sat in her plane, discovering the locations of her friends and other survivors, and experiencing the binding void that attempted to hide itself from her.

Growing daring in her efforts, she began peeking into homes in search of the one she was connected with. She wanted to know just how distracted they truly were while interacting with her. Twenty different homes of varying sizes were laid out in a seemingly random way. Each one had a door facing a different direction and was positioned away from the others at unpredictable distances and positions. Cautiously she looked into several homes and found them to be empty. Her seventh attempt provided success as she peered into a home with an alien sitting with crossed legs in the center of the igloo, its eyes closed tightly, and its head resting in its top set of hands. It sat with its left side facing toward the door.

I know I will make it back safely, she reminded herself as she watched from outside the entrance. She slowly made her way inside. Each movement forward was a more difficult force of will than the last. The alien remained in a pose of fierce concentration, unresponsive to her presence. Inches turned into feet as she made her way farther into the igloo. She eventually reached a position close enough that she could see the water around the alien move back and forth as it slowly breathed. A momentary distraction captivated her as she wondered if the alien was breathing oxygen from the water or some other element. She immediately threw the thought out of her head and focused on what was before her.

She had now moved to within a couple of feet from the alien and felt confident that it was unaware of her presence. She had just one more test to perform; she must touch the alien. Though the alien was sitting in a position that faced Shannon's left, because of the two sets of eyes it had, with one on each side of its head, it had a closed eye that faced directly at Shannon. The eye before her rolled around beneath its translucent lid as it attempted to search her mind for information several miles away. Slowly, regretfully, Shannon moved the collara's hand forward. Despite how close she had made it without being noticed, each inch forward was gained with the utmost terror. She once again reminded herself that she already knew she had made it out alive, and in a moment of courage thrust her hand out and touched the alien.

Instantly, the eye that faced Shannon shot open in a mixture of shock and hatred. Its mental focus, she knew, was pulling away from herself and turning toward the collara before it. With the current contact, it attempted to enter the mind of the collara and seize control.

Shannon, nearly twelve hours and a few hundred miles away from this moment, felt a sudden presence within her own mind as the alien fought to control the collara's consciousness. Repulsed by the sudden awareness and strength of Shannon's presence within the collara, the alien recoiled in horror and pain as Shannon regained control of the collara and immediately turned to retreat.

For several hours she watched her back closely as she pushed herself at full strength in her escape from the aliens. She never observed a pursuer. They had not given chase to her.

Chapter 23

The plane sloshed on the water with just enough force to rock Shannon awake. Warm rays of light splashed across her face, forcing her to squint as she greeted the new day.

She had been flying for four days, and had pushed herself as hard as she could to try and catch up to Brenda. She worked over the math in her head. The trip to Hawaii took seven days. Brenda had left four days before her, but was going quite slow since she was staying on the water to tow the subs. Meanwhile, Shannon had started her flying each day earlier and ended later than she had when going toward Hawaii, and was confident that her efforts would result in her finding Brenda today.

Shannon prepared her breakfast with the intention of eating while she flew. Her desire to reunite with Brenda was unbearable. Before taking flight, she connected with the collara that accompanied her, reliving the night that had just come to a close four times. One stayed with her at all times. One would back track at night for several hours to make sure no one was following her. The other two would run ahead for a few hours in search of Brenda. None of them provided her with any new information.

Anxiously, Shannon threw the plane into full speed, and, skipping turbulently off the choppy water, eventually bounced into the air. She climbed quickly in the hopes that a higher elevation would allow her to see farther and give her a better chance at finding Brenda.

As the day slowly crawled forward, a tension built in Shannon's chest that threatened to hinder her breathing. Every fifteen minutes, she would check her radio, hoping that she was suddenly in range of Brenda. Her efforts yielded no results. Forced to sit with her thoughts as she desperately searched the vast ocean for Brenda, images of her father would invade her mind and she would suddenly find herself crying. She would quickly reprimand herself and dry her tears.

I can not allow myself to assume the worst about her. She is a far more capable woman than I am. If I can get this far, then so can she, she would remind herself.

Gradually the day carried on, and the warm glow of late evening spread its fiery color upon the water. In a brief moment of desperation Shannon drew her plane upward to expand her view as much as possible. The diminishing light fought against her efforts and made the details of the water difficult to see. She held out as long as she could, but as her plane's battery dipped to critical levels, and the last rays of light threatened their retreat, she knew she must land while she could still see where she was going.

As she began her descent and her focus was removed from her search, a light flashed across her eyes, a quick flicker of the sun that had reflected off of something and drawn her attention. With her heart exploding out of her chest in excitement, she nearly lost focus of her landing and dropped onto the water with an alarming force that kicked water into the air.

"Brenda, are you there?" screamed Shannon into her radio.

No answer.

Shannon didn't care. She turned her plane in the direction she thought the glare of light had come from and started taxiing in that direction. She could see nothing ahead of her as the last glimpse of light set behind her. The sound of her plane rose and fell as her batteries squeezed out what little power they had left. Rifling through her bag, she grabbed a flood light, cracked open her door, and pointed the light out ahead of her. Sweeping the light back and forth, she hoped to see another glare indicating Brenda's location. Suddenly her light bounced back at her and she corrected course in that direction. She pulled the light back inside her plane and focused on her new heading.

A hundred feet away and the light of the moon brought just enough detail to be able to identify Brenda's plane clearly. The power of Shannon's plane grew and sank more rapidly until it died out completely. Despite the buttons and levers that Shannon had at her disposal, none of them functioned. Her plane was dead. It continued with its previous momentum for a brief moment, and then suddenly its speed dropped. Brenda's plane, now fifty feet away, inched closer more and more slowly, until, at twenty feet, the movement of the ocean's waves took control and the two planes ebbed and flowed in parallel. Shannon yelled out of her door, but there was still no response. She grabbed her light again and leaned out as she pointed her light at the plane. Her heart sank.

The light revealed a plane that appeared perfectly intact. The door to the aircraft swung back and forth lazily with the flow of the water beneath it. From her current distance, Shannon could see all of Brenda's items still on the plane. Everything looked as she would have expected it, except that the pilot was missing. Brenda was gone.

Tears poured down Shannon's face. Her grip grew weak, her hands shaking as she rummaged through her items to find a rope. Struggling to search as she wept, the plane rocked back with sudden force. She looked out and saw the collara towing her plane. In a brief moment, her plane bumped into the other aircraft. Having finally found her rope, she moved along the outside of her plane and tied the two aircraft together. As she used the rope to anchor the two planes to each other, she noticed that only one of the personal submarines remained. The other five were gone. She quickly went to the cockpit of Brenda's aircraft and searched for any indication of what might have happened. All the samples were intact. All of her clothing and gear were still present.

Shannon sat in the seat of the plane. She started it up to see the charge. It was full.

The plane must have been here for a while to have recharged completely.

There was no note, no sign of struggle. She closed the door, and then gave it a push. It stayed closed.

She couldn't have just fallen out while sleeping.

She opened the door and looked down at the black abyss below her. One by one, the collara popped up nearby. She laid hands on each of them and had them pull her plane in the past and then sent them down into the water to search for any sign of Brenda.

The water was far too deep and dark. Regardless of the time of day, she knew she would never find Brenda if she were in the water below her. There was likewise no sign of the other subs.

Her body let out an uncontrollable shudder. As much as she couldn't bear to think or act in any fashion, she now knew she had two options. Either she waited here, hoping that Brenda was still alive and was just gone using a submarine, or continued moving to prevent whatever had happened to Brenda from happening to herself.

What if everything was left here as a trap after the aliens took her?

She wanted to stay. She wanted to hope that somehow Brenda was still out there being the strong woman Shannon knew her to be. She wanted to compromise her position and attempt connecting with the aliens so she could find Brenda's location. She wanted to ignore everything she knew Brenda would be screaming at her right now.

There was no way Brenda would voluntarily get in the water; she had made that very clear. Either something bad happened to her naturally, or she was in some way attacked. Regardless, there were too few scenarios where she was alive, and there were too many scenarios where

Shannon had just stepped into a trap. Her gut was telling her she needed to move.

She grabbed a nearby jacket and bundled it around her face as she screamed into it, releasing the frustration, panic, and sadness that shook her to her core. In that moment she stuffed her pain down cramming it lower and lower until it was in her feet. She then stomped her feet in impotent rage before throwing the door open and standing up.

Unwilling to relinquish any of her resources, Shannon stepped out of the cockpit and tied her plane so that it would trail behind Brenda's at a distance. She checked the line connected to the submarine to make sure it was still secure, and then climbed back into Brenda's plane. She fired up the engine and threw the throttle into the taxiing position. The plane lurched forward and then rocked backward when the line towing the other plane became taut. She checked her compass and confirmed she was moving in the right direction.

She had to leave that place, salvage what she could, and get as far away as possible. She wouldn't stop until she fell asleep or her plane died. She needed to be on land, away from this water that had taken too much away from her. That was the only way she would feel safe enough to hunt for answers, if any were to be found.

Chapter 24

Exhausted and overwhelmed, Shannon drove her plane onto the beach. Having slept only when she could go on no longer, and immediately resuming her travels when she woke, she had returned to land at nearly the same time as she had expected to when flying. She had been able to alternate with the two planes, one towed while the other charged. With a singular focus, she had made her way to the coast, and, having now arrived, she stumbled her way out of her plane, and collapsed onto the beach, crying as she sprawled out.

For the first time since discovering Brenda's plane, Shannon allowed herself to process the loss of her friend. Her emotions had threatened to overpower her in waves, but she had fought to suppress them until this moment. It had been so sudden, something she simply hadn't seen coming. She struggled to believe it was real.

She pulled off her necklace in hopes of finding answers now that she was safely on land. She waited for her mind to be intruded. Nothing happened. She continued to wait. There was no sign of anyone. She closed her eyes and attempted to push her mind outward in search of an alien to connect with. Still, nothing happened.

Is this because of what happened with the collara at the alien village? Are they avoiding me now, thinking that I might have set up a trap for them?

Several minutes passed, until eventually Shannon admitted defeat and replaced her necklace. Her tears poured so freely that her cheeks felt raw. The four collara instinctively placed themselves in protective positions around her as she cried herself to sleep.

The sun hung overhead, warming her as she slept for an hour, until the hunger from her own neglect outweighed her fatigue and sadness. Upon her waking, a coldness seized her. Expelling her anguish, she focused on the nearness of her brother and Chris. She would have to return and deal with her conflict with Matt and the others. She wondered how Brenda would have handled this situation. *Far more confidently than I will*, assumed Shannon. *I need their help moving forward, so I will have to try and make peace with them.*

For an hour she secured her planes farther inland than the beaches. There was far too much to carry, and she couldn't remember just how far the new settlement was from the ocean. She would have to return with help, if she could get any. To prevent coming off as threatening or creating any confusion, she placed her hands on the collara and requested that they remain at the beach rather than follow her.

It was nightfall by the time Shannon reached the settlement. She approached cautiously, hiding out of sight behind large debris. Activity was slowly dying down as people began settling in for the night. To her delight, she saw Billy, Jenny, and Chris at different points throughout the evening as she waited for her chance to approach. She was relieved by how much better Chris looked from when she had last seen him, still very much injured, but moving around freely.

After a long delay of waiting for everyone to go to sleep, Shannon lost her patience and began throwing small rocks at her brother. After several misses, one finally connected with his lower back. To Shannon's pleasure, he reacted quickly but quietly. Immediately sensing the meaning behind the surprise attack, he jumped to his feet and made to run toward the perimeter of the camp before regaining his composure and casually strolling away. He looked around blindly in the dark as he made his way toward Shannon. As he neared, she peeked out of her hiding place and grabbed him, pulling him into a hug.

They embraced quietly for a moment. She wondered if he had gotten a little taller since she had been gone. Her head rested comfortably against his chest. He had clearly been eating well; he had maintained his athletic physique. And his once short, blond hair now hung down to his chin, shining in the glow of nearby fires.

"I had started giving up hope I would see you again," spoke Billy, at last. He maintained their hug.

"I'm sorry I was gone forever. I didn't mean to make you wait so long. You won't believe how much I have to tell you." Shannon's voice was mixed with relief and sadness.

Billy rested his hands on Shannon's shoulders and pushed her to arms length as he looked her over, making sure she was okay. His face looked older to Shannon. It now had the seriousness and maturity of someone who had experienced pain and struggle in life. Lines and a tan had developed from working outside. He then glanced around, looking for her companion.

Shannon shook her head. "I don't know what happened. We traveled separately on the way back. I found her things, but she was just gone." A shakiness grew in her voice as she spoke.

Billy pulled her back into a hug and reassuringly pet her hair. "It's okay. I'm here."

"How has it been since I've been gone?"

"Well, the good news is that Jenny and Chris are getting better. Jenny was really upset when you left and latched on to me even harder than before, which is fine by me. However, she is still opening up more and is starting to return to normal a bit. Although, she still stays far away from other men. Chris is up, and most of his bones seem to have healed. I gotta say, he pulls off the eye patch look pretty well. Phil keeps yelling at him to take it easy, because he keeps wanting to get back into shape. I think he really had faith in you that you would return, and he wanted to be ready to help you when that time came.

"The bad news is that Matt is to this settlement what Dillon was to the last one. Everyone is surviving, but we're all miserable. I've been on the team doing beach runs every week. He thinks I have the same luck as you with the land demons. Although, I have to wonder if it isn't true, because ever since you've been gone, they haven't been attacking us."

"I think I know why that is," responded Shannon. "I sort of figured out how to tame them."

Billy's eyes opened in surprise. "Okay, it sounds like you do have things to tell me."

Shannon nodded. "First, though, what do you think my reception is going to be like?"

"That's a good question," responded a gruff voice from behind Shannon.

Shannon whipped around in shock and found herself staring down the barrel of a rifle. It took a moment before she remembered the name of the man holding it. Frank. A look of disappointment hung on his face.

"This was obvious. We didn't even need to keep a lookout for you," said Frank. "Of course you would try to contact your brother if you came back. We just had someone always keeping an eye on him. I think this is the first time I've seen him more than five feet away from his girlfriend since you left."

Frank looked around. "Where's Brenda?" He asked with disdain.

"She didn't make it," responded Shannon flatly. Her expression was cold, concealing her emotions. She wasn't going to give him the satisfaction of seeing her true feelings.

Frank gave a hateful smile. "You've made it too easy for us. Getting your own friend killed. It will be easy to justify getting rid of you now."

Wounded by his words, Shannon took a step back. Billy pushed her back farther and stepped in between her and the gun.

"Put the gun down," demanded Billy loudly, alerting others from the settlement. His blue eyes were fierce and protective.

Investigating the commotion, Chris came running up and stopped short as he saw what was happening. "What the hell are you doing, Frank? You hurt them and I'll kill you." Though he had lost a lot of weight, he was still well built and towering over Shannon. Like her brother, his hair had grown out and he now kept it slicked back. His eye patch made his words all the more threatening.

"No, you won't," said Matt as he shoved his rifle into Chris' back.

Chris raised his hands instinctively.

"Thanks for showing us where your alliance stands," said Matt. "That makes this easier." He glanced at Frank, "Brenda?"

"The girl says she's dead."

"You hear that everyone? She sneaks away with our supplies, abandoning us when we needed the most help, and then gets our leader killed," announced Matt. "She's a threat to everyone here. For all we know, she's led the land demons here and we could be under attack at any moment." Matt shoved Chris forward so that he was standing grouped with Shannon and Billy. "Even if she didn't bring the monsters with her, it's only a matter of time before these three work out a plan to steal our things and attempt a coup."

Matt lowered his voice and leaned toward Shannon. "It's about time you got what was coming to you before you ran away." To the settlement he spoke again, "They can't be trusted and they can't stay here. Frank and I are going to escort them to the beach and see what happens. If the land demons attack them, then they will get what they deserve. If they don't, then we will know that she is on their side, and we will kill her as our enemy." Matt leaned in once again and, through clenched teeth, spoke in a quiet hiss. "I want to watch you pay for what happened to Steven."

Shannon couldn't help but feel disbelief over Matt's rage. Though it hadn't actually been that long since Steven had died while retrieving supplies for the current settlement location, to Shannon, it felt like a lifetime ago. Combined with the searing pain she was enduring for the loss of Brenda, she couldn't feel any connection to Matt's anger.

Matt stepped away and gave orders to the two others with guns to stay and keep guard while he and Frank were gone. He anticipated returning quickly.

"It's really too bad that we have to do this," said Matt casually as he strolled behind Shannon.

Chris was in the lead position, followed by Billy, then Frank, with Shannon and Matt in the rear.

Matt continued. "A good looking girl like you, there aren't many left in this world, and throwing one away, such as I am, seems like a waste. Unfortunately, you've already done too much damage, proved yourself to be a serious threat, and for some reason, you gain the loyalty of the people around you. I'd love to just lock you up in storage and keep you for my entertainment, but I think it would upset too many of the others and make them harder to control."

Shannon kept her mouth shut. Things were predictable as they currently were, and she didn't want that to change by upsetting her captors. Billy, however, agitated by Matt's words looked back to say something, but was stopped with a quick head shake from Shannon. He faced forward again, but not before Matt took notice.

Matt gave a menacing smile. "It's not all bad, though. Jenny seems like she will be a real treat, and in her broken state, I'm sure I won't even have to force her. She'll submit willingly."

Chris quickly slowed his walk and grabbed Billy's arm before Billy had a chance to react.

"Keep it cool, things are stable right now," said Chris, echoing Shannon's feelings.

Before Matt had a chance to continue, the sounds of the waves breaking on the sand ahead of them finally indicated their approaching arrival at their destination. The debris was much worse around the beach as the ocean continually deposited its waste and pushed it inland. They carefully climbed over the mounds of trash and detritus.

As they walked out onto the beach, Frank stepped back and joined Matt in the rear, a safe distance from the water. He provided just one command as he passed Shannon. "Keep walking."

"Death just seems to follow you," yelled out Matt when Shannon and the others had reached the water.

She turned around as he spoke.

"If you hadn't returned, two more people would still be alive this evening, but you killed them," he continued.

As Shannon watched Matt speak, she saw faint movement from the mound of debris behind him. In an instant, four collara leaped into the air and landed on the two men before they had any realization of their ambush. A single shot rang out into the air, but was fired in surprise and was aimless. The collara were ruthless in their attack, and the men were dead and in several pieces before they ever had a chance to defend themselves. When their targets had been eliminated they waited triumphantly over their victims.

"So, remember how I mentioned that I tamed some land demons?" Shannon said to her brother as she gestured to the waiting animals. "Also, Brenda and I decided to call them collara."

Shannon made her way to the collara and rested her hand on them one at a time, reliving the ambush from four different angles. The only part she had control over was their positioning before they came into view for their attack.

Billy and Chris approached cautiously.

"How tame are they?" asked Chris, not attempting to mask his concern.

Shannon gave a knowing smile. "More than you can imagine."

Chapter 25

With the help of Billy and Chris, Shannon was able to bring everything she needed from her planes back to the settlement. Chris and Billy had also grabbed the guns from their deceased captors, and, through minimal planning and effort on the part of Chris, had quickly and decisively overwhelmed the two men who had remained on guard at the settlement. The other settlers were equally speedy in embracing their new circumstances and greeted Shannon's return warmly.

The settlement had developed quite a bit in Shannon's absence. An agglomerate of materials had been used to assemble makeshift buildings and furniture that gave the place a much needed sense of permanence and comfort. She meticulously unpacked her items into one such building that Billy insisted he had built for them to share. The space was rather small, no more than twelve feet in either direction, and felt even smaller with three beds in it. She was, however, in no position to protest after everything she had put her brother through. Jenny seemed almost as excited for Shannon's return as Billy was. She had embraced Shannon for a long time before finally letting her unpack her things.

There was a light knocking at the entrance to her new home before Phil let himself in. There was no door. His white hair and nice clothes were disheveled and dirty from labor. Though his appearance conveyed a long day of hard work, his expression was relaxed and happier than she had remembered him being previously. "I'm relieved to see that you've returned," he said with a warm smile. "Do you have any injuries that might need tending to?"

Shannon gave a tired smile and softly shook her head. "I'm fine."

"I'm sorry about Brenda." He lingered in silence for a moment as he contemplated his next words, taking a moment to comb his white hair back. "I believed you, you know, that she was one of the good ones. I believed you," he said as he trailed off into silence.

Shannon appreciated his words, suppressing a knot that grew in her throat, but she continued with her efforts to organize her things, unwilling to get into a conversation on the topic of Brenda.

Phil stood and watched her continue to unpack. "Bits of soil and vegetation with labels... are those samples?"

"Yes. We collected them while we were in Hawaii doing reconnaissance on the aliens. I'm not sure what I'm going to do with them yet, but somehow I'll figure out a way to test them."

Phil stroked his chin as he looked at the samples. "If you want, I have tools and solutions to test your soil for pH and EC values, and we could do titration with the food. If you think that could help."

"While my gut tells me to be excited because you said that you can help, I have no idea what those things mean or what they offer me," responded Shannon.

"Well, the pH and EC values will essentially tell you the health of the soil, which in turn tells you what the plants growing in said soil have access to. Titration is a relatively crude method we can use to determine the nutritional values of the food. Basically, get a solution that reacts to vitamin C, D, Zinc, or whatever you are wanting to test for, and see how much of the food you have to put into the solution before it reacts to the vitamin or mineral present in the food. I wish we had the tools to perform high performance liquid chromatography, but we wouldn't have the available power to run those machines anyway."

"I'm guessing that is a fancier way of testing nutritional values, but, honestly, I'll take what I can get at this point, because I am grasping at straws," responded Shannon, gratefully.

Phil shrugged. "We have all this stuff sitting in storage because we will need to test our own food and soil throughout the years as we establish our farms. In fact, I already did some of this work at the last settlement, and should probably be doing it here as well, since we don't know what impact all of these recent events have had on our soil. There's no harm in some additional practice. Tomorrow I'll swing by and you can help me move your samples into storage so I can start testing them."

"That would be amazing," responded Shannon.

The evening carried on and Shannon found herself resting in her bed as Jenny slept and Billy sat up looking at nothing specific while he was deep in thought. His face was cast in shadow from the light that trickled into the room from the fires outside, making his look of concentration appear more brooding.

After a long silence, he spoke. "So, what's your plan?"

Shannon rolled on to her side, propped herself up on an elbow, and rested her head in her hand. She shrugged. "I haven't figured one out yet. I have a bunch of pieces to a puzzle, but still have no idea what the picture is."

"That doesn't sound like you at all, especially for how long you were gone. You must have some ideas," responded Billy.

Shannon's long blond hair was pulled back into a ponytail for sleeping. She pulled it out. Her mind was too active for the restrictive feeling of her hair being pulled back. She shook her hair out; it now came halfway down her back. "Still too much missing information, I think."

"I always knew I would have to be the smart one between us," said Billy. "Tell me everything that happened while you were gone and I'll figure this out."

"It's late, I'll tell you in the morning."

"No way. Tomorrow you'll just be busy doing something else, plus I'm never going to be able to sleep unless I know what you were up to for two months while you were gone."

Shannon conceded, secretly happy to have a distraction from her thoughts about Brenda, and for several hours she recounted her experiences to her brother in great detail as he was prone to asking questions otherwise. Billy rested his head on his pillow. For a moment she thought he had finally fallen asleep after she had finished her story.

"We may not know where this train's final destination is, but I think we do already know a couple more stops it has to make along the way," whispered Billy. Without waiting for a response from Shannon, he continued. "It sounds like you need to figure out what this 'binding void' is, and if we have a fourth type of alien to worry about. We also know now that there are nearly 12,000 people out there, and we need to find a way to contact them. They might be the army we need if we ever have to go to war with the aliens, since we know we would have them outnumbered."

"I guess you're right," responded Shannon.

"Thanks for telling me all that," said Billy.

After a moment of silence, Shannon could hear the soft breathing of her brother sleeping.

Shannon carried her samples into the storage room. Tucked in the back, behind rows of shelves, was a small desk shoved into a corner. The space was brightly lit with small but bright, white lights that were positioned around the desk, upon which were beakers, test tubes, and various solutions. The desk was cramped, but she was able to find space for everything she had collected. Phil stood over the different liquids that covered the desk and examined their labels, confirming that he had collected the right items.

"It could take me a while before I can get you results," said Phil. "You do have large enough sample sizes that I can divide them up into multiple tests. But preparing the vegetation does take time, and each solution will need controls and multiple tests performed to get accurate results. With all of my other obligations, I would think it could take me a week to get through all of your samples."

"All of this would have been a dead end if not for your help, so take as much time as you need," replied Shannon.

Phil walked her out of the storage room. He spoke with a bit of excitement. "Some of this stuff I've definitely never seen before. I'm not sure exactly what these tests will tell us, but with so little information available to us, everything we learn will paint a fuller picture."

"Thanks again," said Shannon as she turned away in search of Chris.

Shannon soon found Chris clearing out a new area for additional farming. The sweat that covered him seemed to indicate he was giving his body far more of a workout than was appropriate for his still healing injuries.

"If Phil sees his patient straining himself like this, he's going to lock you up and force you to rest." Shannon approached him with a cheerful smile.

Chris set down the heavy debris he was carrying and jogged to Shannon, his face full of warmth and happiness to see her. "Come sit down and talk to me for a bit while I finish. I would love the company. Plus, if Phil does see me, I can claim you as an accomplice."

"I'll sit down, but if you get me in trouble, I will throw you under the bus in an instant. I'll tell him how I begged and pleaded with you to stop and you yelled at me," she quipped playfully as she sat down and tucked a strand of hair behind her ear.

"Sounds fair," responded Chris as he turned back to clearing debris.

Shannon sat and watched Chris work. She admired his tenacity. Despite the discomfort she knew he must still be enduring as he worked, he moved around with the same smile he always had when she was around. He was noticeably thinner from his lack of exertion and eating while he had been injured, but he was still far larger than men she typically found attractive. She had also thought he was a bit too pretty when she had first seen him. His leather eye patch, however, gave him a ruggedness and imperfection that endeared him to her. As he continued to work tirelessly in front of her, she felt a nagging feeling in her chest that she could no longer deny. She had begun to develop feelings for him.

Chris sped through his remaining labor and dropped to a sit next to Shannon. He attempted to control his breathing, hiding how winded he actually was.

"Thanks for coming to spend time with me," Chris cheerfully piped. "You've been so busy since you got back, and I knew that your brother and Jenny needed time with you. I didn't want to interfere, but I was definitely hoping for a turn."

"You've always been so persistent. I knew all that space you were giving me was probably killing you inside," she teased. "I do appreciate the space you gave me so I could reconnect with my brother, but..." she lingered, more to drag out the suspense rather than to find the right words, "it's okay to be a little greedy. I wouldn't mind."

Chris' face lit up with a boyish grin that reminded Shannon of when they had first met. He kept his mouth shut, however, to not risk pushing his luck. After silently enjoying his moment of triumph, he eventually spoke.

"After all that time that you had been gone, I was just glad that I knew where you were again. Compared to the two months I waited just to know if you were still alive, a day or two of waiting while you are safely within sight is nothing."

"Well, maybe as a reward for your patience I can join you with whatever project they have you working on. Everybody else seems to have tasks already assigned to them, and I don't have anything to contribute yet."

"That would be great! I've just about cleared this area, but I still have a ton of work ahead of me to slope the land and set up proper drainage," responded Chris. His green eyes shined excitedly.

"It looks nice and flat to me, don't you want it that way?" asked Shannon.

"Normally that would have been fine, but apparently, the land was basically given a salt bath from the tsunamis. So, to prepare the land properly, we have to make sure that the water drains away from it so that when it gets rained on the rain will strip it of the excess salt. We did something similar at the last settlement and it worked perfectly."

Chapter 26

Two weeks passed while Shannon and Chris worked tirelessly to set up multiple locations for farming. Chris had settled into the habit of spending the evenings with Shannon, Billy, and Jenny. A brief moment of peace had found its place in Shannon's life, and she enjoyed it without reservation. Many of her recent experiences had been in near isolation and she was glad to spend time doing something that others could see and appreciate. She knew this time would be short-lived. The lingering burden of finding out what the binding void was had haunted her throughout her brief reprieve in action, but she allowed herself to ignore it as she waited for the results of her samples from Phil.

Clouds lay overhead, moving lazily, painted in bright orange and purple as the early evening slowly gave way to night. Shannon had just finished a long day of work, and she knew it was about time to check in with Phil. Their schedules had been quite full since her return, and they had not run into each other much. She made her way to the storage room where she often saw Phil entering or leaving.

The heavy door swung open with a loud squeal that she knew had given away her presence. The large room was poorly lit but for a strong glow of white light that emanated from the back corner of the room where Phil's desk was. She could see him working as she approached, though he did not acknowledge her despite the commotion she had made as she entered. As she came to a position near him and observed what he was doing, he finally turned his attention away from his work and looked up at her.

"Sometimes the smallest detail can make the biggest difference," spoke Phil cryptically.

"Does that mean you've discovered something useful?" asked Shannon with excitement.

"I have no idea," responded Phil confidently. "I have information, a fair amount of information that I think tells us some interesting things about our unwelcome guests. Is it even remotely useful? Possibly not. It depends on what you can think of to do with it."

"Then stop leaving me in suspense and get on with it," bantered Shannon playfully. "What have you learned?"

"Alright, we'll start with the simple stuff. I couldn't gather too much information from the ocean sand samples you provided. I don't think that's too surprising. There isn't much that can change there with so much salt water constantly covering it. The soil, however, has really high pH and EC levels. The simple explanation is that electrical conductivity, or EC, is a measure of the mineral salts present, which provide everything from Boron to Zinc for plants. The pH determines what of those elements are most present in the soil and how easily the plant can absorb them. So the most shocking thing about the high levels is the quality of the food that grows in it.

It should be damaging to the food, but everything has obviously grown well. Though, with a composition that both makes sense with, and contradicts the quality of the soil. Which I'll explain next.

"All of the food that was being grown, especially the items that are not original to this planet, had ridiculous levels of vitamin D. *That*, I think, could be very telling of our visitors and their biological needs. Which, I also think is confirmed by the extremely high levels of vitamin K, magnesium, and zinc present in the food samples, all of which are known to aid in the absorption of vitamin D. The contradictory elements I had alluded to being magnesium and zinc, since a high pH will increase the availability of magnesium but should create a zinc deficit. Unfortunately, I don't have any tools available to me to analyze the bacteria in the soil. I think that is where the magic is occurring."

"There is bacteria in the soil?" asked Shannon. "I guess I should have heard about that since my dad was a farmer, but I wasn't particularly excited about that stuff."

"Yes, all good soil has bacteria in it. However, just like how these aliens have brought some animals with them, they have apparently brought some bacteria with them, which are producing results that seem otherwise impossible. That's all I can really tell you about that," said Phil with a defeated shrug.

"So," voiced Shannon as she processed the information. "We have aliens with an extremely high vitamin D intake? Is there some way we can use that against them? What would depriving them of that do to them?"

"I asked myself the same questions. What I know off hand is that vitamin D, in humans at least, can have a big impact on depression. There are definitely portions of the brain that depend on it for at least emotional stability. I know you have mentioned the extreme mental capacity of these aliens, so it is possible that they require it for those powers. What I think we could expect, if we deprived them of that resource, would be any of the symptoms affiliated with depression. Mood swings, diminished clarity of thought, poor health, preference for isolation, lack of ambition, all of these are possible outcomes.

"Which obviously leads us to our second question. Is there a way to deprive them of vitamin D. The short answer is yes. I looked through documentation I had on my phone and found different drugs that could prevent the absorption of vitamin D. The long answer, of course, is that we can't just go up to them and ask them to take pills while promising that it is totally good for them and not secretly a sinister plan to kill them."

"And if we had access to their food source?" questioned Shannon.

"We would need people smarter than myself to figure that out, though it might be possible to tamper with it in a meaningful way."

Chapter 27

Another day of hard work had passed and Shannon, Chris, Jenny, and Billy sat at the table in the center of the home that Billy had built. The top of the table was the hood of a car that he had worked to flatten; the legs were sections of metal that had likely made up the walls of a tall building in the past. A quietness hung in the air that seemed odd to Shannon. The four of them were usually quite lively when the day was done, especially Chris, who was always very talkative and eager to learn about the lives the three of them had before the comet. Shannon watched as the other three gave each other knowing glances.

"Someone needs to tell me what's going on," Shannon finally said when she felt that no progress would otherwise be made.

Billy tapped on the table lightly, thinking of how to begin. "Remember the dreams about dad that you were having, where he told you to go into the water?" Billy spoke quietly.

"Obviously..."

"Well, all three of us have been having dreams the past couple of weeks. We each individually thought nothing of it at first, then they kept happening. Still, no one said or did anything about it. I think we all were just trying to understand what was happening. After a little over a week, Chris was the one to finally mention it to me." Billy's movements were tense, anxious.

"Chris is having dreams about dad?"

"No, I've got my own ghost that haunts me," answered Chris. His look was distant, visibly shaken by the thought.

Shannon immediately remembered his fiance. "I'm sorry."

"Mine were with my mom." Jenny spoke on the verge of tears, her brown eyes glossy and sad.

"I suddenly feel like my tone was a bit insensitive. I'm sorry guys," said Shannon.

Chris shook his head and made a face that said it was okay.

"Are you being told to go into the water?" asked Shannon.

"No," answered Billy. "We're being told to take off whatever it is that's preventing the alien from connecting with you."

"And because the message is about me, that's why no one has come to talk to me about it yet. Are all three of you getting the same message?" asked Shannon with a look of concern.

"Yeah, and what's weird is that he doesn't try to trick us," added Billy. "He immediately says that he is the one who connected with you in the past, and that the last time you two interacted something happened to him and he needs to talk to you again."

"What happened?" asked Chris.

Shannon shook her head in confusion. "I don't think anything specific happened. I was sitting on my plane and I connected with him to get information. When I was done, I flew home. Did he give either of you any hint as to what he is referring to?" Shannon asked as she looked toward Billy and Jenny.

"I tried asking him," answered Billy. "He just said that something had changed."

"But he didn't say what?" Shannon tried to remember the details, but nothing specific stood out.

"When I asked him what exactly had changed, he just said he wasn't sure." Billy's expression made no attempt to hide his concern for his sister. "I honestly got the impression that he was as confused as you are. He seems to want to talk to you because he also is looking for answers."

"I don't think that's a good idea." Chris blurted out, nearly cutting Billy off. His brow furrowed, his eyes looked anguished.

Shannon could see the tension on Chris' face, a deep desire to protect her. She couldn't fault him for his feelings. She knew she would feel the same way if the roles were reversed. She leaned over and laid a hand on his knee.

"I haven't decided to meet with him, but even if I did, there is no risk of anything bad happening. I've learned to control my interactions with him. But if you are really concerned, you can stay close by and pull me out of it if you want." Shannon spoke as reassuringly as possible. She looked at everyone as she spoke, but her attention was focused on Chris.

Chris relaxed slightly, but still showed concern.

"What are you thinking?" asked Billy. His expression was not much different from Chris'.

The loss of his carefree attitude had changed him from the boy he had been less than a year ago to a handsome man. Shannon knew her dad would be proud to see him as he was now, though likely saddened, as she was, that his innocence had been so forcefully removed.

Shannon took measure of all the different ideas and pieces of information that swirled in her head. "Of all the things I know, I still feel like I have more questions than I have answers. There is something—or someone—big out there, hiding. I got just enough of a glimpse of it to not doubt myself, but little enough that I still feel like I know nothing. We can't really move forward until we truly know what we are up against. I don't think I really have a choice. If he is somehow indicating—through words and actions—that his tactics or intentions have changed in some way, then I need to play along. Who knows? I might be able to just ask him directly and get an answer about who or what I felt."

"It sounds like you've already made up your mind," delivered Chris with a slight pout as he sank deeper into his chair.

Shannon extended out the necklace of magnets that hung around her. "This obviously works," she said, looking directly at Chris. "I mean, he had to go to you guys to get the message out to me. If you think anything is going wrong, or I take too long, then dropping this on me is an immediate emergency brake. But yes, I think I have made up my mind."

Chapter 28

Two days had passed since the dreams of Shannon's companions had been revealed to her. They had decided today would be the scheduled day for her meeting with the alien, and Billy and the others had made sure to convey as much to the alien when he met them in their dreams. They had taken advantage of the delay to determine questions to ask and information to gather. Her top priority was to find out as much as possible about the entity she believed she had encountered. Her secondary mission was to get as close to the exact locations of the other survivors as possible. They knew it was important to establish contact with the other survivors, regardless of the aliens, though the presence of the aliens made it all the more imperative.

Chris paced anxiously outside Shannon's home as noon—the designated time for the meeting—approached. He occasionally popped in to ask questions or offer assistance. "Should I light some candles or something?" He asked as he popped his head into the room.

"It's not a seance," chuckled Shannon.

"Sorry," responded Chris, before promptly ducking out and resuming his pacing.

Shannon stood, stepped outside, grabbed his arm, and stepped back inside, placing him in the seat next to hers.

"You're not helping me by being a nervous wreck." Shannon rubbed his leg. "Sit here, be confident in me, and reassure me that you have my back. That's all I need right now."

He nodded in response, but remained quiet.

Laying on the table in front of Shannon were two of Billy's tablets. Both tablets had world maps on them. One was intended for her to mark the locations of the other survivors, while the other tablet was designated for the locations of the aliens. Billy sat on the other side of Shannon with his phone in hand, ready to record anything that Shannon might say. He checked his phone for the time. "It's noon," he announced.

"Don't be quick to use this," said Shannon as she took off her necklace and placed it in Chris' hand. "It hurts like hell to have the connection forcefully severed. Plus, I've done this before, and I know what I'm doing."

"I trust you," assured Chris with a gentle smile.

Immediately, and with alarming strength, Shannon felt the entrance of an alien in her mind. The presence had a clarity unlike anything she had felt before, and a strength almost identical to that of when she had been in the colossal shark's mouth. However, that had been—in her understanding—due to close proximity. There was no water around to allow for an alien to get close enough to her now, though.

Who are you? Shannon asked, hoping that her thoughts did not betray her attempt to mask her fear.

The presence combed her mind, like fingers through hair, in search of something. The sensation was oddly unpleasant and invasive. Shannon closed her eyes to concentrate as she struggled to isolate her invader.

Who are you? She persisted.

I... I don't know. The presence responded with a voice that Shannon could have sworn she had heard in her own ears.

Are you the one I met before? Shannon grew tense as she considered the idea that this was a new, and stronger, alien attempting to contact her.

Yes, but something has changed. I need answers. The voice bordered between panicked and angry. The desperate probing of her mind continued.

Despite her best efforts, the alien persisted in his attempts to search her mind, freeing himself of her mental blockades. A searing pain shot through her head like a sudden migraine as her memories were urgently and violently sifted through. Several seconds passed as Shannon was held captive to her pain, unable to think or move as her consciousness was accosted. Quick flashes appeared in her mind as memories were traversed; sudden snippets that came and went, like flipping through the pages of a book.

Suddenly her pain exploded as fireworks, shooting waves of electricity throughout her body, frying her nerves, and throwing her out of her chair onto the ground. Fire ran down her spine, through her arms and legs, and forced her fingers and toes to extend uncontrollably as her body panicked from the pain. Then a new pain, dull in comparison, squeezed her mind, and the agony that had poured from her head to the rest of her body shut off like a faucet. Her eyes shot open in agony as she saw Chris standing over her, his hands around her face as he held her necklace to her forehead.

For several minutes she convulsed on the ground as the shock and pain receded from her body. Her fried nerves felt like the lingering uneasiness of turning off vibrations after long exposure. A low drone, accompanied by a high pitched squeal, blocked out all other noise. Tears streamed from her eyes uncontrollably, though she was hardly aware of them. If she could still see, her mind was in no condition to register it. Her thoughts had been reduced to only those that were necessary for survival. Sweat soaked her clothing. She settled into a fetal position before her mind regained the strength to see or hear the others around her.

Distantly, she heard her name being spoken; a far away echo.

"Shannon," spoke Chris loudly.

Ten minutes had passed and she finally looked in Chris' direction.

"You saved me," whispered Shannon.

Chris leaned over, lifted her into his arms, and embraced her.

Chapter 29

Several days passed, and no one mentioned what Shannon had gone through. Each morning Chris greeted her at her door with a smile and escorted her to the fields they were working on. He worked tirelessly to prevent her from overexerting herself. When their work was finished, he would follow her around wherever she desired to go. He would prepare her food for lunch, eat with her when she had dinner with Billy and Jenny, and linger a short distance away if she requested to be alone. She recognized his intent. It was never a burden on her. After he had rescued her, she felt a security with him that was reminiscent to that which she had felt with her father.

Billy had remained quiet the first day, giving her time to recover, but she had noticed him in the mornings after that waking up seeming angry. He would mask his emotions with a disingenuous smile when he would look at her, but she knew something was troubling him. She lacked the energy or desire to press him on the issue, and hoped that in time he would open up to her about whatever he was dealing with. The last two nights, she heard him and Jenny whispering to each other as she was arriving home from working the fields. They promptly stopped and moved on to other topics. Shannon was not sure if that was related to his mood in the morning. She hoped rather that it was a sign of their relationship developing.

Shannon sat on a large stone near the field they were clearing, evaluating her work in between thoughts of her brother. The glow of the sun diminished as it dropped below the rising land behind her, throwing the field into a darkness that made it hard to continue examining her progress. Chris settled next to her, their legs gently touching. His efforts to sit slightly closer to her each day had not gone unnoticed, though she had no intention of making it easy on him by letting him know his advances were welcomed. Watching him work for it amused her.

"I wonder if Billy and Jenny's relationship is progressing," pondered Shannon aloud.

"I would think that is obvious, as devoted to her as he is," responded Chris. "What makes you question it?"

"Oh, the last couple nights when I got home, he and Jenny were whispering and stopped when they noticed me. Normally I would consider that unmistakable proof of their relationship. However, in the mornings he seems upset and distant, which would belie that assumption." Shannon gave a dismissive shrug, an admission of defeat.

Chris cleared his throat and shifted in his seat. "Has he mentioned anything to you about why he might be upset?"

"No, and I don't really want to press him on it."

"Probably for the best. If he is having girl trouble, it could be awkward talking to his sister about it. I'll check in with him and see if everything is okay. Sound good?"

"If you think it will help."

"It's worth a shot. It's time to be done for the day anyway. I'll walk you back and have a little chat with him. I'll see if I can get any info out of him." Chris stood and then helped Shannon to her feet.

They sauntered toward her home. As she arrived she walked in while Chris stood pensively at the door. Chris caught Billy's eye and gave a subtle nod toward the outside, indicating he wanted to talk. Billy threw a quick glance at his sister, and then made his way toward the entrance without speaking. The two stepped out of sight of Shannon, leaving her to wonder about their conversation.

"What's up with them," asked Jenny curiously.

"I think Chris is asking about you two," she responded with candor that surprised herself.

Jenny chuckled. "Why?"

"You know, it never occurred to me that I could talk to you. My brother is so glued to you that the idea of talking to you privately entirely slipped my mind. I just noticed you two whispering the last couple of nights when I've gotten home, but Billy has seemed upset the last few mornings so I was worried that he had done something to upset you."

"How nice of you to assume it would be his fault," laughed Jenny. She wore the same yellow dress that Shannon remembered seeing her in when they first met. She was still as thin as she had been before, so the dress fit her perfectly.

"What kind of sister would I be if I didn't assume that *everything* was his fault?"

Jenny got up from sitting on her bed and placed herself in the chair next to Shannon. Her smile drifted away. Her brown eyes, reflecting the light of a nearby candle, were hesitant. She lingered in silence as she passively watched the entrance, her mind clearly somewhere else. After a moment she gave herself a reassuring nod. Her face flashed with determination as she turned toward Shannon.

"We've been having more dreams," breathed Jenny so quietly that Shannon almost didn't register what was said.

At that moment, Billy and Chris walked into the home. Shannon was still facing Jenny.

"He didn't want to tell you," mouthed Jenny rapidly before facing Billy with a slight expression of guilt.

Shannon's expression dropped to disdain. "Spill the beans, idiot," she snapped at her brother.

Jenny groaned and closed her eyes at Shannon's brashness.

Billy gave an angry glance toward Jenny.

"She didn't say anything," lied Shannon. "I was eavesdropping."

"No," he answered flatly. He stared at Shannon directly. His expression was one of resolve.

Shannon looked to Chris, eyebrows raised.

He quickly threw his hands into the air in a pose of surrender. "Don't look at me, this seems like a family issue." He took a hesitant step back.

"Okay," delivered Shannon with an icy stare. "If you won't tell me what your dream was, then I'll just take my necklace off and find out for myself." She reached for her necklace.

Chris lunged forward, arm outstretched. "No!" He shouted.

Shannon's hand clutched the magnets, her grip tight, ready to pull. "Then tell me."

"Fine!" Billy threw his chair back and sat down angrily. He looked at his sister sternly as he mulled over the thoughts in his mind. "He appeared in my dream, told me he wanted to talk to you again, and I told him to screw off. The end."

Shannon turned to Jenny. Jenny looked away, unable to meet Shannon's stare. Shannon moved her attention to Chris. Regardless of any feelings he had toward her, his military experience strengthened him, and he held his focus on her, but said nothing. His face gave no indication of his current thoughts.

"And let me guess," began Shannon. "He just left without putting up a fight or saying anything else to try and convince you. 'I'm proud of you for standing up for yourself. You're so strong and handsome. How could I possibly ignore such rugged manliness?'" she said in a mocking tone.

Billy didn't concede a visible reaction. "You forgot about the part where he asked me to show him how to strengthen his gains in the gym, but you got the long and short of it."

"Why must you be so obstinate?" Shannon's voice rose as she spoke.

"Why?" responded Billy, his volume exceeding his sister's. "Because I would rather have you hate me and be safe, than to let you do what you always do; ignore me and go off on your own. I could handle it when dad was around, even if I did always miss you more once mom was gone. I can't handle it now."

Shannon's impetus to fight abandoned her. She slunk back into her chair, bowled over by this revelation. Guilt washed over her as she thought about all the times throughout the years that she had left her brother behind, giving his feelings no thought. How he must have felt when she left for college.

He had my dad before, but now I'm all he has left.

Thinking of her dad reminded her of the first time she came back to visit after leaving for college.

"Remember what dad said the first time I drove home from college?" asked Shannon.

Billy shook his head.

"He said it was like we were connected by rubber bands. When we all lived in the house together, we didn't actually spend that much time with each other. But, when I left and pulled those rubber bands tight, I came back as quickly as I could. The farther away I got, the more likely I was to come back." Shannon looked at her brother with sympathetic eyes. "I wish..." A sigh stuttered out of her as she worked out the words. "I wish I could be someone else. I wish that I could leave tomorrow's problems for tomorrow. I wish I could leave them for someone else to deal with. I wish that I could be content not knowing the answers. I wish that I could promise you that I would never leave you alone again, but I can't. I can't let all of that go. I can't stop searching. I can't stop trying to fix things. I can't replace mom, and

I really can't replace dad." A quiet sob burst from Shannon's lips as she spoke.

Shannon reached out and grabbed her brother's hand. "The only thing I can promise is that the farther away I go, the more I desire to come back. Because of that, I always have, and I always will, come back."

Billy pulled away his hands and wiped at his eyes before tears had a chance to reveal themselves. He stared at Shannon for a long while, attempting to maintain his mask of anger. "He said he'll tell you about the thing you refer to as the 'binding void.'"

Chapter 30

Much to Chris' chagrin, he once again found himself ready to throw magnets on to Shannon if she needed rescue. She could see the anguish on his face as she prepared herself emotionally for the endeavor of meeting with the alien once more. He gave her a pained smile of reassurance.

Billy and Chris had been in agreement that no meeting would occur until after they had a chance to talk with the alien in their dreams at least once more and warn him that he would have no more chances to meet with Shannon if he did anything to hurt her again. She fully supported their decision and felt a little safer knowing that the alien hopefully understood that no more infractions would be tolerated.

Shannon lay down on her bed, desiring to not fall to the ground like last time should anything go wrong. Shannon rested her hand on Chris' hand. "Everything will be fine because you are here to rescue me just like last time." She gave his hand a squeeze.

Without delay, she removed her necklace and handed it to Chris. The alien's presence entered quickly, but lacked the forcefulness of the previous occasion.

I gained the answers I was seeking through our last encounter, announced the alien.

Before she could be distracted by the alien she searched for Brenda. He had had the opportunity to find his answers and this was the answer she had wanted. It only took a brief moment to confirm what she had already assumed. Brenda was gone. There was no trace of her. A pang of sadness shot through her before she quickly shook it off and focused her attention back to the alien. Once again, she would have to deal with her emotions some other time.

What answers did you find? Shannon could not help but be drawn in by her curiosity.

I know what powers you have gained. I understand now what happened to me. The remaining question is how *it happened, which neither you nor I know yet. I now also believe that we have the same mission.* The alien's voice in Shannon's head was clear, calm, and methodical in its delivery.

You keep referring to what happened to you, but I don't know what you are talking about. Shannon knew she was gaining more questions than answers.

When I came into contact with the creature you call a collara while you were controlling it from the future, it severed my connection to that which you know as the 'binding void.' I have been freed from my imprisonment.

The alien's delivery remained balanced, but Shannon thought she had heard a hint of either anger or excitement at the end of his sentence.

What is it? The question had consumed Shannon since the moment she had first discovered it. Her excitement grew at the prospect of finally gaining answers.

Much like how my kind controls the collara, there is one that has taken my kind captive and controls us.

The vague language irritated Shannon. *What do you call your kind? What should I call you?*

We do not speak any language you know and have no name you would understand. The voice in Shannon's mind paused. *You can call my kind Simas. I, therefore, am a sima and I will be called Lysander.* A tinge of pride could be found in his otherwise stoic delivery. *As for what it is, if you will close your eyes and let me have more control, I will show you.*

The fact that Lysander offered, rather than forced, gave Shannon courage that something was different this time. She closed her eyes and relaxed, breathing long and deep. A twinge of pain struck her and then immediately faded. In an instant, notwithstanding her eyes being closed, she could see. She was underwater, floating effortlessly. Despite the depth that she could feel she currently inhabited, she could see through the black water. Lysander, his limbs moving effortlessly to maintain his position in defiance of his imposing form, was next to her.

"You can feel where we are," announced Lysander.

He was correct. Shannon could feel that they were in the southern portion of the Pacific Ocean near Antarctica.

"Yes." Her voice was somehow clear, even though she felt as though she was underwater.

"You have seen the food we grow. Simas have multiple farms such as that around the world. While we are permitted to eat a small portion of what is grown, especially from that which is grown in the ocean, the vast majority of it is delivered here. I have been here several times. What you are seeing is from my memory."

As Lysander spoke, Shannon was startled as she noticed a couple other simas swimming down into the ocean depths past them, carrying food. They were coming from different directions and moved quickly. As if pulled by her own curiosity, she and Lysander began moving downward with the other simas. The shadowy depths below her grew in clarity as they moved downward, though her range of sight was still limited to roughly fifty feet.

Slowly, a long fin broke through the shadowy abyss below. As Shannon descended, a monstrous creature was revealed to her that far exceeded the distance she was able to see in the water. As she moved lower in the water, the fin she had first seen the tip of grew to fifteen feet in height and appeared to run the distance of the creature, at least from what she could see. It protruded from the back of a horrible beast covered in large scales. The color of which was between dark blue and black, but had a shimmer that Shannon wondered if she would have been able to see without the assistance of the sima's eyesight. The body continued below the fin for over thirty feet. Gradually they moved along the enormous body, reaching strong formidable arms that reminded her of a Tyrannosaurus' arms, though the hands seemed more dexterous.

Still they continued onward. She was confident they had covered more than four hundred feet when the ghastly head of the detestable creature finally came into view. The neck was meaty, but allowed the head to sway back and forth and looked like that of an alligator. The face was domed, similar to a killer whale, though there was no designated area for eyes. The mouth was filled with teeth that were three to four feet long, thin, and menacing. There were rows of them like in a shark's mouth, though their length appeared to make them impossible to grow straight. They curved, coming to hateful points that faced in all directions. They did not appear practical to use.

Sensing her observations, Lysander spoke. "They are not used for chewing. They are for defense, though he has no need for them here."

One by one, the simas would move in front of the beast and toss their food into its mouth. Each one would then make a hasty retreat. The food, floating freely into the jaws of the abomination, seemed to just disintegrate.

"It can do that with its mind," clarified Lysander.

Shannon was dumbfounded by the gargantuan size and grotesque nature of the behemoth before her. The idea that this creature existed anywhere was sickening. The fact that it was on her planet was maddening. In pure shock, she uttered just one word, "Leviathan."

As if responding to its name, the beast whipped its head in the direction of Shannon and lunged forward.

A scream burst from Shannon's lips as her eyes shot open and her body catapulted into a sitting position on her bed. She was instantly met with Chris' embrace and the security of the magnets. The revolting image of the creature hung in her mind. She wasn't sure if she wanted to keep screaming or throw up.

Chapter 31

Two tablets sat on the table in front of Shannon, maps on display. A soft blue glow emanated from the screens that added a sterile quality to the light in the room as late evening set in.

After the startle that Shannon had given Billy and Chris, it took until the next day to convince them that it was okay to meet with Lysander again. In both of the meetings she had with him, she had been unable to gain any of the information she had intended, other than about the creature she now called Leviathan. She had, however, gained many more questions, not the least of which was what Lysander thought their shared mission was exactly.

Feeling confident that Lysander was no longer at risk of being hostile, Shannon lacked the nervousness of her previous encounters with him. Without hesitation she removed her necklace and set it on the table. Chris sat by anxiously, but she knew that only time would reassure him.

Lysander's presence was immediate. Shannon closed her eyes and was transported to the beach, a familiar location from their previous encounters. Lysander stood before her.

"Are we at risk of being caught by Leviathan?" asked Shannon.

"Regardless of what you think you saw, that was just a memory," answered Lysander.

"But I was able to look around. When I view the memories of the collara they have a fixed perspective. I shouldn't be able to explore things within a memory that you didn't experience."

Lysander gave a dismissive wave of his hand. "The collara are simple creatures that are only controlled by Simas. They have only one experience, their own. Simas, on the other hand, when connected to Leviathan, can experience the perspectives of others."

"Does that mean you can see anyone's memory?" asked Shannon.

"Not everyone's, only those with a shared experience. If we were both connected to Leviathan, then I would be able to remember this conversation from your perspective, my own, and from anywhere that our two perspectives overlap."

"It seemed like Leviathan had turned directly toward me, as if I was the target of its attention." Shannon knew she could not be convinced otherwise.

"There is not enough data to draw any conclusion other than coincidence," delivered Lysander dismissively.

Shannon decided to move on. "You said previously that we have a shared mission. What exactly do you think that mission is?"

"We both desire to find freedom and peace for our people. You used to believe Simas were your enemy, and safety meant eliminating them as a threat. You now understand that they too—like the collara—are controlled. It is only a matter of time before Leviathan finds a way to control humans as well. We now have a shared enemy. Simas will desire peace once they have gained freedom."

"So, we both want to eliminate Leviathan. Do you think that is possible? Do you have a plan?" Shannon asked her questions with sobriety. Her curiosity did not outweigh her fear that she was pursuing a challenge that was unbeatable.

"I have but just escaped my prison. I have had neither the time nor the faculties to pursue this endeavor on my own. I have also become aware that you have gained capabilities that far exceed my own. I do not think I could accomplish this task without your assistance. My best idea is that which I am doing now, seeking your aid."

Shannon observed Lysander as she contemplated his words. Unlike in her previous visions on this beach, where she talked with her dad, who acted natural, Lysander was stiff and nearly unmoving. He seemed to make no attempt to lure her in with calming, casual gestures. His rigidness was almost reassuring. Shannon shook her head. Even with Lysander's odd behavior serving as a distraction, her thoughts kept returning to Leviathan's reaction to her. She needed to test it, to understand her enemy more.

"I am willing to work together, but I need to test something. I want to go back to Leviathan. The same memory, starting from the same spot."

In an instant, the world around her was the deep black and blue that she had seen before. Again she descended, and the imposing fin that ran the length of Leviathan revealed itself first before leading to the massive body it was attached to. She observed the same shimmer on the scales. Everything seemed identical, including the other simas that swam around. In the path that she retraced effortlessly she tested her movements; they were not restricted, she was able to move to different areas than the first time she had been here. Finally, she reached the head of the beast.

This time around, Shannon worked her way to the other side of Leviathan's head. Lysander followed. She then waited. Her heart beat furiously in her chest. Eventually the same sima she had witnessed before swam forward and tossed in its offering. Shannon grew anxious to watch from a new perspective.

Suddenly, Leviathan whipped its head in the opposite direction from Shannon and burst forward.

Seeing the same results as before, Lysander commented. "See, it's the same results as before. Nothing changed. Do you believe it was a memory now?"

"Yes," conceded Shannon.

Again, as though responding to her voice, Leviathan swung its impossible mass to face her direction and lunged forward, its horrific mouth open in anticipation.

Shannon's reflexes overpowered her as she shoved her hands forward. Her eyes opened as she pushed against the table in front of her and her chair tipped backwards, throwing her to the ground.

"It definitely noticed me," gasped Shannon. *Let's not do that again.*

Chris jumped to his feet and stood above Shannon with the magnets ready, a look of terror strewn across his face, yet this time he hesitated. With Shannon's eyes open, and her having just spoken, he didn't want to act too quickly.

I can't understand how it's possible, but I'm willing to believe he noticed you, conceded Lysander, still present in her mind.

Can we go back to the beach?

Yes, responded Lysander.

Shannon picked up her chair, straightened out her clothes, gave Chris a reassuring smile, and sat down again. She waited a moment for heart to stop pounding in her chest and her breathing to calm. When she was ready she closed her eyes and found herself back on the beach. Lysander had taken up his previous position.

"What do you think would have happened if I had not opened my eyes and escaped?" asked Shannon.

"You are asking me for clarification on something that I am not capable of comprehending." Lysander's demeanor was affectless.

"Can you hazard a guess? What do you think the possible outcomes could have been? Why would Leviathan bother lunging toward me if it would have been without result?"

"The obvious possibility is that it could have killed you. It is also possible that if your minds had inhabited the same space, he could have gained access to your frequencies and patterns and been able to control you."

The idea gave Shannon a shudder. She had gained the answers she needed, but in hindsight, the risk may have been more than she should have gambled. She quickly began feeling exhausted.

"This is all a lot to take in. I think I'm going to need to rest soon, but I have information I need to get that I have failed to retrieve with our last two meetings." Shannon opened her eyes. *Can you see what I see?*

Yes, answered Lysander.

For fifteen minutes, Shannon worked with Lysander and documented the locations of the remaining people, the simas, and of Leviathan.

Chapter 32

"When I recently made a trip to the beach with Chris, I tried sending the collara down to investigate Leviathan and they wouldn't go. The only assumption I can make is that they would die, and therefore never come back for me to take control of them, so they never left to begin with." Shannon sat in the musty storage room at the desk that was occupied with Phil's experiments. She fought her urge to fiddle with the items in front of her as she idly contemplated the situation. Chris, Billy, and Jenny stood around her and Phil, who were sitting.

"From what you have explained," began Phil. "It would seem that you can't sneak up on him, because he can sense where everyone is."

"Correct."

"He is also the primary consumer of this," he gestured to the remaining tests and ingredients on his table.

"Also correct."

"You can't just distract him if he has that level of awareness. Due to his size, it also seems unlikely that we have the resources to eliminate him just by drugging him." Phil tapped the table as he mulled it over. Strands of white hair hung over his lined and weathered face. "You might be able to do both. Neither one, individually, would be strong enough, but combined, it might make him vulnerable enough to attempt an attack. Although, I don't know what we could do to kill him. There are plenty of places in a human body that you can stab someone and they won't die. A creature as large as you described, even if we had a weapon big enough to hurt him, it could be very easy to miss anything vital."

"I might have an idea for the weapon," chimed Jenny timidly. "I was digging through all the information Billy had on magnets, since you said that you released the collara with magnets, and you defend yourself from invasion with magnets. I came across something that described how to make liquid magnets, and it's all ingredients that we probably have. If you can drug and distract him like Phil mentioned, then you could maybe inject him somehow with liquid magnets, which might disrupt his ability to do all his telepathy. If he can't do that, then it sounds like he wouldn't be able to feed himself, if it didn't just kill him right away."

"That is a great idea," responded Chris. "With all the equipment we have for animals, both in and out of water, I'm sure I could make something from a tranquilizer dart."

Shannon gave a small smile. "So we have a potential weapon. If we can take advantage of his vitamin D dependency, then we have a potential drug. I think there are several ways we can make a distraction, which, like Phil was saying, could be an easier task if he is drugged." Shannon knew the distraction would work best with other people involved. Though, she had some ideas that she would keep to herself until the time was right. She let out a deep breath of relief. "It's nice to feel like we have a direction to move in again. I think we need to start recruiting help."

"I'm coming with you," said Chris with a look of determination on his face. He and Shannon stood outside of her home.

At six feet and four inches, Chris had eight inches of height on Shannon. With as close as he now stood, she had to tip her head back significantly to look him in the eyes. "But you can't fly with only one eye."

"They're two-seaters, and I will cram myself into the back."

"As tall as you are, I'm not sure you could fit in the front seat, let alone the back." Shannon actually wanted him with her for the journey, but couldn't imagine the logistics of making it work.

He shook his head, refusing to concede. "You're going to Austria. I speak German. We've also seen the kind of horrible people in positions of power that you can't seem to avoid. I may only have one eye, but I am still more than capable of being a body guard and a translator."

"What about the people here who need you?" asked Shannon halfheartedly.

Chris let out a snort. "Seriously? I'm just a mule, and honestly, they are just giving me busy work. We could be gone a year and they wouldn't have put to use all the space you and I have cleared."

Shannon appreciated how adamant he was. She truly wanted to find a way for him to come. However, she had built up the habit of teasing him whenever she could. This was just as good of an opportunity to have fun at his expense as any. Playfully, she continued teasing Chris, enjoying seeing him upset. "I'm sure someone there speaks English." She gave him a dismissive look. "But fine, if you can fit inside the plane, then maybe I will consider it."

Jenny walked up to Shannon and Chris and handed Chris a necklace with magnets in it. "I made three, so we each have one for the trip." She noticed Chris' sour look. "You are coming, right?"

Chris whipped his head toward Shannon, his face in a brooding scowl. "As long as I can fit on the plane," he delivered with a growl.

"Where there's a will, there's a way," responded Jenny in a chipper voice as she gave him a pat on the back.

The two girls gave each other smiles as Jenny turned and left.

"If you're so confident that you can fit in the plane, then how about you come with me as I retrieve the third plane. If you can't fit, it will be a lonely hike back to the settlement by yourself."

"I'll be ready before you are," retorted Chris with a grin.

"It's an eight day hike there, plus time to check the plane, fly it to the other planes on the beach, and finally hike back to here from the beach. So, pack everything you've got. We'll be gone for a while." Shannon gave him a pat on the chest before turning into her home to pack her things. She could only imagine how giddy he must be at the idea of being alone with her for ten days.

"You're sure I'll be able to fly a plane?" Jenny nervously asked when Shannon entered the room.

"It is shockingly simple. You'll be able to manage it. No problem," reassured Shannon.

"How long is the trip going to be?" asked Billy.

Shannon closed her eyes as she worked through the math. "My trip to Hawaii was roughly 2,500 miles long and took about seven days. The trip to Austria is just over 6,000 miles. So, assuming we maintain a consistent speed, and don't have any issues along the way, we could get there in about two and a half weeks. Though, when I flew to Hawaii, we had enough water for the trip. We only distilled water when we were already choosing to land, assuming there was still sunlight. We did that just to keep our stock of water healthy the whole time. For a trip this long, we may need to actually dedicate a day, every now and then, entirely to replenishing our water supply."

"Do you really think it was necessary to pick somewhere so far away?" asked Billy.

Shannon shrugged. "It's the largest collection of people on the planet, and they are located near several smaller groups of people. It will be easy for them to disseminate the information to others."

"It will be nice to go for a bit of an adventure," said Billy. "Being stuck at these settlements for the last few months has started getting a bit boring."

"It will be nice to have you two along this time around." Shannon added.

Chapter 33

"We'll meet you back here in about ten days," said Shannon as she gave Billy a hug.

"Don't you dare think about running off without us," threatened Billy in a tone that failed to mask his genuine concern.

"I won't," assured Shannon.

Phil and several other prominent people within the community who had formed a committee to help guide the decisions and planning of the settlement were also present to see Shannon and Chris off.

Phil leaned in close to Shannon and spoke in a whisper. "I know you have your own reasons for going, but I got the support of these guys because I told them this was about forming communication with others globally, for the sake of keeping things simple. They weren't exactly happy about not having a say in who goes on this trip of yours, so make sure you seem grateful. I know you'll be back in a few days, but it's best to start sucking up to them now so nothing changes between now and when you fly out for Europe."

"Thank you for providing us with your support," said Shannon with a smile as she turned to the other leaders.

"Not that we had much of a choice," grumbled Lupe, a short but stout man in his mid forties, with jet black hair, dark tanned skin, and black tattoos that covered his arms, which he kept crossed in front of himself. He spoke often of the restaurants he used to run. Shannon always thought he did an amazing job now with as few ingredients as he currently had access to. To his left stood Karen, the psychiatrist and seamstress of the settlement, a chubby woman with pale skin, wild brown hair, brilliant green eyes, and an odd combination of facial features that individually were attractive but combined in such a manner that left Shannon confused as to whether or not she was beautiful.

"If you happen to find anything in the hangar that seems useful to us, bring it back as a peace offering," suggested Phil, quietly.

"We weren't of much use to you anyway. So if you had to send anyone, we were the most expendable," said Chris as he turned around and began walking away.

"I guess we're off," said Shannon as she threw her arm around her brother one more time before running to catch up to Chris.

Shannon lingered one final moment as she looked down the path she had last traveled with Brenda. Though she had been busy lately, she never actually stopped thinking about her. A pain welled in her chest, sadness for the dear friend she lost, and fear that this trip could have similar results. Doing the only thing she knew to do, she stuffed her feelings down to be dealt with later.

"I guess if you're mean to them, then it makes me seem even nicer in comparison," joked Shannon as she caught up to Chris and settled into a brisk walk.

"I've never liked that guy," responded Chris. "He always tries to short me on food and complains that I'm stealing resources from others by eating too much. I played it off as a joke at first, but it never stopped. It's not my fault that I have, like, a foot on him. I'm here specifically because of my size and strength and he just never appreciated how much food I brought in from all of my trips to the beach, which were sometimes only successful because of what I offered."

"Well, I'm sorry. I remember having growth spurts when I was an early teenager where I ate all day. My dad would try to stop my snacking for fear of it ruining my dinner. I hated having someone who was trying to cut me off from food when I was starving." Shannon fell silent as she briefly mourned the loss of her dad. "Anyway, this is not how we should be starting our trip. No need to ruin things by being upset."

Shannon quickened her pace and used her new speed as an excuse to grab Chris' hand to pull him forward to match her speed. He made sure not to let go. His frown immediately grew into the goofy, boyish smile she was used to seeing on him when she was around.

After four hours, they reached the gulf and were greeted by Shannon's four collara. It was noon, and they decided they would stop for lunch. While Chris reluctantly prepared the fish that the collara had provided, Shannon ran through the memories of each collara. She saw nothing of significance, and was relieved to have no new revelations to process.

"I know I've seen you do that a couple times now, but it is still really weird to see you touch them," said Chris in between bites of food.

"You'll get used to them over time."

"That's what I'm afraid of. Pretty soon all of this stuff will just seem normal. I'll end up forgetting what life was like before all of this happened."

"Maybe that's for the best," responded Shannon. "There's no point in longing for a world that no longer exists, and possibly no longer *can* exist. Forgetting may be the easiest way to simply be happy with what you have now."

Chris thought about it for a moment and then gave a shrug. "I think I will be happy whether I remember the past or not, as long as you're around," he said as he gave her a smile.

"Smooooth," laughed Shannon.

"It's worked so far."

"I thought it was the eye patch that worked," teased Shannon as she ate her fish.

"Meh, it was my spare eye anyway, but I'll take it. A win's a win."

They finished eating and quickly resumed their journey. The collara retreated to the water and followed from a distance. The remainder of the day's efforts passed without incident, and as evening set in and the cool light of the moon shed its rays upon the water, they set up camp.

The time they had spent together working on field preparations had given their relationship the strength to work in silence next to each other or talk casually without it ever feeling forced or uncomfortable. However, Chris rarely let the silence go on for long. Over time they had learned about each other's experiences before, during, and after the impact, and with each new detail revealed, they grew closer.

With camp set up and their stomachs full of freshly cooked fish, they climbed into their sleeping bags, which Chris had meticulously positioned so they were close to the fire; their heads were positioned in a way that they could still look at each other, and be as close to each other as possible. Shannon rested with her face looking up at the stars. With the beginning of spring and temperatures slowly warming, she left the top of her sleeping bag folded back and her arms rested on top of it. The excitement of having a task before her counterbalanced the fatigue she felt from the day's exertion, leaving her with just enough energy that she couldn't fall asleep immediately.

The deep, ever-expanding space above her felt open, and she suddenly had the feeling that she was lying on the bottom of the earth and that at any moment she could simply fall off into the endless expanse before her. The sensation of loneliness and helplessness brought a burning to her chest, a feeling of urgency combined with impotency. Her thoughts drifted back to her father.

"What was your fiance's name?" asked Shannon suddenly.

Chris cleared his throat, obviously caught off guard by the question. "Lin."

"Do you miss her," asked Shannon. Her voice was quiet.

"Uh..."

"It's not a trap," said Shannon quickly.

Chris thought about it for a moment and then let out a deep breath, choosing to believe her. "Yes and no."

"How so?"

"I've actually thought about this a lot lately, for obvious reasons. At first there was a lot of guilt. A feeling that I was betraying her. She died with me in her heart. She committed herself to me until her very last breath. So I had to come to terms with the fact that she gave me something that I couldn't give her back. I had to question if our loves for each other were equal. Did she love me more by dying while in love with me? Was I lying back then when I said I loved her as much as she loved me?"

Chris released a shaky breath. Shannon could hear the ache in his heart in it.

He continued. "I thought: If I say yes, that I do still miss her, the implication is that I have needs that she fulfilled that are currently not being met. But there is no reason that should be the case. It would only be through a denial of my own potential happiness that I could claim that my needs are unmet. That wouldn't be what she would want for me. She wouldn't ever want to know that she had become the source or reason for my lack of love, happiness, or companionship in life. That probably sounds more mechanical, or sterile than I am intending. It's not just that I have a potential replacement for the things she offered me that makes me not miss her. It's that our time together, including losing her, has changed who I am, what I think, how I feel, and what I need, down to my very core. In that sense, she will still be with me forever, because I will never be the same because of my time with her. It's all very confusing and hard to think about without feeling like I'm the worst person in the world."

"I'm sorry," inserted Shannon.

"I don't miss her, because I feel like everything I had with her has made me who I am today and I am extremely grateful for that. What I think I feel sadness for is the lost potential. The hopes and dreams that were washed away. Do you miss lobster when you are currently full on steak? No, your stomach is full, and you ate something delicious, but you may still miss the potential of lobster."

Chris paused, but Shannon could sense he wasn't done.

"Maybe none of that made sense. Guilt, coping, regret, and happiness don't blend well together, and every time I think I have finally figured myself out through senseless ramblings, I only have to wait a couple minutes before I reflect on my conclusions and realize that they make no sense. I guess this is why I talk so much during the day and I dread laying in bed by myself, forced to listen to my own thoughts."

Shannon could hear Chris sniffing in, holding back his tears. Without speaking, she worked her way out of her sleeping bag and crawled over to Chris and climbed into his. She put herself next to him with her head on his arm as she curled up into his warmth.

Chris remained quiet, not questioning her actions or intentions, and they fell asleep.

Chapter 34

The fleeting sun drew long shadows onto the ground as Shannon and Chris pushed on, attempting to reach the hangar after eight days of hiking. The lake, the circumference of which they had spent their journey traversing, was now behind them. Mangled building materials, fragments of trees, and an agglomeration of trash laid waste to the path before them. Chris turned on his flashlight as they continued.

For nearly an hour they progressed slowly over the debris until Chris' light illuminated the building that Shannon recognized. With relief, she made her way into the building while Chris collected wood for a fire. It pained her to enter and find that things were still in the same condition as when she had left them with Brenda. An unexpected wave of sadness struck Shannon as small memories over insignificant items stormed her mind. One thing that did calm her slightly, however, was seeing the third plane they had painstakingly salvaged, still sitting where she had remembered it. Taking the needs of the moment as inspiration to escape her emotions, Shannon went about rummaging for MREs to eat while Chris started a fire.

"They claim to be spaghetti," said Shannon as she handed Chris a meal.

"This is one of the few that is hard to get wrong," he responded with a smile.

With ferocious appetites they consumed their food. They had taken few breaks to eat as they had attempted to cover a great distance throughout the day. When Shannon was finished, she leaned back in grateful satisfaction and watched the plumes of smoke from the fire lazily rise into the air and escape out of a nearby hole in the ceiling of the hangar.

"Do we know if that thing will fly?" Chris asked as he gave a nod toward the plane.

"Brenda had worked on it to make sure it was functional, though we hadn't given it a test run. The bigger question is if you think you can fit in there?"

Chris gave a slightly worried look. "I'm going to admit, I don't remember the planes on the beach being that small."

"With the wings collapsed it does look smaller, not that it makes the cockpit any larger with them up."

"There's only one way to find out," he said as he stood up and made his way to the plane.

Shannon joined him, helping him raise the wing that blocked the door. With much groaning, he climbed in and over the pilot's seat. His fingers searched the cabin walls for purchase as he attempted to lower himself into his seat. Slowly he slid and wiggled his way into the cramped area, his legs protruding in multiple directions as they struggled to crumple up in an organized way and his head slumped forward against the ceiling.

"Told you I fit," he exclaimed. "Is it possible for your seat to move up at all?" He asked casually.

"I might be able to do something," responded Shannon as she adjusted the levers on the side of the chair. Her seat slid forward five inches.

"Oh, thank you, Lord," said Chris in a relieved breath as he slid down in his seat enough to give his head clearance.

"Okay, *this* I can do for a few weeks, no problem." Chris reached his hand out of the door and gave a thumbs up. He shifted in his seat, his confident expression quickly drained. "I may actually be stuck in here."

Shannon laughed. "That's one way to make sure that you get to come along." She grabbed his hand and pulled with all of her strength until he was able to mount the chair in front of him and exit the plane. "After seeing you in the plane, I don't think we can do this all in one trip. I'll have to fly you to the beach, drop you off, and come back for the other items we want from here. Speaking of which, it might be nice to collect them before we go to sleep."

In a short time, Shannon had collected for Chris, Billy, and Jenny the same winter clothing she and Brenda had worn when they had traveled north. Chris gathered a harpoon gun and a tranquilizer gun, with as many spare parts as he could find, hoping to be able to combine the two for use against Leviathan. Lastly, Shannon gathered seeds, solar ovens, new tooth brushes, and spare cloth, in an attempt to satisfy the members of the committee that Phil was a part of.

Shannon looked upon the pile of loot that they had gathered with satisfaction. Meanwhile, Chris prepared their sleeping bags, which were now consistently right next to each other. Shannon had to give him credit. He was smart enough to not push her forward too quickly, and self-aware enough to know that it wasn't wise for him to rush forward as he worked through his own emotions. However, he was careful to not give up any progress he had made with her either. They both knew that the development of their relationship was simply a matter of time, and neither of them had any intentions of separating from each other, so they were both willing to enjoy each phase as it progressed naturally.

Shannon eased her way into her sleeping bag, settling in between the warmth of the fire on her left and the warmth of Chris on her right. For several minutes she thought to herself of the plans she had for the coming day until she noticed the slow, relaxed breathing of Chris as he slept. She was amazed by how quickly he was able to shut out the world and escape into slumber. In the last few nights, she had already grown to enjoy his presence as she fought off the remaining concerns of the day. With the comfort of his companionship and protection, each night became easier than the last to shed her burdens and fall asleep.

"This isn't bad at all!" Chris exclaimed as Shannon settled into the seat in front of him. The snugness of the cabin made it feel to her as though she was practically sitting on his lap.

"Oh yeah? Think you can handle this for a few weeks?" asked Shannon. "I mentioned how we have to sleep like this when we are on the water, right?"

"Well, I'm basically just hugging you right now. If staying in this position for three weeks kills me, then at least I will die doing what I love."

Shannon could feel him grinning from ear to ear without turning around to see it.

"I've never understood why people say that," she said with a chuckle. "He died while skydiving. 'Well, he died doing what he loved.' You mean, he loved failing at the thing he enjoyed doing, to the point of death? I think what he loved was succeeding at that thing, not failing at it."

"I will admit that under normal circumstances that is an odd thing to say. However, in this situation it would be true, since I would never have failed in any way while being this close to you. I simply would have done it so much, for so long, and enjoyed myself so extremely that my body simply gave out."

"Well, don't enjoy yourself too much back there," responded Shannon with a laugh.

"Why must you question my pure and saintly ways with your baseless and sinful accusations?"

"Said no man ever."

"Yeah, probably," he conceded.

They both laughed.

Shannon started the engine of the plane, giving them a jolt as the propellers spun to life.

"Please don't kill me," whimpered Chris.

"If anything is going to bring this plane down, it will be the extra two hundred and fifty pounds sitting behind me."

"Please doctor, work on your bedside manner. That's not helping my anxiety."

Shannon threw the throttle forward and the plane slowly began picking up speed.

"Do or die time," announced Shannon.

"Not helping!" yelled Chris.

The plane bounced on uneven ground as it picked up speed. "Don't worry! I'm mostly confident that we will survive this."

"Mostly?!" cried Chris.

"Like, fifty fifty."

"You have to stop or the heart attack I'm about to have will kill me, if this plane doesn't."

"Hey, at least with how compact we are, and the fact that there aren't any airbags, when this thing inevitably goes down, it should be a quick death." Shannon couldn't resist teasing him.

"Inevitably," he repeated with a groan. "That's it. I can't go on. I've died."

"Well. I've never had to resuscitate someone before. I know it's called mouth-to-mouth, but I've never had to do it. I'm assuming it's just another name for a kiss. I'll just have to try giving you a kiss when we land to see if you come back to life."

"I think it's worth a shot."

It took longer than Shannon was used to, but the plane picked up speed, eventually allowing her to pull back and launch the plane into the air. She climbed to a safe altitude and then leveled out. The bright blue sky revealed the world below them. Shannon could see small patches of green where grass and other plants were developing in the early spring warmth. A sense of hope rushed into her as she became confident that the earth would eventually escape the brown and dismal hell she had been surrounded by since surfacing so many months ago.

Four hours passed and the anxiety that Chris had slowly released came rushing back as it was time to land the plane.

"I'm going to land on the water," declared Shannon.

"Why the water?" asked Chris with concern.

"I think it is easier and a little safer than the uneven sand that tries to stick to the tires." Shannon swung the plane over the ocean. "Just close your eyes. Think about the fact that we are traveling at less than forty miles an hour, and it will be over in no time."

Chris remained quiet as Shannon gently lowered the plane onto the water. The plane landed with minimal turbulence. She then taxied onto the sand and made her way to the other planes, coming to a gradual stop.

"You survived," declared Shannon.

"Oh, thank goodness," responded Chris with relief.

Shannon threw open the door, climbed out, and stretched before turning around to help Chris. Leaning back into the plane, she grabbed his hands and pulled him over her seat. He dangled half in and half out, holding himself back from falling out of the plane as Shannon eased in and gave him a quick kiss on the lips. Shock made him lose his grip as he tumbled out of the plane and into her arms as she struggled to prevent him from crashing to the ground.

"That's not fair. I wasn't ready," pouted Chris.

"Well, too bad, because that's all you get. I have to hurry back to retrieve our stash of things if I want to get back before dark. It's nine hours round trip, and it's ten o'clock now. I need to grab one of the other planes so I have a full charge."

She quickly examined the nearest plane, mimicking the actions she had seen Brenda do dozens of times. When she was satisfied with what she saw, she opened the door and climbed in. She fired up the engine, which started without delay.

"Come here!" She yelled at Chris, who stood a safe distance away.

"What do you need?" he asked. His face was right next to hers so he could hear her over the engine.

"Get everything prepped while I am gone, okay?"

"No problem," he answered.

Shannon quickly leaned in and gave him another kiss before shoving him away from the plane and slamming the door closed. She taxied to the water before pushing the plane to full speed and taking off into the air.

It would be nine hours before she returned with her plane full of goods, and the last hint of light peeking above the horizon as she landed. She was greeted by a massive bonfire that Chris had started to help draw her attention and cast as much light on the surrounding area for her as possible. She nervously landed her plane and was relieved to be on solid ground, knowing that she had made a risky decision to fly so late into the evening.

Chris welcomed her back with food, which she consumed greedily. He quickly sorted the items that they would take back to the settlement in the morning, and then found a seat next to Shannon. They stayed up late into the night talking and enjoying the remaining time alone that they would have before embarking on their voyage with her brother and Jenny.

Chapter 35

Billy was found waiting near the edge of the settlement in anticipation of the return of his sister. He greeted her with an excited smile as he eagerly ran up to her, and relieved her of the things she was carrying. She couldn't tell if his enthusiasm for her return was his fear of her leaving him again, or his excitement for the upcoming trip. She hoped for the latter, but thought the truth was likely somewhere in the middle.

Entering the settlement, they were met by many who were desiring to enjoy their gifts, snatching them away hungrily. It was only a short moment later when Shannon learned that the items she had brought to serve as bribes were successful in their purpose, as a conversation between Chris and Billy, turning toward the upcoming trip, was met with no resistance.

Phil, seeing Lupe, the stubborn chef, struggling to hide a smile as he examined the solar ovens now at his disposal, leaned in toward Shannon and quietly spoke. "You did a good job."

"Whether they are actually happy with me or not, I guess, doesn't matter as long as they stay distracted long enough for us to leave," responded Shannon. "Though I would like to believe that this brought me a little closer to them actually liking me. Eventually I need to be able to settle down here."

Phil gave her an encouraging pat on the back. "I think they would like you a lot more if you did settle down. Most people can't even handle being around this much adventure or adversity. They want to know that you are someone they can depend upon, especially since you have been rather unpredictable so far. That's why I tried to bring them into the loop as much as I could before you leave this time, so they don't think you are going rogue again."

"Thanks," said Shannon as she gave him a smile.

"We will take two days to rest and gather any remaining supplies," said Chris, speaking to Billy.

"Does that timing work for you?" asked Shannon to Phil.

Phil gave a nod. "I think that will be fine. I know that if you tell me these magnet necklaces that Jenny made for us for while you are gone will work, then they will work. But we are planning on leaving for the beach tomorrow and we will be back before you are gone. So, it will give everyone a chance to learn first hand that they will be safe without Chris' protection, or Billy's aid. It will also strengthen their confidence in you that you know what you are doing, and can be trusted to make good decisions. That being said, we are losing, hopefully only for a short while, the youngest and most able-bodied people we have available to us. It's a scary proposition to risk losing you guys permanently, should something go wrong, regardless of when you choose to leave."

"Thank you for all your guidance with the politics of all this," said Shannon.

Phil gave her a fatherly smile and placed his hand on her shoulder. "Just remember what I'm good for when you take over leadership one day. Now, go get some rest. I'm sure you need it."

Shannon had not realized how fatigued she had become from her exertion during her trip until she woke up half way through the day, fourteen hours later. With her blond hair still in a wild nest, she groggily stumbled outside to find Chris sitting nearby, holding a small stack of papers, waiting for her.

"Don't worry, I also just woke up a little while ago," responded Chris when he noticed her look of concern.

Shannon dropped into a sit next to him and gave a hard yawn. "What do you have there?" she asked, gesturing to the papers he held.

"A whole list of questions and information to provide to the people in Austria." He handed it to her.

"Anything I need to know or worry about?" she wondered as she thumbed through it, seeing stats and graphs that looked difficult to understand at a glance.

"Not really. It's mostly technical stuff from our communications specialist. We have a few different ways to try and communicate with them, but they all require a lot of specific information on both ends. That stuff is all way over my head. Then there are a few more general questions that people from the committee have, personnel, information, and resource sharing. We obviously have our own questions to ask as well, but none of those are in there."

A small group of people gathered around to send off the four travelers. With as few people as the camp had, and the nearly insurmountable amount of work to be done, most people could not afford to stop their duties long enough to wish the group farewell.

"Do you need any help?" Chris asked as he effortlessly shouldered two large bags.

"I think you have more than enough. I can handle my own bags," responded Shannon as she slung her bags over her shoulder.

"Don't be reckless out there," warned Phil. "If things get hard, for any reason, just come back and we can regroup. I would rather have embarrassed survivors than proud victims."

"We'll be as careful as we can," assured Shannon. "The planes are small, simple, and slow. I doubt they will give us much trouble. Plus, with the magnets we have, we should be relatively invisible. Don't worry. We'll be back in no time."

Shannon leaned in and gave Phil a hug, who returned it happily.

"We'll be waiting for you," said Phil.

Chapter 36

After two exhaustive days of flight training, both Billy and Jenny felt confident for the long trip ahead of them. The group had awoken early in the morning and prepared their planes, eager to get started. Billy and Jenny's planes were as full as they could manage, and every plane had additional items attached to the outside of the plane to compensate for the limited capacity of Shannon's aircraft with Chris in it. Chris had been extremely careful to manage weight evenly across all three planes.

Shannon went to each plane, with its respective pilot sitting ready for flight, and examined everything. She made sure that they all had a flare gun sitting nearby, and that the gauges and electronics were working properly. She then went back to her plane, jumped into the pilot seat, with Chris looking cramped yet as happy as ever to see her.

"You remind me of a dog," said Shannon, intentionally not clarifying the statement.

"Um, what? Care to elaborate?" asked Chris.

"Nope, not really."

"Then I assume it is because I am cute, loyal, protective, and nice to cuddle. Complement accepted," responded Chris with his usual enthusiasm.

"I was thinking because you always seem irrationally excited to see me, but I guess those other things are true also." Shannon gave a chuckle and then picked up her radio. Speaking over the radio, "Remember that if you have an issue, land your plane immediately. Use the radio as soon as possible, and if communication isn't possible for any reason and you have lost sight of the others, then wait two minutes for us to notice and turn around, and then fire off your flare so we can find you. Can everyone hear me properly?"

"Yes," responded Billy and Jenny.

"Great. Now we will do it like we practiced yesterday. The takeoff order is me, Billy, Jenny. We each circle back after taking off to give room for the next take off until our flight order is reversed, with Jenny in the lead. Remember, we are heading northeast at 325 degrees."

"Let's do this!" cheered Billy. The radio crackled from his volume.

They each turned on their engines and, bounding down the beach, leaving deep tracks in the sand, launched into the air after bouncing wildly on the uneven surface.

"You did well this time," commented Shannon to Chris.

He inhaled deeply after releasing a breath he had been holding. "Hopefully I'll get used to it over time. I've always hated flying, but this just seems so much worse, even if it is probably safer than a big plane."

For four hours, Shannon and Chris talked to each other while peacefully enjoying the views around them. Much of the landscape remained decimated by the fallout of the comet, and was littered with debris from a lost era; but everywhere they looked, small patches of green could be found. Nature was slowly fighting to erase the signs of humanity that had previously worked so hard to destroy it.

The radio stayed quiet for most of their initial flight due to Jenny being too nervous to want background noise as she flew. They eventually landed near the border of California and Nevada for lunch. Jenny, over time having settled into the activity of flying, exited her plane proud and confident. She conveyed a sense of composure that Shannon hadn't seen in her for a long time.

"It's liberating being up there and in control of your own life, isn't it?" asked Shannon.

"I've felt, ever since we emerged from the bunker, like a feather being forced to go wherever the wind sent me, as though I had no control over what puddle or mess I landed in. There is obviously no better example than my mom's murder, which only served to make my feelings of helplessness worse. Being up there, feeling like I was moving under my own motivation and strength, I think it's the therapy I need." Jenny gave a big smile as she wiped away a couple of tears.

Shannon gave her a hug. "I'm so happy for you."

Billy struggled to control his excitement as he came bumbling out of his plane toward them. "I can't believe I just flew two hundred miles! That was amazing. Gosh, Dad would have loved that! I mean, I thought we were going to be thrown into the stone ages after the comet, and here I am flying!"

"Just wait until we are flying over the water for a few days. You'll be sick of it in no time," said Shannon with a grin. She turned around and looked for Chris.

Chris had promptly left the plane when they landed and went about stretching. Unlike with their previous flight, he did not complain. Shannon assumed he would keep it to himself until the trip was over rather than be negative during their journey. She was confident he would milk his pain and suffering for attention once they got back, though. After several minutes of stretching, he went about preparing lunch for everyone. Everyone ate standing up, knowing they had plenty of sitting ahead of them. After an hour of resting, they got back into their planes and continued flying.

They would continue their tour over the destroyed remains of the United States for five days before eventually reaching the northern tip of the new east coast of North Dakota. Over those five days, as they flew, more patches of green revealed themselves on the desolate earth below them, promising hope of an eventual revitalization. They had first flown north, until snow became an unavoidable issue, which forced them to move east, remaining at a latitude that left portions of bare ground to land on. They then finished their northern ascent while following along the coast, freely landing on and taking off from the water. Through repetition they each settled into their routine, the novelty of the experience gradually wore off.

Chapter 37

Chris maintained a large fire for two days as the group rested on the coast of North Dakota. The land was covered in the remains of winter snow. Chris was able to find enough wood buried under the white blanket that he never worried about staying warm. He gladly cooked the fish that the collara supplied, and enjoyed not being stuffed inside the plane.

Shannon used the collara to investigate the ocean and beach nearby, but found nothing of significance. It would still be several months before it became the same time of year that they had first started noticing signs of the collara after surfacing from their bunker. She wondered if they had a migration pattern that ran along this coast, and if it would be the same from year to year. It was entirely possible that they came from a world with completely different year lengths and seasons, and that the animals had very different migration patterns on their home planet, or possibly had no need to migrate in the past. There was so much she wanted to study once larger threats were removed from the picture.

Despite the pain of the ice cold water, they made sure to bathe themselves, choosing to avoid the task in the coming days as they flew over the ocean. Shannon abhorred the idea of getting into the water while out on the deep ocean, as well as the idea of trying to get dry and warm without a fire. She had been tempted to explore the surrounding area, but discovered quickly how dangerous it could be to walk on snow-covered debris. A couple close calls as her feet would sink impossibly deep between dangerously shaped objects, and she decided the best thing to do was remain near the water.

On their third day at the beach, they packed their items and prepared to set off as the inviting glow of the sun broke over the east horizon. Jenny had become used to the experience of flying, and the three pilots settled into their routine without much thought. Shannon looked down as they left their camp grounds behind them. A collection of rocks had been formed into numbers by Chris and Billy, to signify the year, and location that they had encamped there. She wondered if they would be washed away before anyone had a chance to find them again. Wisps of fog rolled in from the warming air on the icy water, sweeping over the beach.

"I've suddenly realized why I like having you crammed in the backseat like a sardine," spoke Shannon.

"Oh yeah? Why is that?" asked Chris.

"You keep it warmer in here. My own personal space heater," answered Shannon.

"How sweet of you," responded Chris sarcastically. "Even if you are making a joke at my expense, you still acknowledge that you like having me around. I don't care why, I'll take the complement. I'll always be around to keep you warm."

"I'm sure you will," chuckled Shannon. Without thinking, she ran her fingers through her hair, straightening it out slightly.

"I could say the same thing. I like having you be my pilot, because from back here the view is always nice."

"I didn't know poorly washed blond hair was your thing," responded Shannon.

"It's the best."

"I'm glad you think so, because we'll be sleeping on the water for the next two nights, which means my gross hair will only get worse, and you won't be able to escape it."

"There's no place I would rather be." His tone conveyed the smile Shannon knew he had.

The water slapped against the pontoons of the planes as Shannon, Billy, and Jenny worked to tie them together into a triangle. Jenny moved cautiously over the black water below her, cinching up her last knot. The last hints of orange and pink painted clouds shrunk in the distance as the light diminished. Billy helped them both, double checking that everything was secure. Shannon, knowing exactly what was in the water, worked as fast as she could.

Shannon climbed back into her plane, eagerly escaping the edge of the cliff she felt she was otherwise standing on, which was waiting for just one wrong step so that it could consume her. Chris had scraped himself out of the cocoon of the backseat and still stood on a pontoon stretching.

The collara popped their heads out of the water near Shannon, giving Chris a startle that left him clutching at the collapsed wing of the plane so that he didn't fall into the water.

"That almost killed me from shock." Chris gasped. "Somehow they have to do that differently next time."

"You'll be okay," reassured Shannon. She reached out and connected with each of the collara. There wasn't anything specific she was looking for, but she investigated the surrounding area in an attempt to comfort herself that there would be no surprises from colossal sharks. When she felt confident in her safety, the collara dropped into the water and swam away. If they had been the cause of the previous incident when she was flying with Brenda, then she didn't want them anywhere near her while she slept. They would come back in the morning.

"I think I'm ready to be safe inside the plane," said Chris when she finished with the collara.

"Sounds good," responded Shannon as she climbed into the backseat so that he could have the leg room of the pilot seat while he slept.

"You don't have to do that," he said in response to her actions. "I'm of no use until we get to land. If you'll sleep better in the front, and it will help you fly better, then I'm okay in the back."

"I'm small enough that it's just cozy back here," answered Shannon with a smile.

"You don't have to tell me twice." Chris jumped into the front seat, reclined the chair, and leaned back, his head stopping next to Shannon's. "You sure I'm not going to crowd you too much?"

Shannon wrapped her arms around his chest. "Nope, this is just fine."

Chris smiled big, pulled his feet into the plane, and close the door.

They flew for two more days, seeing land at the end of the second day. The islands of Quebec. After a day of rest they then continued on. The islands were all nondescript. Covered in snow, they appeared completely inhospitable. The frigid air, combined with the feet of snow that blanketed anything that protruded from the water, made them eager to leave after they had time to stretch their limbs.

The most notable characteristic of the far north to Shannon was the white tendrils of snow that the wind would pull off of the land, snaking through the air before settling into another mound of snow. There was a constant movement that masked the lifeless land beneath it. While she was happy to have seen it, she was also happy to leave it as soon as possible. It was not the experience of traveling the world that she had envisioned for herself as a child.

Chapter 38

The coast of Greenland neared. It was no different from the last set of islands they had seen. The snow covered land presented an uninviting image to its approaching guests. It didn't appear any more appealing the closer they got.

"You two land while Chris and I run a pass over the land to do a little investigating. We'll only take a few minutes," said Shannon over the radio.

"Sounds good. See you in a bit," answered Billy.

Shannon brought the plane down low. A white and smooth mass presented itself below them, smooth and calm from a brief reprieve of the strong winds they had been dealing with.

"I think I see tracks," announced Chris.

"You can't possibly determine anything about the tracks, can you?" Shannon struggled to see below her as she focused on flying the plane.

"No, they're too far away," he answered.

"When we get back, we will want to investigate more. Hopefully we aren't placing ourselves in danger by camping where we are."

Shannon attempted to look out her window and see what Chris saw, but it was too difficult while maintaining her attention on flying. Shannon circled back and joined the others as they began setting up camp. She tied up her plane while Chris went about his routine stretches. His disdain for the cold weather could not outweigh his excitement to spread out his legs and back.

"We saw some tracks that we are going to investigate. Don't get too settled in, just in case we are invading someones territory. I would rather run than defend our position," said Shannon to Jenny and Billy as she and Chris turned in the direction of the tracks and began their trek.

"Do you have reason to be concerned?" asked Chris.

Shannon struggled to walk through snow that regularly collapsed under her weight. She was quickly winded. "Not entirely. From what I noticed when I went north with Brenda to collect the collara I have now, they seem to be like turtles that lay eggs and expect the babies to make it on their own to the water. My hope is that the tracks are from the mother leaving after laying the eggs, with no intention of returning, let alone defending the eggs."

After several minutes of exploration they found the tracks they had seen from above. The tracks consisted of a deep and wide center portion where the torso was dragged and small punches in the snow from the collara's hands as it used them to move forward. Chris examined the track and compared it to his own.

"When you compare this track to ours," he began, "it doesn't have the same crispness. The edges are soft. It leads me to believe that they aren't new. There doesn't seem to be any wind and we haven't seen any snowfall. Since we are unable to know for sure what the weather has been like around here, I can't make any solid determinations. The track could be an hour old with mild wind, or three days old if there has been no wind or fresh snow."

"Let's follow it and see if it leads to a nest," responded Shannon.

The track continued for two hundred yards before coming to a stop at a small mound in the snow. Carefully Shannon approached. Disturbing the mound as little as possible, she reach into the snow and touched an egg. She had the same sensation as her previous experience and could feel how much longer the eggs needed to incubate.

"These seem rather new. They won't hatch for a few weeks. I think we are safe. Just to be sure, though, it would probably be wise to fly to the east side of Greenland before taking a day to rest." Shannon removed her hand from the nest, gently packed snow into the hole she had made, and began her way back to Billy and Jenny.

The walk back was slow and exhausting. They remained quiet, reserving their energy.

"What's the verdict?" Billy asked as Shannon approached.

The phrasing and the delivery of his question reminded her of her father and a brief pang of sadness jolted her.

"I think we are in the clear, though we did find a nest. We can play it safe and leave first thing in the morning," answered Shannon.

"Are you sure it's wise to wait? I've gone on the fishing trips before, back at the settlements. I know how nasty they can be. I would hate to be camping in their known tracks." Billy seemed nervous.

Shannon gave him a reassuring smile. "I have reason to believe they aren't coming back any time soon. I also have reason to believe that simas don't control the collara when they are tending to their eggs. When I tracked down eggs previously, the collara I was using to find the nest had all of its memories intact, which meant it wasn't being controlled at the time. Collara that aren't being controlled do not seem to be aggressive. Plus, it is far too late now to fly anywhere. I don't want to try landing the planes on water when it is dark."

Billy conceded to her arguments, but was packed and ready when dawn came around. He hadn't been able to sleep much throughout the night, and every wave that created more noise than average got his attention.

"You have far more reason to be trusting toward these animals than I do," said Billy when he saw Shannon's questioning look as she woke up in the morning surprised by his readiness.

"Hopefully you got enough sleep to be able to fly," responded Shannon.

"Only one way to find out," he answered as he loaded his plane.

It was a half day of flying for them to reach the other side of Greenland. Once again, Shannon made a pass over the blanket of snow, and this time she found no evidence of collara.

"I don't think I would tell him, even if I did find more tracks," admitted Shannon as she made her way back to camp.

"That would have been the right call," laughed Chris.

They rested the next day without incident. Though the temperature on the island was as freezing as anything else they had experienced so far, when the sun hit Shannon directly she could feel the warmth of the coming spring. With it came a sense of hope that fought against the oppression of their current surroundings.

When the next day arrived they began making their way toward the small islands that remained of the United Kingdom.

"I've got to say," said Chris as he thought back to his view of the debris and snow-covered island of Wales. "I'm really not looking forward to flying back after we are done in Austria."

"At least we'll know that it's over after that," responded Shannon. She packed up her gear in preparation for continuing flying.

"I never thought I would hate touring the world. However, visiting places that I've been to dozens of times, and being forced to accept that it truly was the entire world that was destroyed, and not just my little area in California, has been surprisingly upsetting." Chris looked over their campgrounds to confirm that nothing had been forgotten.

Shannon shrugged. "I guess some places you visit to see the land, the beauty of it. Other places you visit for the people that inhabit the land, to experience the culture, the beauty of the people. Neither of those are possible at the moment, unless you find snow, or mud, or barren desert worth visiting."

Two days of travel had passed after leaving what remained of the United Kingdom. Flying over the continent that now lay largely submerged under hundreds of feet of water, an extra layer of debris and trash seemed to cling to the region, hinting at land and life that once lived below. As Shannon finally gained a glimpse of the western coast of Switzerland, her body grew anxious. After reaching land today, she knew she had only one more day of flight before reaching her destination. They would finally be on the same chunk of land that the settlement they were heading to was on, and she could walk the remaining distance, if she really felt like it. She was almost certain that Chris would choose to walk, if presented with the option.

Even from a distance she could see strong hints of green. The fertile European lands were in stark contrast to much of the desert regions that North America still contained. It was early evening by the time they reached land, and Chris could not contain his excitement at being nearly done with their journey. They flew farther inland than they had on their previous landings because

Shannon knew she would have to remove her magnets to talk with Lysander, and she didn't want to be within range of violent collara on the coast.

When Shannon was sure she was far enough inland and had found a place to land, she came in quickly. The strip was narrow and short, forcing her to come down at a sharp angle and endure a bumpy ride as her tires ground to a stop. Chris' groaning didn't stop for several seconds after the plane had come to a rest. Shannon quickly jumped out of her plane and helped Chris escape what he occasionally referred to as his "flying coffin." He proceeded to shake his arms, legs, and head as he paced around, forcing the adrenaline out of his body.

While the others set up camp, Shannon made herself comfortable on her plane, took one last glance out of her window to assure herself that she was far away from the coast, and removed her necklace. Lysander joined her immediately, having anticipated her arrival. Shannon closed her eyes and allowed Lysander to send her to their usual place for conversation, the beach.

Compared to the freezing cold weather she had been enduring, the sudden warmth was a shocking contrast that her body quickly embraced. Lysander stood a short distance away and began talking without waiting for Shannon to adjust to her environment.

"They will be expecting your arrival," announced Lysander.

Shannon was surprised. She had known that Lysander would attempt to make contact with the Austrian settlement, but had yet to hear about any progress.

"Have you been successful in persuading them toward our cause?" asked Shannon.

"With your arrival they will have the confirmation they need that the dreams I have been giving them were genuine," answered Lysander. "They will not be difficult to convince after that."

"How much have you told them?" asked Shannon.

"They know that we need a chemist. They apparently have the tools and ingredients needed to create a wide variety of medicines, including what we are asking for. I don't think that they have started anything, though. Because—as you know—I have to present myself as someone they have seen before, it is hard to convince them that they aren't just having a regular dream when I speak to them through the form of someone they know. I can tell they understand that something unique is happening, but they still have too many doubts to take action. You showing up tomorrow will be the proof we need for them to cooperate."

Chapter 39

Several people stood below, waving to the planes as they flew overhead. Shannon was relieved to have finally reached her destination. The view of the snow-capped Alps in the distance had provided a scene of beauty that most of the environments they had seen lately lacked. A large area had been cleared of wreckage and provided a perfect place for landing. The planes touched down, shaking and bouncing on rough land as they slowed to a stop. People came running up to the planes as soon as they stopped, not waiting for the occupants to exit their aircraft first. Their hosts eagerly greeted them with baskets of fruit and bread.

"Halli hallo! We have been expecting you. Willkommen! I am Franz," said an energetic man in his fifties with a strong accent. He had lightly tanned skin, faded blue eyes, medium length gray hair that was combed back, and a full, but not heavy, face. At five feet and ten inches, he stood significantly lower than Chris, whom he greeted with surprise and a strong handshake. "Sehr groß!" He exclaimed with a smile.

"Which of you is Shannon?" asked Franz as Billy and Jenny joined them.

"That would be me." Shannon raised her hand, then lowered it, gesturing toward each other person as she spoke. "And this is Chris, Billy, and Jenny."

"Wunderbar!" He shook their hands excitedly. "Many of us have been quite worried, having dreams predicting your arrival. It was rather startling. It is quite lovely to see that, other than your sehr groß freund, you are not intimidating or scary at all. No offense, mein hübscher Riese!" He said as he gave Chris a wink and a hard pat on the back.

"What was that last bit?" whispered Shannon to Chris.

"He said 'my handsome giant,'" answered Chris.

"You just got yourself a new nickname," responded Shannon with a smile.

"Please, come this way. I'm sure you need some rest. I know there is much to discuss, but our talks will be more fruitful if you are well rested." Franz gestured to them while looking to the people who accompanied him. They quickly jumped forward and shouldered the bags that Shannon and the others carried.

Shannon followed as they began walking along a path that was surprisingly clear of debris.

"I do hope you guys have been here before. I would hate for this to be the first time you are seeing the Alps. It has lost so much of its splendor, being ripped clear of most of its trees. The few that are left are obviously burnt and hideous. We are working diligently to restore it as quickly as possible, but these things will take years, and may likely never fully recover." Franz threw up his hands in a sign of defeat. "Such is life. At least we are alive to complain about it!"

Shannon was in shock as she approached what she could only refer to as a town. She had known this was the largest group of people still alive on the planet, but what she saw far exceeded what her mental picture of a settlement could be. Unlike everything she had seen thus far, the entire area was clear of waste. The place was completely clean. There were two dozen buildings running in two lines with a center road dividing the rows of buildings, like pictures she had seen of towns in the wild west. Each building had solar panels on top and looked like a very modern home.

"How do you have standing buildings?" asked Shannon in awe. "They even have glass windows!"

Franz laughed. "We Germans are known for our building kits. We have had these for a while now," he declared triumphantly. His chest stuck out proudly. "Don't let my Austrian companions say otherwise. They always like to take credit for the things the Germans do, and blame the Germans for the things that they created."

"How did you have space for all of these?" asked Chris.

"You would be surprised by how compact you can make them when they are not assembled. Plus, space wasn't really an issue for us. The B8 Bergkristall was more than large enough for everyone and these buildings," he said, somewhat mournfully. "Who knew something so tragic would lead to something so fortuitous?"

Surrounding the buildings were a mixture of gardens, animal pens, and large tents that felt a bit more reminiscent of what Shannon had experienced. There were also people everywhere. Compared to what she had known for the past year, the place felt crowded.

Franz led the group into one of the buildings. It was two stories tall. The front door had a large glass panel in it with the word "Apotheke" written on it. Inside, the house had been converted into multiple offices and chemistry labs.

"Wir sind zu hause," announced Franz to no one in particular. "This is my office. I am the head chemist and pharmacist here. After you have had a chance to settle in, I will be the one you will meet with to discuss what you need developed. Please follow me upstairs and I will show you to your room. I hope you do not mind, but we only had one spare room, which was being used as storage. I had it cleared out and filled with cots in preparation for your arrival. I wish I could be more accommodating on such an amazing occasion, but such is life."

While the outside of the home had looked finished, the inside was still made of basic building materials. Shannon was not surprised that they hadn't wasted space or time storing and then installing flooring, which currently consisted of plywood. The walls were lined with unfinished drywall. When they reached their room, they were greeted by a twelve by twelve foot room with four cots that lined the walls and was otherwise empty. The space smelled of sawdust and cardboard boxes, revealing its original use, despite having been emptied out.

"Please come down when you are settled. We can eat and talk about everything that is happening then." Franz gave a nod of satisfaction and left them in their room, closing the door as he went.

Jenny set her things on a cot, turned back to the door, opened it, and closed it again. She stood there silently before opening and closing the door one more time. Her hand lingered on the door handle before she went back to her cot and sat down. Tears slowly ran down her cheeks. "I didn't realize how much I missed being in an actual home, with a real bedroom, and a door. It's so familiar, yet it seems like it's been forever."

"It does feel like we've stepped into another world," agreed Chris. He dropped his items onto the ground and threw himself onto a cot, stretching his arms out and dangling his feet over the edge. He closed his eyes with satisfaction.

Shannon set her things on the ground next to a cot and lay down. She let out an exhausted breath. She tossed briefly from one side to another, attempting to find a comfortable position. Her body buzzed with excitement. After a moment she sat up. "I know I could use a break, but after all the waiting I just did in the form of traveling, I just want to get things done. Are you coming, my handsome giant?" Shannon extended a hand to Chris.

Chris gave a look of resignation. "Of course," he said as he took her hand and stood up.

Chris let out a hard yawn. Tears welled up as he stretched. Several hours had passed while Shannon and Franz had talked, discussing everything she had gone through, as well as the questions and information that

Phil had provided her before she had departed. Chris had contributed very little, but had served as a translator just enough that he never felt comfortable leaving.

"Okay!" Franz said as he rubbed his hands together excitedly. "Give me a week and I will provide you with what you need. It will need to be a multi-step attack! We can lower the calcium in the soil to prevent the plants from absorbing as much of it, since calcium helps absorb vitamin D. We can also provide a couple different drugs that will help prevent vitamin D absorption."

Franz glanced at his watch. "Oh my! If we don't hurry we are going to miss dinner." He stood up. "I will get you as soon as I have made the appropriate drugs for you. However, there will be others that will want to discuss things with you while you are here. Please talk to them while you are waiting."

Franz led them outside to one of several areas where food was being served throughout the town. They quickly found Jenny and Billy, who greeted them with smiles. They were accompanied by a man in his late thirties with a short, dark beard, well-manicured hair, a medium build, and dark, serious eyes. He promptly put his hand out as Shannon and Chris approached. Chris quickly caught his hand for a firm shake.

"My name is Tamer Dogan," he declared in a husky voice. "I'm the current elected leader of this community. It's a pleasure to finally have the chance to meet you. I understand you have already taken the time to speak with Franz."

"Yes," answered Shannon. "Thank you for your hospitality."

"Not a problem. I am only sorry that I couldn't have taken the time to greet you upon your arrival. Please, enjoy your evening here and we can discuss everything tomorrow morning when you are well rested."

Before they had a chance to talk to Tamer anymore, others came up to him. Their desire to talk to him appeared urgent. He listened to them momentarily, his face still carrying the same serious expression he had greeted them with, and then he turned away and followed the others away.

"He is a very busy man," observed Franz. "I am glad no one pushed for my nomination for that position. When you are too busy, you don't actually get anything done."

Rows of folding tables filled a clearing and were occupied by swarms of people who talked loudly. Shannon was served a meal of fish, rice, and fresh greens. The items weren't much different than what she was used to eating, but they were prepared in a way that she knew could only happen when a community is large enough that the cooks could be completely dedicated to their task and not divided among other responsibilities. It was one of the best meals she could remember having.

Chapter 40

A light flashed before Shannon and she quickly hit a button. The task was simple, and she'd done it a dozen times, but the assortment of doctors and scientists that were observing her reaction times seemed interested with each iteration of the test. They had already performed a similar test with audio.

Though she should have guessed it, she was surprised to find that people were more interested in studying her than they were in hearing her story. However, that didn't stop her from having to explain her experiences to more people than she could remember. Yet, with everything they asked of her, they always treated her kindly and never expressed any doubt about what she told them. She didn't think they had much reason to doubt her after the way Lysander had prepared them for her arrival.

As much as she loved being around people that had an equal interest in research as she did, her favorite part of the community was the chance to interact with other girls her age. There were only a handful of them, but the settlement had very specifically expanded the ages of its members to include teens and young children so that there would never be a large gap between children and adults as newer generations were created and raised. In the long term, it meant that there were young people available for work at all times, but for now it meant that Shannon had people her age to spend time with, what little time was available to her.

Franz shook his head in disbelief. "I have no idea what I was expecting, but I am nonetheless surprised to find no noticeable impact—positive or negative—on your cognitive abilities from your interactions with the aliens. They didn't add anything, like upgrading a computer, to give you the abilities you have gained. Yet, wherever in your head those new skills lie, they don't interfere with what is already there. It is truly a mystery."

He handed her papers with results on them. Without a proper understanding of the baseline, she had no way to interpret the information. She smiled and handed the papers back.

"The idea that a large percentage of your brain is just sitting around not being used is an old myth," explained Franz. "That is why it is so shocking that they somehow reconfigured your brain's wavelengths—which we have observed—and pumped you full of new skills like mind control and a sort of time travel, yet left no sign of the change for our tests to measure."

"I'm sure something has changed and we just don't know where to look yet, or how to measure it," assured Shannon. "When I have a chance to come back in the future, we can figure out new tests to perform.

A week passed from her arrival in Austria and Shannon was relieved to be preparing for her departure. Each day had been full of meetings. Discussions had been had to fully document the locations of other groups of people, ways to implement long distance communications, methods for preventing what Tamer referred to as 'mental hijacking' from the simas, and other things she struggled to even remember. The work that Lysander had done to prepare the way for her had made her job quite easy. Not only did everyone believe Shannon about what needed to be done, but they had been prepared on what questions to ask and how to best utilize the time they had.

Work was being done to create magnets for each of the members of the town. She had been supplied by the communications specialist with equipment and instructions for receiving skywave radio signals so their two communities could communicate. Much of the equipment, and the conversations that had occurred around them, exceeded her understanding. They had left no detail unattended, and she had a pile of documentation to prove it.

Jenny gave one last longing glance at the room the group had shared as they stood at the door to leave. The morning sun poured in through a window and lit her face brightly, illuminating her sad brown eyes.

"I'll build you a proper home someday," Billy declared confidently.

"I'm sure you will," responded Jenny with a contented smile. She was the last to leave the room. She gave the door handle a couple extra turns before fully closing the door, savoring the sensation one last time.

The group made their way out of the building, walking through the hallway lined with labs that now seemed so futuristic to them, and were met by Franz and Tamer, as well as a group that would help carry the additional equipment they were meant to take with them.

"Do you have everything you need?" asked Tamer. His demeanor was professional, but not entirely cold.

"You have been extremely generous in your hospitality. I believe we have tended to everything that was necessary. With your help, we should be able to communicate between our two communities and resolve any other issues that way. Thank you," answered Shannon.

The two shook hands.

"I apologize that I had not greeted you upon your arrival, but I will once again need to rely on Franz to see you to your planes. With the plans we have discussed and the locations of others that you have provided to us, I have much work ahead of me that I must start on immediately. Please feel free to visit again, hopefully under more favorable circumstances." Tamer gave a warm smile and then dismissed himself.

Everyone took one last longing look at the buildings that surrounded them. The environment felt more controlled, stable, and less reactionary than they had been able to enjoy for the past year. Though they each desired a different aspect of what the community offered; Jenny, the familiarity of it; Billy, the stability to have a family; Shannon, the chance to perform more thorough studies and experiments; they all yearned for it equally, nonetheless. Led by Franz, the group began their hike back to their planes.

"Shannon," began Franz. "You have the heart of a scientist! It was such a pleasure having these past few days to talk with you. There is a whole new world to discover out there. If our plans come to fruition, you must come back so that we can do research together. You have gained abilities through your experiences that must be studied and understood." Franz's face grew into a grin. "I wouldn't mind trying to replicate your experiences and seeing if I can yield similar results. All of our equipment would be useless then," he said with a laugh.

"I'm dreading the flights ahead of us," interjected Chris. "It might be a while before I can stomach the journey back here."

"I couldn't possibly come without my handsome giant," laughed Shannon. "I'll convince him to come back soon enough," she assured Franz with a smile.

"With the way he looks at you... I'm sure you will." Franz let out a loud laugh and gave Chris a hard pat on the back.

Chris was unfazed by Franz's joke.

The hike passed quickly. Their excitement to return home, unhampered by the long trip ahead of them, made the effort of the hike unnoticeable, and before they knew it they were loading their planes. With a final sigh of resignation, Chris tapped his hand on the door and then climbed onto the plane. Franz and his companions stood nearby and waved as the three planes came to life.

"Auf wiedersehen! Tschüss!" yelled Franz.

The familiar rumble of the plane shook Shannon's bones. *How quickly my body had forgotten the sensation,* she thought to herself. She listened to Chris as the plane picked up speed, noticing his hands that extended past her on either side. He had finally learned to remain calm during takeoff. As the bouncing of the plane became softer—the aircraft floating more with each drop—and she eventually pulled back, raising the plane into the air, she wondered if she really would have the luxury of coming back some day.

Will life settle down enough that I can consider traveling for research, rather than survival? By the time I'm done, will I even want to travel again?

The group flew for several days without incident. They spoke excitedly as they flew. For a brief moment they had set aside their future plans, and reveled in their success with their current task. The gloomy surroundings that had lowered their morale on their way to Austria, now shined white under the sun, appearing clean and hopeful. Even Chris' spirits, despite his grumbling over his cramped sleeping arrangements, seemed to rise the closer they were to home. Shannon thought that part of their enthusiasm came from seeing what was still possible. They were going back home with hope and inspiration. When they landed in the evenings, Shannon could often hear Billy talking with Jenny about what he would build for her as a home.

Chapter 41

Shannon and Chris took a short hike away from the coast of Greenland, with the various concoctions that Franz had developed in Shannon's hand. She trudged through snow carefully, making sure that she always paid attention to her steps and avoided the traps of hidden debris. When she felt like she was a safe distance from the coast, she stopped. She prepared to remove her magnets. Not wanting to draw any undue attention to the Austrian town she had visited, she waited until she had arrived at a remote location before contacting Lysander to hand off the various chemicals for poisoning Leviathan. With rising tension, and a lingering fear that she hadn't come far enough inland, she removed her necklace and closed her eyes.

The familiar sight of the California coast greeted her. The sand was warm, brightly lit under the afternoon sun, and accompanied by the gentle sounds of the ocean waves. Not entirely removed from her actual body, the sensation of the conflicting feelings were almost sickening in the way they confused her senses. An aching homesickness bit at her subconscious. Looking down at her hand, she saw that she still had the items she was holding before closing her eyes.

Lysander stood nearby. Though Shannon had become used to his form, he still remained an unreadable statue. He made no attempt to greet her.

"Are we at risk of being attacked right now?" asked Shannon before progressing.

"I do not believe so," answered Lysander. "There are only two collara, several miles from your location, and they are not responding to your presence."

"Good."

Shannon reached out her hand to show Lysander the items she held. "I have a big one back at my plane that you will pour on the ground around the crops to change the soil." She then nodded to her hand. "One is a gel that can be injected into the crop after harvesting that shouldn't dissolve in ocean water. The other is a pill that can be mixed in with the food. According to Franz, the pill is the most effective method. The gel is a safety net, in case the pill is spotted or for some reason falls from its hiding place after you place it."

"Okay," responded Lysander.

"After I put my necklace back on I will move to the coast directly south of me to give you these things. Are you sure they won't be too much for you to take?"

"No, they will be easy to carry, and I can make the trip faster than if you—" Lysander stopped and his head cocked to the side, as though something had caught his attention. "The two collara that are currently south of you have begun moving in your direction."

Shannon's eyes shot open. She turned to Chris, panic on her face. "Collara are coming. We need to get back to Billy and Jenny!"

Shannon placed her necklace back on, hoping it would deter the collara from continuing to pursue her, and then began running back to the planes. The deep snow seemed to fight against Shannon with every step. The more effort she exerted, the more her footsteps sunk into the snow, swallowing her attempts to produce speed. Painstakingly, she struggled to return to the planes. Her lungs heaved, burning from the freezing air that they desperately pulled in.

As the beach neared, Shannon began yelling. "Collara are coming! Get into the sky!" Her voice—out of breath and weak from the cold air—struggled to cover the distance. The planes remained menacingly out of sight. The ground covered in snow, dropping significantly before reaching the water, kept her planes and companions below her view. She and Chris kept yelling.

After much struggling and a burning of her lungs and muscles that could only be overpowered by her fear, she reached the top of the slope before descending down to the water. The planes were visible, and Shannon could see Billy and Jenny attempting to board their planes.

Without warning, a collara burst from the water next to Jenny's plane and ripped Jenny into the water. A second emerged just a moment after, but Billy had already dove into the water. Shannon let out a scream, and, attempting to run down the snow, lost her footing and tumbled down the hill. Regaining her feet, she ran to the edge of the water with Chris chasing to catch up to her. He grabbed her just before she could dive into the water.

"You'll just get yourself killed!" Chris yelled in an attempt to stop her.

"How long has it been? Thirty seconds?" pleaded Shannon. Her voice was strained and frantic. She fought against Chris' powerful grip.

"I'll go in, not you," answered Chris.

As he began removing his cumbersome clothing, Billy surfaced, followed by Jenny. Shannon let out a sob of relief. Chris rushed toward them and removed them from the water. They shivered uncontrollably.

"Are you hurt?" Chris asked as he ran to grab towels and blankets.

Billy shook his head. "No, but they got our necklaces. They dropped like flies when they grabbed them, but I couldn't get them back." His teeth clattered as he spoke.

Jenny and Billy began removing their wet clothes.

Shannon removed her necklace and thrust it in Billy's face. "Put this on, now," she said sternly.

Billy pulled back slightly and looked at her with concern.

Shannon turned to Chris. "Give her yours," she demanded.

Chris' expression was serious, but not defiant. "Are you sure?"

Shannon continued holding her necklace in front of Billy. "You are putting these on and getting into the air immediately. The heater packs in your planes will warm you up once you are in the air. I am not discussing this with you. If you don't have these on, then you are at risk and we will be at risk if we are with you. If you have these on and fly ahead of us, then only we are at risk. Get in the air and go!"

Shannon refused to wait for a reply and put her necklace on her brother. Chris complied and did the same with his necklace for Jenny. He was concerned for Shannon's safety, but dared not fight with her on the issue.

"Are you okay to fly?" asked Billy.

Jenny nodded.

"I will never forgive you if you don't make it back," said Billy as he stared at his sister coldly.

"We need to wait for Lysander to give him the chemicals anyway. We will leave after that. It should give us enough distance to keep you safe. Now go!"

With anguish Billy helped Jenny get onto her plane before getting onto his. His movements were slow and labored. Shannon watched him talk to Jenny over the radio before she launched herself into the air. Billy was quick to follow. He gave one last saddened look toward his sister as he pulled away. Shannon and Chris waited silently, watching the two planes fly away.

"Couldn't we have divided up the magnets in our necklaces so we could all be safe?" asked Chris.

"There are so few magnets within each necklace. I have no confidence that dividing them would have been strong enough to work. I've lost enough as it is. I will not be responsible for losing them as well." Shannon spoke in a tone that indicated she was done talking about the topic.

Several minutes later and Lysander surfaced from the water nearby. He had launched out of the water with surprising force, using his lower arms only to assist mildly in climbing onto land. He was similar in height to Chris, but appeared much larger with his second set of arms. Chris, having never seen Lysander before, viewed him with fear and intimidation. He hesitantly moved forward, unwilling to abandon Shannon's side as she approached. Shannon handed Lysander the necessary items quickly. He held them easily with two of his four arms.

Why are you not wearing your necklaces that hide you? asked Lysander inside Shannon's mind.

The collara attacked before we had a chance to flee into the air. We lost our necklaces, answered Shannon.

Lysander paused for a moment. *The collara that attacked appear to be retreating. It is possible that whoever was controlling them believes that you have a method for neutralizing them and doesn't want to pursue you with them anymore. The magnets are quite painful to interact with.*

My concern is for the colossal sharks. We will be traveling for four days over the water, responded Shannon.

Lysander paused for a moment. *I estimate that the nearest colossal shark is at least two days away. They do not prefer colder water*

Then I better not linger here any longer and give them time to catch up to me. Shannon turned to Chris, who still observed Lysander with open concern, and mild confusion since he had not heard any of their conversation. "We are safe for now, but we need to go before colossal sharks have a chance to catch up to us."

Chris forced his attention away from Lysander. "Okay," he said with a subtle nod.

Lysander, carrying his items, slipped back into the ocean, sunk beneath the surface of the water, and disappeared.

I wonder if he was holding his breath just now, thought Shannon. She shook the idea from her mind, refusing to be distracted. "Let's get in the sky quickly. We don't have much time."

Chapter 42

Two days and nights passed without any sign of a colossal shark. Shannon's anxiety grew with each passing moment, fearing the inevitable. However, they had begun their third day without issue and were safely in the sky, away from the dangers of the water. Chris, in an attempt to allow Shannon to focus on flying—which she struggled to do—kept his eyes on the ocean below.

After six hours of flying, with the sun now overhead, they decided to land for lunch. There was still no indication that a colossal shark was near, and Shannon knew that this might be her last chance to fully charge the plane and have a moment of rest. Her heart raced as they touched down on the water. She swept the surface of the ocean with her eyes constantly, yet felt no relief when her search yielded nothing.

"Here, eat," said Chris as he handed Shannon food.

She brushed it off. "I would rather keep my eyes on the water while you eat and rest. I'll eat second."

Chris was exhausted from intently watching the water and had no desire to immediately resume the task. He ate without argument. Though he desired to eat slowly and enjoy his moment of relaxation, he nonetheless ate quickly, and after several minutes finished his food.

"Are you still wanting to watch the water?" asked Chris.

Shannon listened to the light sloshing of the water around the plane, and the peaceful passing of the wind, and let out a defeated sigh

"I'll eat now," she answered. She knew she could only go for so long while denying her hunger.

Chris handed her food and then leaned forward as much as the space would allow and watched out the windows. The plane rocked back and forth rhythmically with the water. Reflected rays of sunlight danced on the plane. Shannon ate, but kept a portion of her attention on the water.

Suddenly, Chris sucked in a breath as he leaned forward, shoving against Shannon. He squinted as he peered out the window intently.

"Is that something?" He asked as his large arm shot forward and pointed.

Shannon couldn't see anything specific. The water had a choppiness to it that made picking out definition from its surface difficult.

"I can't see anything," she answered.

He remained focused on a specific point outside, not accepting her initial answer.

"That," he said, tapping on the window as he pointed again. "At first it just looked like another wave, but it seems to be rising too high."

Shannon followed his finger and squinted. She still couldn't make out any definition, but his concern was more than enough to make her feel that they were risking too much to remain on the water. She faced forward and brought the plane to life.

"Oh, that's a thing," exclaimed Chris in awe. "That's definitely a thing!"

Shannon threw the throttle forward before stealing a glance and seeing a fin rising into the air two-hundred yards away. The plane bounced on the water as it picked up speed. Another glance, and the fin of the approaching colossal shark was now one hundred yards away. Shannon rocked in her seat, urging her plane to accelerate faster.

Chris let out a groan, emotionally preparing for impact.

Shannon didn't waste any more time looking at her pursuer, and focused on her speed and the water in front of her. The familiar feeling of the plane floating on the water slowly took over, and she yanked the plane into the air as quickly as she could. The plane tipped backward as it shot into the air, her grip on the controls fierce as her heart rattled in her chest.

A sudden thud was heard and the plane lurched forward slightly, throwing the aircraft off balance. Shannon struggled as the plane weaved side to side; she was forced to diminish her ascent as she fought to level out.

"We're clear!" Chris shouted as he punched the ceiling of the plane in excitement.

Shannon loosened her grip, allowing blood to return to her fingers. She forced herself to breathe, having held her breath during most of her ascent. She continued to raise the elevation of the plane. Having seen colossal sharks leap out of the water in the past, she wanted to be sure that she was clear of any other surprises.

"What can we do about this?" asked Chris. He attempted to control the tone of his voice as much as possible, masking his fear. "It appears to be following us."

"I'm not sure," answered Shannon. Her mind ran through all of the concerns she knew she would have to address in a few hours.

"Is there some way we could lose it? Isn't that one of those things that gave you a ride in its mouth? How did you control it?"

Shannon shook her head as she thought about her previous experience. "It's currently being controlled by a sima. Pain is the only way to force them to disconnect. I stabbed the one that had captured me in its mouth with the knife you had packed for me. But I have no idea if that would work from the outside. Its skin could be too thick or strong for a knife to do damage to it, and I'm not about to let it eat me so I can stab its mouth again."

"I'm not particularly a fan of that idea either." Chris sifted through some nearby items and produced a knife that he handed to Shannon. "Just have it on you anyway. I would love to think of some other way to deal with that thing, but we only have one proven method. Better safe than sorry."

"As much as I abhor the idea of keeping a six inch knife on me so I can perform close combat with the second largest creature that has ever existed on this planet—a sentence that sounds equally stupid in my head as it does out loud—I'll do it anyway." Shannon took glances at her body as she flew the plane, trying to find somewhere to store the knife that wouldn't put her at risk of hurting herself. After several failed attempts, she contented herself to just set the knife across her lap. "Thanks."

Several hours passed. The colossal shark continued to follow them closely. Its dark, ominous shadow trailed behind them, the tip of its fin peeking out of the water on occasion.

"I was hoping that flying would allow us to outrun that thing," commented Chris.

"Yeah. Unfortunately, this plane goes tragically slow. At least now we have learned that they can swim at least forty miles per hour."

"That's a fast fish," exclaimed Chris. "It honestly doesn't seem like it's exerting itself that much either. I bet in short bursts it could reach fifty or sixty."

"That sounds horrifying."

The two became silent for a moment, neither desiring to build up the monster in their minds anymore than they already had.

"So," began Chris, breaking the silence. "When we eventually have to land, do you think it will try to kill us or capture us?"

"I don't know. Maybe it just wants to scare us."

"Hmm... so 'Bang, Marry, Kill,' monster edition?" asked Chris.

Shannon let out a burst of uncontrollable laughter. "I shouldn't be laughing right now," she said in between gasps. "I just got the mental picture of several of the colossal sharks facing a computer screen, with a picture on it of us fleeing, and like a bunch of idiot teenagers, they're discussing whether they want to scare, capture, or kill us." Shannon continued laughing. "The absurdity of it was exactly what I needed right now." Shannon fought to stifle her laughter. Bursts of giggles would rise each time she thought she had brought them under control. Eventually she calmed down.

With a sigh of relief, she spoke. "So far, they have shown every intention of keeping me alive. I think they have made too much progress with me, and had too much success with their previous experiments, to give up."

Chris thought it over. "You had previously thought your plane was at risk when they attacked you and Brenda. They clearly didn't seem to be concerned about her. The thing also hit our plane as we escaped. So I think we can draw some conclusions, assuming they do want to capture you. First, I don't think they will have any issues hurting or eliminating me. They only care about you. Second, they have no problem damaging the plane to get access to you. In fact, they might intentionally be trying to remove you from the plane, or at least trying to disable the plane so that you are essentially captured by not having a method of escape."

"So the risk is that, in an attempt to gain access to me, the colossal shark could destroy the plane or kill you," spoke Shannon as she thought out loud.

Chris glanced out the window. "Um, it's gone."

"What?" exclaimed Shannon.

"There is no sign of it," reiterated Chris.

"I don't know if that is good or bad." Shannon hated not knowing the location of the enemy, even if that meant that her surroundings were hopefully clear.

Chris observed the darkening sky as late evening set in. "At the moment, we are almost out of sunlight and will be grounded, so maybe this is a moment of good luck."

"You don't think they believe we aren't going to land any time soon, and so they gave up, do you?" asked Shannon.

"It's been following us for hours, not to mention that it started pursuing us several days ago; maybe it got hungry," responded Chris.

"Or it's a trap. Either way, I'm going to fly until the last shred of light threatens to leave the sky. I think we can fly for another thirty minutes. I'll feel safer if we still don't see any sign of it after that much time."

Chris watched the water intently, examining every shadow and ripple in the water. There remained no sign of their pursuer.

Eventually, the sun lowered, the orange and red sky feeling more ominous than ever before. Shannon brought the plane down slowly over a long period of time, attempting to coax their follower to the surface. She nervously flew well within range of the colossal shark— should it jump—for several minutes, but nothing happened. She finally decided to land.

For a while, Shannon waited, struggling not to hold her breath, anticipating a sudden attack. Nothing came. She forced herself to relax.

"We don't have much choice right now," said Chris. "We can't fly. Our plane is exhausted. *We* are exhausted. If we don't rest right now, we might not have a chance later, and we won't be in any condition to fly tomorrow." He pulled out some food. "Let's eat and rest. What comes will come. Whether we are staying up all night or sleeping, the results will be the same regardless."

"Okay," responded Shannon. She thought about the discussion they had while flying, wondering if the colossal shark really did just want to capture her.

They ate quickly and quietly. Shannon was too anxious, desiring to listen to her surroundings rather than talk. Shortly after eating, they attempted to sleep. To Shannon's surprise, Chris fell asleep immediately. *He must really be used to high pressure situations,* she thought to herself. She forced herself to close her eyes, knowing that she couldn't see anything of value outside in the darkness of night anyway.

For an hour she tossed and turned. The tension that dug its nails into her mind prevented her body from finding a comfortable position. After a while she eased the door open, making sure not to wake Chris. A wave of fresh ocean air poured in. She stretched out through the opening. The moon was not present. The stars above offered little hope of seeing the water well. Leaving the door open, she swung her body back into her seat and closed her eyes again.

Suddenly, chills shot through Shannon's arms and legs; her eyes shot open. Outside she heard moaning. The sound was distant and faint. Several minutes passed until she heard the noise again. It was now much closer.

A wave of thoughts rushed over Shannon, her breathing suddenly rapid. Her body shook. A third moan and the distance seemed impossibly close. In an instant, clarity came to Shannon. She turned around and kissed Chris on the cheek. He stirred mildly. "I'm sorry," she said, before turning toward the door and stepping out of the plane. She moved down the length of the pontoon until reaching the end. She tucked the knife Chris had given her into her waistband and patted it to make sure it was secure. Looking down at the black depths below her, she took a deep breath and then plunged in silently.

The freezing water shocked Shannon's body, sucking life out of it. She felt enveloped in a straitjacket of ice. For a brief moment she sank, the cold seeping into her bones, unable to force movement into her limbs. Her determination slowly won, and she began swimming away from the plane as fast as she could. Though she struggled with all of her might, it took longer to surface than she thought she would be able to bear. She sputtered and gasped as she finally reached the open air. She continued swimming, putting as much distance between herself and the plane as possible. She couldn't risk anything happening to Chris or the plane.

When she had reached a distance that she believed was safe, she stopped and waited. It was only when she stopped swimming that she heard Chris frantically yelling for her, but the noise was soon drowned out by the sound of rain. The water suddenly dipped beneath her before rising up. Instantly, the mouth of the colossal shark came down over her at shocking speed. It closed itself around her with a force that tossed her mercilessly in the water that it had also captured in its mouth. She tumbled around helplessly, unable to get her bearings. She crashed into the mouth of the beast repeatedly, causing shooting pain in her shoulder and hip. When her fear began to subside, she remembered her plan and fumbled for the knife she had placed in her waistband before leaving the plane. The turbulence of the water was enough that she almost dropped it, but she managed to maintain her grip. Unable to predict her next impact, she held the knife out with both hands as firmly as possible, hoping that she wouldn't accidentally injure herself. Several more times she bounded into the mouth of the beast, hitting her back and head. Still, she kept the knife out. Suddenly the water threw her forward and the knife plunged into the animal.

Immediately, Shannon was expelled from the mouth of the colossal shark. The shark—suddenly freed from its mental captivity—then plunged into the depths below. Shannon found herself in the black abyss of the ocean, entirely disoriented. She lingered where she had been ejected, unsure of what direction was up, or if she could reach the surface—even if she knew where it was—or if it was too far away. As she began to panic, she felt hands gripping her. A new fear consumed her as she felt herself being pulled, unsure of where she was going. She quickly remembered the vision she had so long ago. These were her collara and they were rescuing her. With urgency they pulled her toward the surface. Her lungs burned, yet she fought the urge to suck in air that she knew wasn't available. She squeezed her eyes shut forcefully, willing herself to deny her urges and keep her air in. They burned so badly that she was becoming afraid she wouldn't be able to breathe out so that she could then breathe in fresh air. Finally, she burst out of the water at a shocking speed and gulped in air before falling back into the water.

Her lungs still ached. She reached the surface again and gasped with each breath. Her lungs felt like fire, her throat dry, as she kept taking in deep and panicked breaths. Eventually her body calmed and her breathing settled. Shannon trod water as she looked around. There was no sign of where she was. With her burning lungs now recovered, she realized she hadn't thought about how she would get back to the plane. Shannon felt a tug on her leg and she sucked in a deep breath before being pulled under the water. The collara swam, continually surfacing just long enough for Shannon to get a fresh breath of air and then pulling her back under. After several minutes, she could see the plane again.

"Oh, thank God," shouted Chris.

The collara pulled her quickly to the plane and Chris yanked her out of the water and handed her a towel.

"You have no idea how worried I was, or how mad I am," said Chris after a long silence. "I knew not to expect anything different. This is how you work. You make a decision and just go for it without talking to anyone. Now I know how your brother feels." His tone was filled with anger.

"It would have done anything to get me and you and the plane would have suffered if I hadn't left. There was no point in talking to you about it. You never would have let me go." Shannon dried as quickly as possible.

Chris gave a shrug and shook his head without saying anything. His face was anguished, his body filled with impotent rage, but he knew she was right.

Screams of exuberance filled the tiny cockpit as Chris and Shannon watched the color of the water below them change as the land rose up from below, blocking the colossal shark's pursuit. Land was finally within sight, and for the remainder of their journey they could confine themselves to the safety that land provided. As the land drew nearer, an additional wave of relief washed over Shannon as she saw the camp of Billy and Jenny. They waved to the plane excitedly from below.

Shannon brought the plane down quickly and landed with a bit more speed than Chris was happy with, eager to rejoin her brother. The camp was well established, with benches placed around a large and inviting fire, the crackle of which was music to her ears as she opened the door to her plane.

"Are you both okay? Did you run into anymore trouble?" Shannon asked as she made her way out of her plane.

"We're fine," answered Billy. "Once we were in the air, we didn't have any issues. Though Jenny was sick for a couple of days from not getting dry fast enough. Just a minor cold, though."

"I'm just glad you're safe," said Shannon.

"Fortunately, your collara have been here providing us with fish, so we have had an easy couple of days while we waited for you."

"I was honestly wondering where they were, since I only saw them once while we were flying. It makes sense though. Now that I have a chance to connect with them, I'll just have them stay clear of the commotion. I have a pretty strong feeling that colossal sharks like to eat the collara."

After the harrowing journey it took to get back to the new East Coast, Shannon was eager to rest. She and Chris set up camp with Billy and Jenny and allowed themselves the chance to rest the following day. Though she was eager to return to the settlement, she was too exhausted, drained both physically and mentally, to continue immediately.

Chapter 43

The roar of rushing water flooded Shannon's ears. A thousand memories, feelings, fears, washed over her as painful recollection consumed her. It was dark. The headlamp she wore cast insignificant rays that died out quickly. Water was rising around her and had reached her chest. The urge to wade kicked in, despite still being able to stand.

She was in the bunker. Glancing around, she could see that she was alone. There were no bags or life rafts to lift her to safety, and she didn't have any oxygen on her. Regardless of how unprepared she found herself for the situation, the water continued rising, unabated.

With the water climbing toward the top of the room, it grew eerily silent; only the light sloshing of the water in the corners of the room and her panicked breathing could be heard. She now had to tip her head up to reach the last sliver of air that remained in the bunker. Feeling helpless and yet understanding that this must be a dream, she allowed herself to sink. She waited for the burning in her lungs to force her to suck in water. The aching of fire flared in her chest. The pain was far too real for a simple dream. A fear grew in her that she had somehow made a mistake. She beat at her chest to fight off the pain, her terror preventing her from willfully drowning herself.

Finally, as the pain exceeded her last ounce of fighting strength, she desperately sucked in water.

The pain lingered. The aching fought within her chest, yet the water did not bring relief, nor did it kill her. Slowly the pain subsided and the dark hell that was the water began to lighten.

"Amazing," spoke a voice, hidden down the dark passageway to the bedrooms. The voice had a low, rumbling quality to it, and she could hear it perfectly, despite the water she was under. "I do not have to parade around in the grotesque abomination that is a human body. You've seen my kind before."

A sima slowly emerged from the hallway. The details of the appearance seemed slightly different from what she was familiar with. It wasn't Lysander.

"What do you want?" asked Shannon. The sensation of speaking underwater brought temporary feelings of panic. Her mind struggled to understand that she wasn't drowning.

"I'm just trying to understand my enemy," he answered casually. "I tried getting the information I needed from you while you were awake, but your mind is... fortified. So, I thought I would try it this way, and have a conversation with you. Let's talk."

"I have nothing to say to you," responded Shannon.

"I just need to know what you know, and I can do most of the talking to figure that out," spoke the sima with confidence. His head snapped to the side slightly, as though something had caught his attention. "Interesting, you have knowledge of Leviathan. I quite like that name, actually. We never gave him a name before. There was no need to. With him in control, we knew him so deeply, his very essence so intertwined in ours that there was no need to refer to him at all."

A sudden explosion of pain shook Shannon, her world shaking in response. She was tossed around in the water violently until eventually smacking into one of the walls.

Shannon opened her eyes, her vision blurred from waking and the splitting headache she now endured. Chris leaned over her, his hands clutching her shoulders, his face dimly lit by the dying fire. Beyond him the stars sat peacefully in the sky, unconcerned.

"Are you okay?" asked Chris. His eyes were filled with terror, his brow scrunched. "You were nearly convulsing."

Shannon threw her hands to her head. A fierce headache rolled over her, grinding her brain against her skull. "I'm fine, other than the excruciating headache I now have." She dry-heaved from the pain.

"Can I do anything to help?"

"Don't talk."

Chris waited in silence. Small movements would indicate a sudden thought or desire to help, but he would refrain and settle back into his seat. Several minutes passed as Shannon's headache slowly dissipated.

"Someone other than Lysander was in my dream," whispered Shannon, when her pain had diminished enough to quietly talk.

"I hope it hurts them as much as it does you when you get dislodged from a dream unexpectedly," said Chris.

"Me too." Shannon dropped her hands from her head and leaned back against Chris, resting her head on his shoulder. "I don't think he gained much information from me, which is good. I'm not sure how I'm going to be able to get any more sleep before I get a new necklace, though."

"We'll just have to sleep in shifts. Whenever I see you acting weird in your sleep, I'll wake you up."

"That sounds absolutely awful. Thanks."

"Don't be dumb," said Billy as he leaned up from his sleeping bag, rubbing the sleep from his eyes. "You can have my magnets when you sleep. If it becomes a problem for anyone else to sleep without magnets, *then* we will sleep in shifts. But it will be two people with magnets sleeping, while the other two just wait peacefully. I'm not letting you sleep without protection from the aliens, though."

He tossed his magnets at her and then rolled over and went back to sleep. Shannon placed the magnets against her head and a new burst of pain jolted through her before quickly subsiding. It was then that she realized that her headache was not from being woken up suddenly, but from the alien's presence still persisting in her mind.

"I think I'll be okay now," sighed Shannon in relief.

"I'll sleep better knowing you are wearing those too," responded Chris.

They talked quietly for a short while as they both waited for their adrenaline to wear off, their conversation quickly lulling Shannon back to sleep.

The remaining trip was peaceful. With Shannon wearing magnets, neither her, nor anyone else, encountered any more trouble. Their sense of urgency temporarily subsided as they enjoyed flying, the views around them, and the company of each other. They knew that they had to wait for Lysander to do his work, and yet, much would be expected of them when they returned to camp.

They spent their nights after flying staying up late and talking. Their mornings were spent sleeping in and they lazily pursued each day's tasks, and they took many breaks throughout the day to stretch and even sight see.

They were all also relieved to see how well Jenny was recovering finally. None of them were too interested in putting her back into the old environment that they had only ever seen her struggle in. Billy had hope, however, that she had begun her healing process, and that the effects would be permanent, but he also liked having her mostly to himself.

When they eventually reached the California coast, they decided to rest for the remainder of the day and hike back to camp the next morning, allowing themselves one last celebration for their success as the tight-knit group that they were.

Chapter 44

After two trips to retrieve everything from the planes that had been brought back from Austria, Shannon collapsed onto her bed, exhausted. Phil, desperate for answers, had taken the documents from Shannon greedily, but refrained from hounding her with questions until after she had recovered. With a new necklace securely fastened, she closed her eyes, eager for uninterrupted sleep. Shannon slept for several hours, only waking when she was overcome by a feeling of hunger, spurred on by the smells of cooking that crept into her home.

A steady drone of talking could be heard from outside as people gathered to eat dinner, excited by the items and information they had received. Shannon emerged from the dark cave that was her home into the dying light of evening and the flickering flames of multiple fires. Chris waved, holding out a plate of food for her.

Chris gave Shannon a smile as she sat down and took her food. "I might have spared you the bulk of Phil's questions. He's been grilling me for three hours straight. I can't say that I understood all of the conversations I sat in on with you, but I was able to recall enough to pacify him. He also said that we don't have the kind of equipment that can emit skywave transmissions, whatever those are, but that the original settlement does. He has, apparently, already reached out to them and they are working on getting in contact with Austria."

"It's nice to know that things are moving forward," responded Shannon.

"And quickly," added Chris. "What's next?"

"We will wait for Lysander to return from dropping off all the supplies we provided him with," answered Shannon.

"He doesn't need to remain there to administer them?"

"No. He will do it remotely with the collara. It will actually be safer for him that way. Since he isn't plugged into Leviathan like all the other simas, he is more likely to get in trouble hanging around. The collara can sneak around more easily without drawing attention to themselves."

"And when he gets here?" asked Chris.

"We will train."

Shannon ate her food. Her heart and mind were clear. She had obvious direction and determination.

Phil came by and sat next to Shannon. He had a warm expression, but approached silently. He ate his food for a while, saying nothing. When his plate was empty, he spoke. "You did a good job. The committee members are thrilled with the results of your efforts." He gave Shannon a comforting smile. "You've definitely made my job easier."

"With everything I have to do to prepare for what's coming up, I hope you can return the favor," responded Shannon.

"The work you have done to help this settlement grow and prosper, and the fact that you did it after communicating with everyone, has helped people trust you a lot more. I think I can get them to support you in whatever way you need," assured Phil.

"I'm going to need the freedom to be at the beach a lot in the coming days," said Shannon.

Waves crashed against Shannon as she stood in waist deep water. Summer was threatening to set in as the sun beat upon her, keeping her warm, despite the cool Pacific water. Her eyes were closed. Before her stood the imposing form of Lysander. He was dripping water, constantly submerging himself after several minutes of standing. One of his powerful arms was outstretched, his hand placed on Shannon's head.

For two days they had worked tirelessly to "calibrate" their minds. The pain had been excruciating for Shannon at first. Over time, she became familiar with the feeling and even looked forward to it. With each occasion that Lysander was forced to re-submerge into the water, the connection between them was severed and they would attempt to practice their slowly gained abilities. For Lysander, he worked to travel through, and manipulate, the past of a collara as Shannon could. Shannon worked to control a collara in real time, from a distance. Little by little, they both made promising gains.

The lingering effects Shannon had observed from previous connections also seemed to be persisting longer with the tuning of her mind. Her awareness of her position on the planet and the location of others remained between sessions from one day to the next, but she wasn't sure if it would be permanent.

Lysander released his hand from Shannon and threw himself into the water. Chris stood closely behind Shannon and placed his arms out to catch her. She closed her eyes and thrust her consciousness into a nearby collara, collapsing into Chris' arms. For several minutes he held onto Shannon's lifeless body, observing the minutes slowly ticking by on his watch as the collara ran around in the water. Fifteen minutes passed before Shannon regained her feet and opened her eyes.

"New record by almost five minutes," announced Chris.

"I can feel my mind has almost clicked into place." Shannon said with excitement. "I'm on the verge of being able to maintain it indefinitely."

It should not be much longer, spoke Lysander in Shannon's mind.

By the next morning they had gained the skills they had worked so tirelessly for. Her next step was to return to the settlement and practice her new skills on her own, making sure that she was capable of retaining them without Lysander's assistance. Her gained skills also provided her with the ability to reach out to Lysander from a distance rather than waiting for him to make contact. So she could talk to him whenever she needed while at the settlement.

The energy in the air was electric as the fishing crew returned from the beach. Billy, having been a part of the crew, came running up to Shannon, his eyes wild with excitement.

"Something is happening," he blurted out between gasps.

Shannon gave him an exasperated look as she waited for him to catch his breath. She hated the anticipation.

"Crazy things are happening. On two different occasions a torrent of water just shot into the air from the ocean. It looked like a wall of water, maybe fifty feet wide, shot into the air, maybe half a mile off the coast. I couldn't tell what I was looking at, but other people thought it was shooting three or four hundred feet into the air. There it was, just blasting water into the sky for about five minutes before settling back down as though nothing had happened. It happen twice, about three hours apart. The second one was equally far away, if not farther."

Shannon tried to imagine the imagery that Billy painted for her with his words. "You think it was a clear sign that the poisoning had taken effect?"

"Could it possibly be anything else?" questioned Billy.

"Not really, I just wanted to confirm that you thought the same thing."

"Yes," said Billy emphatically. He swept his blond hair to the side as he composed himself. "But that kind of power... it's terrifying."

"Is there any reason you would think that it occurred intentionally, as a threat?" asked Shannon.

Billy's eyes shot to the sky as he thought it through. Eventually he shook his head. "It *was* threatening, but I don't think it was intentional. It was so far away. If I had that kind of power, and wanted to scare someone, I would do it next to them. It was far enough away that I think it was just coincidental that we even saw it. It was just like seeing the colossal sharks for the first time. It felt like watching a movie, too insane to be real!"

For a couple of hours Shannon went around and heard the events described from multiple people. Each person described it as Billy had, and no one seemed to think that it was an intentional show for them. When she was done, she went and talked with Phil.

"Do you think now is the time to act?" asked Shannon.

Phil rubbed his chin, he was one of the few men who didn't allow himself to grow a beard. "I think we will want to communicate with the other settlements and see if they have had similar sightings. I would like to have some form of measurement—regardless of how anecdotal it may seem—to tell us if these events are new, common, or potentially increasing. It's too soon to act, we would essentially be going in blind."

Shannon gave a doubtful look. "What if these kinds of events have been occurring for a while and they were just somewhere that couldn't be seen by anyone on land. The world is covered in more water than ever before, and there was already plenty of space on the water where things could go unnoticed before."

"I've overheard what the others were saying to you. I think they are correct that this wasn't a direct threat against us. However, I don't think the location of the event is coincidental either. If Leviathan is aware of us through the sima, then it is probable that our location was on his mind. It would make sense then that the chaotic events would happen near us. I think they will also happen near the other settlements, especially Austria, since they have the largest population."

Shannon nodded in understanding. "Even if they haven't seen anything yet, if your theory is correct, they are likely to see something eventually, once they know to keep an eye out for it."

A couple of weeks passed and the sightings of anomalies coming from the water increased with each fishing crew that came and went, until talk of the water was almost entirely what Shannon would hear when walking through the settlement. Large gatherings, such as what was occurring today, generated a buzz in the air, an excitement that Shannon could feel. Each person talked about the tower of water that they had seen, comparing details and spreading rumors. Those who were responsible for communication between settlements would likewise relay stories that had been conveyed to them from elsewhere.

Everyone had been informed of the Leviathan. Shannon had been unable to move forward any further without the help of the entire settlement, which had required informing them of their newest enemy. The people of the settlement had taken the news surprisingly well. They had all seen far too much to remain doubtful when additional details were provided.

Everyone also had a sense that things were progressing with Leviathan, something that could be seen in the anxious movements that could be observed in others. It was far more common than normal to see people pacing, or shaking a leg as they sat, or mindlessly working a random object over with their hands. The time for action was nearly upon them, which was why they were gathering today.

Directions were announced to the settlement about the plan to go to the beach the following day, and the preparations that would be required before leaving. One by one, each person from the settlement met with Shannon and synced their watches with hers. Each person had an anxious look, staring at Shannon with pleading eyes as they met with her, hoping for words of encouragement. She was rarely one to dole out praise, and far too much of a realist to bathe people in optimism, but she tried her best. Chris remained nearby and quickly learned to fill in the gap in conversation that Shannon was leaving.

When everything had been done to organize the individuals of the settlement, Phil pulled Shannon aside. "I just wanted to tell you that I've been thinking things through and I think you should aim for the neck when attempting to inject Leviathan, since it is most likely to have blood flow going to the head, and other places in the body could lead to nothing and be like an isolated infection."

Shannon nodded. Phil had told her this several times already, but people repeating themselves seemed to be a symptom of the nervousness that everyone felt. No one wanted to find themselves, or the people they were depending on, unprepared. Fortunately, Chris had done excellent work adapting several different weapons into a tranquilizer gun that she had already practiced carrying with a collara.

With the hard work that everyone had put into their preparations, she couldn't think of any way that they could be more prepared. At this point, when they arrived on the beach midday tomorrow, all they could do was hope that their efforts had been enough.

The night was especially dark as Shannon lay in bed, unable to sleep. Phil had offered sleeping aids to anyone who thought they would need them. Most of the settlement had accepted his assistance. Shannon had abstained, afraid that any foreign substance might interfere with her ability to interact with the collara. She wondered if she had made the right decision. The gentle breathing of Billy and Jenny was familiar and soothing, but could not shake the tension that Shannon felt. After half an hour of tossing in her bed, she decided to get up. Carefully she tiptoed out of her home and made her way to Chris' house.

The settlement was abnormally quiet. Small fires served as nightlights that dimly illuminated her path. Chris' home was several buildings away from hers. His doorway had a large piece of cloth covering it for privacy. She stood outside briefly—her ear toward the door—and listened. Like her, he had refused a sleeping aid, but unlike her, it was because he knew he didn't need one. His time in the military trained him to sleep whenever sleeping was allotted to him. She listened jealously as he breathed in the familiar, slow pattern that she had memorized from her time traveling with him. She hesitated for only a moment, before deciding that she needed his closeness to calm her and help her sleep.

She pulled the curtain open slightly and stepped inside. A stream of light broke through into the room from a nearby fire outside and Shannon could hear Chris' breathing change. There was a light rustling noise. She remained just inside the doorway. She could see the shift in his body. He was turned toward her, but said nothing.

Her heart began to race in her chest. Thoughts of the day to come, the battle, the hope, the fear, the uncertainty, swirled through her mind. A whirlwind of emotions were rupturing within her as she took a step forward. She had grown close to Chris, had become familiar with everything about him, had developed a need for him. She was in love with him, though they had had very few moments to ever be alone, and too many emotions to work through to properly cultivate their relationship before now. But a yearning was gripping her heart, squeezing it relentlessly. She was terrified for their future, afraid of what tomorrow could bring.

She took another step forward. He sat up in his bed, waiting for her, seemingly saying nothing so that he didn't ruin whatever was happening. She could see his bare chest in the dim light, and see the shine of his eyes that were focused on her. She stepped forward again, now their toes touched. He reached up and gently set his hands on her waist. She removed her shirt, leaned over as she placed her hands on his cheeks, and kissed him.

Chapter 45

Shannon lay in Chris' bed. The sun was not yet up, but a dim light leaked into the room from the approaching day. She closed her eyes and tested her connection with her collara. She had sent one toward Leviathan several days ago, carrying the weapon that would hopefully kill the monster. Her vision jumped into the eyes of a collara swimming furiously. The world was dark, despite her ability to see well underwater; she was too deep, and not close enough to anything to put to use what little vision she had. She could feel that the animal was nearing its destination. She was confident it would be in position on time. She let her mind come back to her own body.

The space next to her was empty. Chris must have already decided to get up. She wondered if that was what woke her, or if it was that she was well rested. She had had surprisingly peaceful sleep. Finally willing to acknowledge the demands of the day, she rolled out of bed and got dressed.

Pulling back the curtain that covered his doorway and stepping out of Chris' home, she was surprised to see how many people were actually up, for how quiet it was. It was as though everyone was afraid to make noise and admit that the day they had so anxiously anticipated had finally arrived.

She could see Chris helping give final pointers on using the rifles they had available. They had been afforded very little practice with the guns because they had been afraid to waste ammunition. When he noticed her, he quickly checked to make sure his weapon was still empty of ammunition before handing it off to someone else to practice with. She laughed to herself. Anytime he held a gun, he seemed to check it five or ten times throughout handling it to make sure it was empty. She wondered if there was ever a time that a bullet magically manifested itself in his gun between checks. His weapons training was too ingrained in him to do otherwise. He jogged up to her and kissed her on the forehead.

"Pretty much everyone is up already," said Chris. "Phil and Lupe are thinking it would be better to leave for the beach sooner, rather than later. It will give everyone a chance to burn off all their excess energy and still have time to rest before things kick off."

"Sounds good to me," responded Shannon. "I'll go gather my things."

The last round of people arrived as the truck came barreling over a sand dune onto the beach. It came to a quick stop and the occupants reluctantly exited the vehicle. It was shortly after lunch time. With the warm sun hanging overhead and a full stomach, Shannon felt tired. She urged herself to keep going. When everything was set up and ready, then she could rest. They didn't have much more to do.

Chris came running up to her. He had taken the submarine to investigate the nearby water. He looked concerned. "The surrounding ocean floor is covered in the igloos you had described for me. I saw at least forty of them. Do you think that alien that connected with you on our way back from Austria was able to glean our plan from you?"

Shannon shrugged. "It's hard to argue that they didn't figure something out. The good thing is that they obviously didn't figure everything out, since we seem to have been successful in our attempts to poison Leviathan. This does complicate things, though. It seems like we may have more of a battle on our hands than I would have liked. I was hoping to spare the simas as much as possible, since we are trying to rescue them as well. Whether they got information from me, or they decided to guard the area when everyone started wearing magnets, I don't know."

"Hopefully having more of them engaged in combat here will help distract Leviathan, at least." Chris gave a weak smile.

"That seems very possible, but also much more dangerous for everyone involved. I'll try and think of something we can do to defend ourselves."

"We're all set," said Phil as he approached. "Everyone is as ready as they can be. We've been in contact with Austria, as have they with their nearby settlements. Everything is good on their end. Even Dillon's settlement will be joining us shortly. All we need to do now is wait for twelve hours."

"Easier said than done," lamented Chris.

The beach lay quiet as over two hundred people anxiously awaited the arrival of 3:00am. The ocean maintained its rhythmic lapping, interrupted only by the random outburst of water. A geyser would let out its sudden cry of anger into the air followed by the heavy sound of the water raining down, followed by the slight change in the waves that would reach the beach. The momentary tumult quickly succeeded by calm.

Jenny, Billy and Chris stood nearby. Shannon nervously looked at her watch. 2:58am. She then looked around and found everyone else with their heads down, watching the seconds pass on their watches. Every plan, every conversation, every detail she had drilled into her mind as being of the utmost importance. She struggled to run through them all as she watched the time. 2:59am. Fear and concern about her plans, whether or not they would align with what was about to take place, made her heart race. *Did I walk these people to their deaths?* 3:00am. In shocking unison, everyone reached for their necklaces and ripped them off, placing them into their pockets.

The best defense Shannon had been able to think of on short notice, and with limited supplies, to fight off the sima was to throw the magnets at them and hope that brief contact was enough to dislodge them from Leviathan.

Instantly, the ocean before them shot into the air. Not just a single stream or bubble, but a torrent that ripped the top thirty feet of water off of the earth as though gravity had flipped itself. A wall of water stood before Shannon that rose three hundred feet into the sky, constantly draining more water from the ocean to maintain its density as the top of the column climbed upward. The sound was deafening. Several seconds passed as the mass of people stood dumbfounded by the impossible sight before them; several stepped back nervously; a couple turned and ran. Then the torrent of water began falling upon them in large sheets that pelted and stung the skin.

In that moment, as the water came crashing down, a violent storm of activity burst from the ocean as dozens of simas rushed onto the beach under the cover of the raining water. As if waking from sleep, awareness struggled to grasp Shannon as she processed what her eyes were seeing. As clarity gripped her, she grabbed at Jenny's sleeve encouraging her to retreat while Shannon turned and ran away from the water.

The distraction worked! I have to act, thought Shannon.

She ran behind the dunes at the back of the beach to hide. Closing her eyes, she focused on the collara she had sent to wait near Leviathan. Her training took over, sending her consciousness into the collara's body. In the body of the beast, she began swimming in the direction of Leviathan, struggling to move gracefully while she hauled the tranquilizer harpoon that Chris had built.

Every moment that she swam filled her with tension. She maintained a panicked alertness, sweeping her surroundings with her vision at all times. After a few minutes, she noticed a collara that seemed to be following her. She quickened her pace, unsure if her guest was a friend or foe. Regardless of the trailing collara's disposition, she knew her only option was to continue. She pushed forward, knowing that at any moment she would lay her eyes once more upon the wretched monster that she hoped to kill.

As she approached, the shadowy depths slowly revealed the outline of the monster's face. Details gained clarity as distance lessened. She gave the vile creature a wide birth as she moved around toward its neck. She moved cautiously, less concerned for the potential enemy behind her, and entirely focused on the known enemy before her. Eventually, the following collara caught up to her and matched her pace just behind her. She stopped for a moment, waiting for any sign that she might be controlling her new partner with future knowledge, but no sign of knowledge, or intent was provided. The trailing collara just stared at her, patiently waiting for her to act.

She refocused her attention on Leviathan. She inched closer, lingered, and watched for any movement that would indicate awareness of her presence or intent. Seeing nothing, she continued.

In an instant, the large body before her shifted away from her, and the ghastly face of Leviathan moved toward her. Its mouth was open and its curled and menacing teeth were brandished hatefully at her. Its eyeless face somehow seemed to be looking directly at her. A moment of clarity struck her, a sense of inescapable inevitability. She understood that this must be why the other collara had been following her. Knowing she had just a second to act, she threw the tranquilizer toward her companion and swam in the opposite direction. With a sweeping movement of its body and a quick lunge forward, Shannon was suddenly inside Leviathan's nightmarish maw. The mouth closed, and an instant of unbearable weight crushed her from every direction.

Chapter 46

The pain was gone, and Shannon found herself floating in darkness. She was entirely weightless. Her world was perfectly silent. She fumbled around with her hands out and felt nothing. She couldn't tell if she was able to twist and contort her body to face another direction or not. There was no indication of her success.

"You've eluded me for so long." A low and layered voice with deep grit spoke at a volume that shook Shannon to her core. "I knew you were there. I knew you were up to no good, but I couldn't control you. You escaped my clutches when I had you in the colossal shark, but now you've handed yourself over. Your resonance is unique, difficult to find and synthesize, but with you under my control, it is only a matter of time before the rest of your kind will fall to me."

The voice rumbled as it spoke. Though Shannon's surroundings remained dark, the explosive noise of the voice shook her, tricking her eyes into seeing colors and lights that did not exist. She could feel nothing, though she had a strong sense that she was no longer in the collara's body.

"You won't live to see your kind succumb to my will. You are the first to ever deny me of my longings, and your defiance can not be tolerated. It is too simple to just crush you, though I could. Now that I have formed a connection with your body, I could pull you apart limb from limb. I could crush you into a ball. I can control your individual cells however I want. But..."

The menacing voice that pierced Shannon's nerves paused. She felt hopeless. She wanted to reply, to argue, to go down fighting despite her sense of helplessness, but she could do nothing.

"I want you to suffer." There was a terrifying level of satisfaction in the voice's delivery. "I want you to watch your own demise."

Two large windows opened, casting light into the black nothingness that had consumed her. Looking through these windows she saw the sand of the beach. She could see her arms, but she could not control the windows. She was looking through her own eyes, but was removed from them; a prisoner inside her own body.

She watched as her body rose from its hiding place, climbed the dune in front of it, and made its way toward Chris. The simas he fought against found ways to escape, to give room for whatever Leviathan wanted her to experience.

"Chris!" She heard her voice exclaim.

Through the windows of her own eyes, she saw him turn toward her. A look of relief washed over his face as he saw that she was okay. The windows continued drawing closer until she saw her arm come into view and slap Chris across the face.

"You abandoned her when she was dying. In your heart you hated her for leaving you. I could never trust you to love me. You would betray me just like you did her."

Shannon felt gutted at what she had heard her voice say. The windows lingered on his face just long enough to see understanding come to his eyes, hurt and betrayal. Then the windows turned away toward the ocean. Shannon's view into her world bounced. She was running toward the water.

"I'll drown you," boomed Leviathan's voice. "I want you to feel what you did to your father. You can feel the helplessness and pain that you inflicted upon him. You could have saved him, but in your selfishness, you climbed to the surface, leaving him to struggle and suffer, and die alone."

Her windows reached the water, and suddenly, though she was removed from her body, she felt the cold of the water. The icy sensation rose up from her feet, climbing quickly. In an instant, the water was up to her chest and she could feel the floating sensation along with the cold. Then, without warning, the windows plunged under the frigid water.

Shannon felt as though she was being choked.

"Think of your father!" bellowed the voice in her mind.

Seconds passed, and a feeling of resignation fought to take control, but she refused to give in to it. She wasn't sure how much longer she could last.

Suddenly, a weight pushed up from underneath her, and she emerged from the water. The windows spun around to see their rescuer. Chris held her in his arms. His cheek was still red from the slap that Leviathan had given him using her body. His face was filled with concern and fear.

"Not you!" She heard her voice scream. She could feel her body struggling to escape Chris' grip.

"What is happening?" asked Chris. "Something's not right here. Help!" He shouted as his grip loosened on Shannon's body. Leviathan controlled her body with shocking strength, struggling against Chris' arms with more force than she could have facilitated on her own.

The windows looked down and Shannon could see her hand reach for a knife that had been tucked into Chris' belt. The two struggled with each other for several seconds until her hand broke the knife loose. Suddenly the knife was plunged into Chris' chest, the blade buried down to the handle.

Shannon screamed in her mind, voiceless, helpless, and terrified from what she was seeing. A useless rage filled her body, its only outlet to force her body into uncontrollable shaking.

Chris's face contorted in agony as he let go of her and stumbled backward, his hands feebly grasping at the blade that looked to have pierced his heart. His eyes bounced between the knife and Shannon, unable to process the events that had just transpired. Without thinking, he struggled to pull it out. His hands weakly fumbled at the handle, sliding off multiple times before finally forming a strong enough grip. The knife slid out and blood gushed from the wound. His feet buckled under him, and he fell into the water behind him and went limp.

In that moment, lightning exploded through Shannon's consciousness, and her world once again went dark.

Chapter 47

Billy had watched Chris enter the water after Shannon had submerged herself, but had been too busy defending himself and Jenny from the attacking simas to immediately follow.

"Run away from here!" Billy yelled to be heard over the cacophony of noise. He pushed Jenny in the direction away from the water. "The distraction doesn't need you. Get somewhere safe. Hurry!"

Without confirming that she was properly retreating, he began running toward the water. Sprinting through the upward torrent, the water stung his chin and threatened to drown him as it worked its way up his nose. He had just reached the edge of the water when he saw Shannon and Chris struggling. The water, which moved toward the beach before rising into the steady stream that shot into the air, pulled at his feet and legs as he fought his hardest to run toward them. His body dragged—as if in slow motion—through the water. It required all of his focus to slowly progress in the water, pulling his attention away from his sister. When he looked up at Chris and Shannon, he was just in time to see Chris stumbling backward and collapsing, and then Shannon gave a terrifying shriek before her body contorted and also fell into the water.

At that moment, the torrent stopped. The ripping noise of the water being forced into the air fell silent, and for several seconds, the only sound that could be heard was the tons of water in the sky falling back to Earth. Then there was silence. Billy's efforts in the water became easier as the water settled. He quickly reached Shannon and Chris. He threw his sister on his back, her body lifeless, while with one arm he struggled to pull Chris. The water ran red around him.

Try as he might, the weight was just too much. Every few seconds his head was forced under the water and he battled the water's attempts to get sucked into his lungs. A surge of effort, and he was back above the surface, coughing out the water. His fear for his sister fought against the idea that he might drown himself in his struggle to rescue them. For what felt like an eternity, he pushed forward, unwilling to give up on either of the lifeless bodies he carried with him. Suddenly, Chris was lifted from the water and multiple hands reached around Billy, giving him strength. Phil, Lupe, and several others were with him, getting Chris and Shannon to shore.

The two bodies were set next to each other on the wet sand. Phil examined them promptly.

"He has no pulse, is pale, and is still gushing blood from his wound," announced Phil as he turned his attention to Shannon. He checked her vitals. "She has a pulse, but her breathing is shallow." He stood and faced Lupe and Billy. "Move him much farther up the beach. We will have to tend to him later and I don't want the water to be able to reclaim him. We need to get Shannon back to the settlement immediately.

Through panic and tears, Billy did as he was requested. Not sparing time to mourn his friend, he ran back to Shannon as Phil brought various objects for a makeshift stretcher. After several minutes of preparation they lifted her up and began the trip back to the settlement. If the battle was truly over or not, they did not know, but they weren't waiting to find out.

Shannon's vitals remained poor as they reached the settlement. Jenny was wracked with emotions as she followed nearby, observing Shannon's lifelessness. Billy remained strong, refusing to concede to the idea that his sister wouldn't eventually recover. With no other place to more properly treat her, they rushed her to her bed.

Phil worked tirelessly over the span of several hours to get her to a state that he felt confident she could recover from, though she did not move or respond to stimulation. Billy waited nearby, guarding over her, continuing to believe that she would wake up soon enough. When Phil stood to leave, Billy looked at him hopefully.

Phil shrugged. "Without a proper understanding of what caused her to become comatose, I can't make a proper diagnosis of her condition or her chances of recovery. For the time being, we are going to have to tend to her the best we can and hope that she wakes up soon."

When the water had collapsed, and the commotion had died down, the simas had promptly stopped attacking and retreated. The battle had ended and it was decided that everyone could return to the settlement. However, a handful of people remained at the beach to watch the water for a few days and confirm that there was no more anomalous behavior to be observed.

The first two days passed without incident. On the third day a sima presented itself peacefully on the beach. The process was slow, and those who had remained acted with extreme caution. But with the help of Lysander, who spoke to the people in their dreams to prepare them, peace was gradually established with the simas. They quickly started providing reports of Leviathan's death, confirming that an era of peace was now upon them.

While there were many who refused, those who were willing began the process that Shannon had undergone to connect with the simas and develop their skills. Though many people expressed concern about the risks associated with so many people gaining these skills, none of them were able to develop them on the same level as Shannon. Phil hypothesized that Leviathan had done something with her initial contact in the whale that the now-disconnected simas were too weak to replicate.

It was only a matter of time before the two races started working together, trading labor and resources to the benefit of both parties.

Two days after the end of Leviathan, curious how the war had ended, Lysander decided to use the technique Shannon had taught him and travel back in time with a collara to watch her. The process was slow as he realized he needed to go back several days before the final battle if he wanted enough time to get a collara there to observe her.

Though he initially attempted to remain far enough back that he would go unnoticed, his efforts failed quickly when she turned around and spotted him. The effects of time travel were still foreign to him, and going back in time while trying not to influence what had happened and simply observe it made the task all the more difficult. When he knew that he had been seen to gave up his endeavors of stealth and followed Shannon more closely.

Knowing how Leviathan had been able to react to Shannon when he had taken her to see the beast in memories, Lysander approached cautiously as the monster came into view. He hung back a short distance, unsure if viewing Leviathan in the past posed the same risk to him as it had for her, since the creature was dead in the future Lysander was visiting from.

He watched anxiously as Shannon approached Leviathan, and recoiled when the massive body pulled away, allowing Leviathan to face Shannon. He was entirely unprepared—having only expected to be a witness to her efforts—when she turned, threw him the tranquilizer, and immediately was consumed by the beast.

The tranquilizer tumbled to the ground just feet in front of Leviathan, narrowly escaping his powerful jaws as he engulfed Shannon.

Leviathan was instantly thrown into a trance, showing no signs of movement or awareness of his body. Several minutes passed as Lysander watched Leviathan, waiting for the moment that the creature would notice him and provide him with the same fate. With Shannon seemingly out of the picture, and the weapon that was intended to kill Leviathan lying just feet away, he drew up the courage to act. Her last action was to give him the weapon. He knew she expected him to do something.

He inched forward cautiously, knowing that he had no choice but to resume where Shannon had left off. When he finally reached the tranquilizer, he pulled it back slowly, hoping to not make any movement that would draw the attention of Leviathan. In his time connecting with Shannon as they trained, he had seen the memories of Phil repeatedly telling her to inject Leviathan in the neck.

With the tranquilizer in hand, Lysander quickly moved to Leviathan's neck, examined the tool to make sure he was using it properly, and plunged it in. The syringe compressed, and he knew that the task was done; the liquid magnets had been injected. Not wanting to push his luck any further, he made a hasty retreat, uninterested in seeing the results of his work.

It took ten days before Shannon finally awoke. She was greeted by her brother, who had no choice but to break the news to her about Chris' death. She wept bitterly. Her tears filled with guilt, not just for Chris, but for every death she had endured, including her mother's. It began a grieving process that she had put off for many years. Deemed a hero by all of the settlers, she was given all the space and time she needed to mourn. Her brother watched over her tirelessly, and as the days and weeks passed, she slowly recovered. Though, Billy would never feel as though he actually got his sister back. The guilt that plagued her prevented her from drawing close to her brother out of fear that she would get him killed as she had all the others. He would forever remain loyal to her, but over time, his attention shifted to his growing family with Jenny.

Shannon remained reclusive. As she fought through her grief, she struggled to find her place in the world. When it came time for someone to volunteer to make deliveries to and from Austria, no one could stop her from taking the position. It would serve as her official rejection of any talks of a position of leadership within the settlement.

Chapter 48

Small clouds hung high in the sky; light blue wisps outlined in white by the glow of the moon. Shannon had built a large fire that roared before her wildly. The fire radiated heat and light, forcing her to set far back from the blaze. She was alone, somewhere in the middle of northern Arizona. She let out a pained sigh. Her vision blurred, the fire doubling, as her thoughts went elsewhere.

Today was the three year anniversary of their victory over Leviathan. The settlement, the first year, had thrown a ridiculously large party and celebrated while she mourned inconsolably for the loss of Chris, Brenda, and her father. She had decided that in subsequent years she would leave before the festivities began. And thus, she found herself in the middle of Arizona, two days into her travels toward Austria, quietly suffering through her sadness, guilt, and regret. This year was better than the last. She had begun settling into a rhythm, something that she could call life, and it comforted her as she reflected on her past.

When she found herself struggling to push forward, pulled down by the weight of her emotions, she would pull out her tablet and write in her journal. She thought of the joy that everyone else must be experiencing now.

Even Billy had found a way to be happy and move his life forward. She didn't fault him for it, but it was hard for her to be around. His success was the clearest reminder of what she had lost. She looked down at the tablet that sat on her lap and began a new entry.

Today is the anniversary of Chris' death. I can't help but wonder if I'll ever be able to forgive myself for what happened. I know Billy says that I wasn't in control and that it wasn't my fault, but I still felt it in my hands. I still remember the sensation of killing him. I know Chris wouldn't want me feeling guilty about it. Even he would tell me that it wasn't my fault.

I still couldn't stay there, though. Billy and I fought before I left. He said I wasn't around when James was born and I'll probably be gone when his second kid is born as well. He was so mad at me when he found out I was going back to Austria. I wish he would stop asking me to stay. He knows my answer, and he knows my reasons, but he keeps asking anyway. He wants me to be around more for his kids, but they are exactly why I shouldn't be around at all. People die when I'm around, and he knows it.

Shannon closed her eyes and pinched the top of her nose between her eyes, attempting to relieve the pressure from the tears that refused to come. She continued typing.

It's been almost four years since dad died. As I'm flying to Austria, I'm planning on flying east first and following the east coast up. I'm going to take it slow as I travel north along the coast. I'm hoping I can find dad's grave. I never really got to say goodbye and the anniversary of his death seems like the right time to do it. I hope I can find it.

If there isn't anything urgent that I need to bring back from Austria, I think I'll stay there for a while and help Franz with research. Plus, Anna and Lia have been begging me to stay longer when I visit. Looking forward to seeing them has really made the last couple of days a lot easier, and the more time I spend with them, the less I want to leave. I know that eventually something will force me back to the settlement. I'll make sure to apologize to Billy then.

Shannon set her tablet down and leaned back onto her sleeping back. She gazed up at the stars. The constellations were still the same ones she had stared at with her father, the same ones she had looked at while lying next to Chris. They were the same ones that she knew her mother had loved to look at. She smiled to herself. The persistence of the stars gave her an odd sense of hope. Life goes on. She had once looked up at those stars with her dad, thinking she would never be able to recover from the loss of her mom; yet, she did. Her growing feelings for Chris had shown her that there was hope after losing her father. And now, as constant as the stars above her, there was hope still. There was a new world still needing to be discovered, and people looking forward to seeing her that she could start over with.

She knew she would be okay.

About The Author

Steven Jaeger was born outside of Chicago in 1985. He spent his formative years in Arizona. He is a devout guitar player and drummer. He currently resides in Oregon with his lovely wife of eighteen years and three children, who he expects to surpass him in greatness soon. He has a BA in Game Design and has spent the majority of his career building imaginary things for the internet. He is now spending his spare time writing imaginary things for you.

www.ingramcontent.com/pod-product-compliance
Lightning Source LLC
Chambersburg PA
CBHW032143190626
46814CB00005BA/1812